ALL THESE BODIES

ALSO BY KENDARE BLAKE

ALL THESE BODIES

KENDARE BLAKE

Quill Tree Books
An Imprint of HarperCollinsPublishers

Library of Congress Control Number: 2021937005
ISBN 978-0-06-297716-8 (hardcover) — ISBN 978-0-06-315774-3 (int.)

Typography by Erin Fitzsimmons
21 22 23 24 25 PC/LSCH 10 9 8 7 6 5 4 3 2 1
❖
First Edition

KNOWN MURDERS AT THE TIME OF
MARIE CATHERINE HALE'S ARREST,
September 18, 1958

MINNESOTA

WISCONSIN

St. Paul

SEPTEMBER 18, 1958
The Carlson Family;
Infant survived.
Black Deer Falls, MN

AUGUST 29, 1958
Stacy Lee Brandberg
and Richard Covey
Madison, WI

AUGUST 8, 1958
(Discovered on the 16th)
Walter and Evangeline Taylor
Sioux City, IA

AUGUST 13, 1958
Merrill "Monty" LeTourneau
and an unidentified drifter
Highway 30, East of Dunlap, IA

AUGUST 24, 1958
Cheryl Warrens
Mason City, IA

Madison

AUGUST 6, 1958
Angela Hawk and
Beverly Nordahl
Norfolk, NE

IOWA

AUGUST 18, 1958
Jeff Booker and
Stephen Hill
*Mobil Service Station
Clarion, IA*

AUGUST 3, 1958
Peter Knupp
Loup City, NE

Des Moines

Lincoln

NEBRASKA

ALL

THESE

BODIES

CHAPTER ONE

May 1, 1959

IN THE SUMMER of 1958, the murders that would come to be known as the "Bloodless Murders" or the "Dracula Murders" swept through the Midwest, beginning in Nebraska and sawing through Iowa and Wisconsin before turning back to my hometown of Black Deer Falls, Minnesota. Before it was over, the murders would claim the lives of seventeen people of different ages and backgrounds. All would be discovered with similar wounds: their throats slit or their wrists cut. A few sustained deep cuts to the inner thigh. Each of the victims died from blood loss, yet each of the crime scenes was suspiciously clean of blood.

Bloodless.

By the end of August, the murders had tracked eastward, closer and closer to the Minnesota border. We'd been following the trail in the papers, marking each new victim on the map. When those two college kids were found killed in an abandoned house outside of Madison, Wisconsin, it was like a sigh of relief. It was terrible, what'd happened to those kids. Richard Covey and Stacy Lee Brandberg had been their names. They'd been graduate students and engaged to be married. We were sorry that it had happened to them. That it had happened at all. But at least they'd been all the way over in Madison. The murders had passed us by, Minnesota had been spared, and whoever had done it—and *how*ever they had done it—they were probably most of the way up to Canada.

Black Deer Falls is only one hundred seventy miles from the Canadian border, back in the other direction. There was no reason for the killers to turn around, to cross another state line. We thought we were safe.

And then, on the night of September 18, the murder spree that had held the country in its thrall for the entire month of August ended here when it claimed the lives of Bob and Sarah Carlson, and their son, Steven.

The only perpetrator in the murder spree to be found would be apprehended that night: a fifteen-year-old girl named Marie Catherine Hale. She was found standing in the middle of the Carlsons' bodies, which, like all of the others, had been drained of blood. But unlike all of the others, we knew where the blood had gone: Marie Hale was covered in it from head to toe.

It was the story of a century. The story of a lifetime. It should have happened in Chicago or New York and been handled by cops and reporters who had seen it all before: the guys in movies ducking past speeding cars, hats pulled down and collars up against the rain. A short, silver pistol tucked up his sleeve and a cigarette burned down to his knuckles. It should have happened there, and been handled by them. Not in rural Minnesota, where nothing ever happened but more of the same, and not handled by my dad and our nearing-retirement public defender. Not handled, unbelievably, by me.

Michael Jensen. Seventeen-year-old nobody from nowhere, who wanted to be a journalist someday but hadn't gotten further than delivering papers. Unqualified. Untested. Take your pick of descriptors that mean a kid in over his head.

But sometimes the story chooses the writer, not the other way around. Or so says my mentor, Matt McBride—he's the editor of our local Black Deer Falls *Star*—and in this case it's especially true. Marie Catherine Hale chose me to tell her story. Me to hear it, when she could have had anyone—and I do mean anyone: Edward R. Murrow himself would have made the flight out.

So this is that story. Her story, taken down in the pages that follow. When we found her that night, in the middle of all those bodies, I didn't know who she was. I thought she was a victim. Then I thought she was a monster. I thought her innocent. I thought her guilty. By the time she was finished, what she told me would change the way I thought, not just about her but about the truth.

Tell the truth and shame the devil. I always thought that would be easy. But what do you do when the truth that you're faced with also happens to be impossible?

CHAPTER TWO

The Night of the Murders

THE NIGHT THAT the Carlsons were killed I was over at my best friend Percy's place. It was a warmish night for September and we'd gone out to their falling-down barn so Percy could grab a smoke without catching a glare from his stepmom, Jeannie.

"So, what do you want to do?" Percy asked. Then he answered his own question as he stamped out his ashes to make sure he wouldn't start a fire in the old hay. "Not much to do."

"Never much to do," I said. I turned around in the barn and picked through one of his dad's piles of junk.

"Beats doing homework."

"I guess." I held up what looked to be a very old and half-empty can of motor oil. "Where does your dad get this stuff?"

"Wherever he can," Percy replied. Most of the barn was full of junk that Percy's dad, Mo, had picked up at auctions or off the side of the road or taken off the hands of neighbors. Everyone in town knew that if you had garbage you took it to Mo Valentine before you took it to the dump.

The Valentine house was a farmhouse, like most others that sat outside town. But it wasn't a farm. It hadn't been a farm in a long time, though they did have one cornfield rented out for someone else to till. The rest had been sold off or turned to swamp or let go back to forest that made for good deer and squirrel hunting.

"I swear he's got some kind of disease," Percy said. "That makes him see worth where there isn't any."

"Like, a fool's gold disease?"

"Yeah, exactly. My old man has fool's gold disease. Did you just make that up?"

I shrugged. Maybe I hadn't; it seemed like something that might really exist. I stuck my head out through the door and looked at the house. Jeannie was still up—I could see her sitting in the living room, paging through a magazine. I wanted to go back inside. Jeannie was nice, and even pretty, but Percy hadn't warmed up. She was Mo's third wife (which meant he'd had two more wives than most any man in town) and Percy's heart was rough now when it came to mothers, after his own ran off and another had divorced Mo and moved across town to pretend like the Valentines had never existed.

"You asked anybody to Homecoming yet?" Percy asked. "I heard Joy Davis say she wouldn't mind going with a certain sheriff's son."

"How'd you hear that? Or did you just ask her for me?"

He grinned.

"Thanks, Perce. But I can get my own dates."

"It hasn't looked like it lately. And now that Carol's stepping out with John Murphy—"

"What does that matter?"

"John Murphy is a senior. He's the football captain. Now that he's got your old girl you've got to—"

"Why do I have to?" I asked. "It's not like I can do any better than Carol anyway." Carol Lillegraf and I dated for almost three months last spring. She was the dream girl: long blond hair, red lips, long-legged, and tall, and dating me was a calculated move. Going out with the respectable sheriff's son was a good way to ease her Reverend father into the idea of dating altogether. I wasn't surprised when she ended things just before summer.

"She's a cheerleader now," I said. "So who am I supposed to date to compete? The head cheerleader?"

Percy came out of the pile red-faced. Rebecca Knox had just made head cheerleader, and Percy had been in love with Rebecca Knox since the fourth grade.

"We'd better get you home," he said, "before you say something you'll regret about the future Mrs. Valentine."

I chuckled. But as he snuffed out his smoke, Mo showed up at the door of the barn with their two black Labradors.

"You boys come on out to the truck." He looked at me. "Your mother just called and said your dad and the boys need help out at the Carlson farm."

"My dad?" I asked as we followed him out into the dark. We got into his pickup and he whistled for the dogs to jump into the back.

"What's happening?" Percy asked. "Why are we bringing Petunia and LuluBelle?"

"She said to bring the dogs. She said they were asking everyone to."

Percy and I looked at each other. The last of the Bloodless Murders had been three weeks ago to the day, long enough for people to start to relax, for the curfews to ease, for the gin-fueled posses sitting around armed on front porches to disband. It was over. That's what we thought. But Mo was spooked. He pulled out of the driveway so fast that the dogs banged against the side of the truck bed and Percy had to remind him to be careful.

It was a ten-minute drive from the Valentine place to the Carlsons' out on County 23, and by the time we got there, we could see it was something bad. Two cruisers were parked in the driveway with their lights on and my dad's old pickup was parked behind those. Other guys had gotten there before us and parked along the sides of the dirt road. They'd all brought their dogs, too, if they had them; I saw Paul Buell and his dad jogging up the driveway leading their friendly spotted mutt.

"Shit," Mo cursed. "I should've brought leashes. Percy, find something to use."

"Find what to use?" he asked, but we got out and looked. All we found was some old, half-rotten bailing twine in the bed of the truck. So we doubled it up and looped it through the girls' collars. Then we got them down and followed Mo toward the lights. I could make out the shape of his shotgun, pointed at the sky.

"Did you notice he had the gun with him?" I asked.

"He must've had it down by our feet," said Percy. "What the hell's going on out here?"

We got up to the house. All the lights were on inside. Across the driveway and yard, they were all on at the neighbor's as well: the war widow, Fern Thompson, lived in a tiny place so close to the Carlsons' that it might have been part of the same property. There were almost a dozen of us gathered in the driveway between the two houses. Besides me and Percy, Paul Buell was the only kid. The rest were fathers and I knew them all. It looked like my mom had called them off a list from church. They were all carrying shotguns.

"What's going on?" Percy asked again.

I looked at Paul and shrugged, but he only shrugged in reply.

I didn't know what it could be that would make my dad drag us out here, but he must have needed us in a hurry, or he would have called in help from the state patrol. It was chaos in the driveway: the dogs were barking, and the men half shouting questions over the top of the noise. Petunia and LuluBelle were excited to see the other dogs, and I kept one hand on LuluBelle's collar, afraid that the rotten twine would snap.

Someone crossed the driveway, headed toward Widow Thompson's place, and the Labrador lunged. It was Bert, one of my dad's deputies, and he was carrying a striped cat.

"Bert!" I called. "What are you doing?"

He ignored me and went on, and Widow Thompson met him at her door. He placed the cat in her arms. Bert was white as a sheet and looked unsteady on his legs, like any minute all two hundred eighty-five pounds of him was going to collapse onto Widow Thompson's front stoop.

"Rick!" one of the men shouted when he saw my dad. "Rick, what's happened?"

I looked back toward the Carlson house. My dad had just walked out of it and came toward us. I scanned his face, but it was no use. He looked like a cop that night. The only trace of my dad was a flicker in his eyes when he saw me, like he was surprised and kind of sorry.

"Thank you for coming out," he said. "We've got a real bad situation in there."

"What do you mean?" Mr. Buell asked. "Are Bob and Sarah okay? The kids?"

"They've been murdered," my dad said. There was a long beat of quiet. A few dogs barked. Especially one near the house, a black-and-brown-speckled hound that belonged to the Carlsons, and after a minute, Bert went over and got him and shushed him up. Those of us gathered in the driveway started to fire off questions again, and I looked at Paul Buell. He was crying. My mom shouldn't have called him. He was too close to Steve Carlson. But she didn't know.

"Listen, this is what I need," my dad said loudly. "Teams of two and three. Armed, no exceptions. Dogs if you have them. I've called in State Patrol and there are roadblocks going up, but if the killer fled on foot, they won't have men here in time. We're the best chance." He counted us off into teams and finished with me, Percy, and Mo Valentine. He gave Mo a longer look to make sure he hadn't been drinking too much.

"I want you out in all directions. When you get to a neighbor, knock on the door but only to let them know you're out there. We don't need the whole county stumbling around in the dark. Check the creek and west toward the tree line." He pointed to Mr. Hawkins and Mr. Dawson. Mr. Hawkins had been in the army. "You two check the outbuildings."

"Who are we looking for?" Mr. Dawson asked.

"It looks like a Bloodless," my dad said grimly.

My hand slipped off LuluBelle's collar and Percy grabbed for her as the rest of the search party mobbed in on my father.

It was impossible to imagine that what my dad said was true. That the Carlson family—Bob and Sarah, Steve, who I knew— was lying in there dead. And not only dead but murdered by the most famous killer in the country.

I stared at the windows, numb. As a hopeful future journalist, I followed the Bloodless Murders in the papers that summer even more closely than everyone else. But the articles didn't satisfy me. It was the same facts, the same victims' names, the same lack of conclusions. Sometimes they used the same word three times in a paragraph or the same phrasing in two different articles, as if the reporters were as terrified as we were, right there at their typewriters.

The curtains of the Carlsons' living room were drawn, and from where we were in the driveway I couldn't see much of anything. My feet slid right, and right another step. I drifted closer to the house until I could peer through the space between the fabric panels. I didn't see anything at first but part of the ceiling and some photographs hanging on the walls. And then I saw someone standing in the middle of the room. She had her back to me, and she looked wet. Like she'd been swimming in her clothes through red water.

I moved a little closer and saw Charlie, my dad's other deputy. He was pacing, farther into the room, and he was holding a baby. He was bouncing her and kissing the top of her head, and he had one hand out like a stop sign toward the girl covered in blood, which is what I realized she was coated in. But except for that hand, he ignored her like she wasn't there at all.

"The baby," I said. Everyone in the driveway looked at me and then toward the windows. "The baby's all right?"

"The baby is all right," my dad said, and held back a few of the men who tried to go past him. "You're not going in there. No one's going in there that doesn't have a star on his chest."

Who is that? I wanted to ask. Who is that girl? But my dad set his jaw. I wasn't supposed to be by the window. And I was supposed to clam up.

I looked back and the girl was staring at me.

It's impossible to describe what I saw in her face, even though I'll never forget what she looked like. She was drenched in blood. Slicked with it. Her hair was saturated, and the blood looked wet in places: on her neck and where it leaked from her hair to run down her cheeks. That was the first time I saw Marie Catherine Hale. We did not actually speak that first night. But I still count that as our first meeting. Sometimes a look is all it takes, and the look that she fixed on me wasn't the look of someone silently ticking off the new faces of strangers. She saw me like she already knew me. I could almost hear her say my name, "Michael. Hello, Michael," in her low, surprising voice. Looking back now, sometimes I think I really did.

My dad ordered us to start the search and I snapped back to attention. Percy and Mo called for me, and the teams went off in their designated directions. I looked toward my dad, but he didn't see me. He called to Bert, who was still minding the Carlsons' dog, and they went back into the house together.

"Can you believe this?" Percy asked when Mo ran back to the truck for a flashlight. "Steve. The whole family. I don't believe it."

"Not the whole family," I said. "The baby's okay."

"And thank god for that. Not even the Bloodless could kill a baby."

"Perce, go help Mo with the flashlight. I'll meet you down at the truck."

He looked at me a minute, holding on to both dogs. Then he dragged them away, grumbling that he didn't know what use a pair of duck dogs were going to be, anyway, when it came to tracking.

I lingered in the driveway a while longer. Just long enough to see Marie be escorted out to Bert's police cruiser. He'd put his jacket over her shoulders, and later he would tell me that he put a blanket down to cover the back seat, but the blood still leaked through. I remember wondering where it was that she was hurt. She was covered in red from head to toe, and I knew that not all of it could be hers. I thought perhaps she'd been cut somewhere on her head, where the blood seemed thickest. But I was wrong.

After they cleaned her up at the station, they found not a scratch on her. Not a single drop of it had been hers.

CHAPTER THREE

A Girl Soaked in Blood

MO LED PERCY and me across the road from the Carlson place, south, toward town. It was the least likely direction that the killer would have gone, and I knew my dad had sent us that way on purpose because of me, or maybe because of the beer on Mo's breath. Petunia and LuluBelle jogged happily beside us through the dead fall grass and underbrush, but I kept looking back at the house. I'd been working at the jail since I was a kid, sweeping floors and washing windows mostly, but I'd been a sheriff's son most of my life. I could've helped, if they'd have let me.

But as the lights from the cruisers and the Carlson house disappeared and the sounds of the other men and dogs faded, I started to pay attention. I realized that we were looking for a killer. Actually hoping to find him, and not just any killer but the most famous killer in the country, who carved up his victims and left no blood behind. Except there'd been plenty of blood on the girl standing in the Carlsons' living room. Maybe that was the secret, and we would find the killer crouched by the creek and covered in it, too.

"You're making too much noise," Percy said to me.

I slowed. Percy and Mo were hunters, with practiced hunter's walks. Even the Labradors knew how to tread softly.

"I should have stayed back," I said.

"I'm glad you didn't. I feel about ready to jump out of my skin."

"Percy," Mo hissed. "Quiet."

But I could hear it in his voice. And I could see it in the way the shotgun shook in his grip. Mo didn't want to go either. There was a lot of nothing south of the Carlson house, just the creek where it crossed back and a lot of trees between there and town for someone to hide in. We'd been braver together in the driveway, when we were angry about our neighbors lying dead in their house. Now we went slow, and then slower, listening for the barks and shouts that meant someone else had found him first.

We got to the tree line, close enough to hear the water gurgling in the creek. And then the dogs refused to go on.

Percy tugged on Petunia's makeshift leash.

I patted LuluBelle. "Come on, girl."

But she only whined and dug her paws into the ground.

"Petunia! Lulu! Get on!" Mo ordered. "It's just water. You're duck dogs you two stupid—" He reached for their scruffs and tried to pull them along. The Labradors whined and barked. Eventually one of them snapped at his hand.

"What's gotten into them?" Percy asked.

I grabbed LuluBelle's collar again and buried my fingers in her fur. "Maybe we should listen."

Mo cussed and stood taller in the dark. The beam of his flashlight cast back and forth, and I held my breath looking into it, afraid that at any moment it would show a face in the trees.

"I guess I'll go myself," said Mo. "You boys stay with the dogs." He hadn't taken more than a couple of steps before something got up and moved, something big that snapped twigs and crashed through the underbrush. The dogs went crazy barking. Neither Percy nor I could hang on. I think the twine broke in the middle but Lulu might have just pulled it out of my hands.

"Petunia! Lulu!" Percy shouted as they ran.

"Goddamn it!" Mo shouted.

We stood frozen. The dogs weren't running toward the sound. They were running away from it. Mo pushed us behind him and pointed his gun at the creek.

"Backtrack to the Carlsons'," he said. "Find the girls and get them into the truck. I'm right behind you."

We found the Labradors back at the road, circling nervously and whining. We caught them and loaded them up, and Mo joined us not long after, breathing hard from running. Then we stood by the truck and let our hearts slow. In the safety of the light cast from the house and the red and blue flashing from the cruisers, it was easy to recover our nerve.

"Percy," said Mo, "drive Michael home and then take the dogs back and stay with Jeannie."

"What about you?" Percy asked.

"I'll go to the house and join up with another search party. You boys shouldn't be out here anyway."

"At least take one of the dogs."

"So I can chase her around again? They're no use without proper leashes."

"But Pop—"

"Just go home and I'll see you in the morning."

Percy and I drove to our house in town with the black Labs between us on the bench seat. When we pulled into my driveway, I said, "You okay? You want to stay over?"

He thought about it, petting the dogs.

"I'd better go home. I don't think Mo wants Jeannie to be by herself."

"Okay." I looked at my house. All the downstairs lights were on, and it looked safe. I knew my mom would probably be heading in to the jail a few blocks away, and I would need to stay home and look after my little sister, Dawn, even though she would already be sleeping.

Before I got out of the truck, I gave LuluBelle a good scratching. Even then when none of us wanted to admit it, I couldn't help thinking that those dogs turning tail had saved us from something.

I went inside and found my mom with her coat already on, ready to go to the jail like I'd figured.

"Are you going to stay the night?" I asked.

"I imagine so," she said. "They're going to book the girl in to stay."

"Book her? Why?"

"I don't know, Michael. Look after your sister." And then she left. She went to the jail to help the doctor clean Marie up. They wiped her down from head to foot, examined her, and found no injuries. Then my mom put her into a bath, and later she told me that even after all the wiping, the water in the bath turned as red as beet soup.

My mom didn't stay the night. The women's cell sat alone, connected to the rest of the jail on the western end of the second floor above the sheriff's office. It was built into the kitchen of our former family home, from back in the days when the sheriff used to live on the premises, and is separated from the men's cells by a few layers of brick and plaster and a good forty feet. We didn't live there anymore; my father, the sheriff, Richard Jensen, built us a new house, in town. Not so far from the jail that he couldn't still walk to work on a nice day, but far enough to keep my little sister from hearing any questionable language from rowdy prisoners sobering up in the cells downstairs. On the rare occasions when the women's cell had an occupant—Mrs. Wilson after being caught a few too many times for intoxicated driving, for example—my mother still stayed there. She didn't like to leave them alone in that drafty place, surrounded by bars and walls, even though most of the female prisoners stayed only one night. Marie Catherine Hale would remain there for one hundred and forty-four, alone for all but three.

After my mom left, I went up to my room. I tried to finish up my homework. I read a little. Mostly, I lay on my back and thought about the Carlsons and the Bloodless Murders.

At the time of Marie's arrest we thought that the murders had begun in early August, that Peter Knupp in Loup City, Nebraska, had been the first. From there, the killings seemed to escalate: a pair of student nurses with their throats cut on August 6, a trucker and a hitchhiker on the thirteenth, an elderly couple in Iowa on the sixteenth. And so it went on, with new victims found every few days until the students in Madison when everything stopped. A week went by. Then another. Lights still burned late into the night and doors that had never before been locked found themselves with new dead bolts, but that would just be the way of things now. Twelve people were dead. Twelve people bled out in their own homes or in their cars, or at their jobs, like that poor gas station worker Jeff Booker, murdered in the service office.

The papers increased their circulation by transfixing us with details: so little blood had been found at the crime scenes and no one knew how or why. The wounds were very clean. Very neat. No one was stabbed. They were cut at the throat or at the wrists, sometimes deep in the leg. "Could it have been the work of an ordinary kitchen knife?" the papers asked. Maybe. But so far, none had turned up missing at any of the victim's homes.

I don't know how much time passed with me lying there thinking. But I was still awake when my parents came home a while later, and I heard them talking softly downstairs.

"The baby," my mother said. "What's going to happen to the baby?"

I thought of that little baby, a two-year-old girl named Patricia.

She had been inside the house, in the very same room when it happened.

"The neighbor said Sarah had a sister," my father said. "I imagine she'll go with her."

My mother is a tall tough woman. An equal to my dad in both heart and height, or so he liked to tease. But when he said that, she started to cry.

I imagined them there in the kitchen: his arms around her back, turning her gently back and forth, his chin resting on the top of her head. She had cried before, when terrible things had happened. When the Ernst family's station wagon had rolled during the blizzard of '54 and killed everyone inside, including their five-year-old boy, Todd, she'd cried for days. But that night her crying sounded different. What happened to the Ernst family was a tragedy. What happened to the Carlsons was maddening. It was terrifying. It was inexplicable.

They came upstairs a few minutes later, and my dad came down the hall after he saw my light was still on.

"Michael, you awake?"

"Yes, sir."

He poked his head in. "You all right? Dawn all right?"

"Yes, sir."

My father looked over his shoulder and stepped inside. He closed the door behind him so my mother and sister couldn't hear.

Before he spoke, he sat down on the foot of my bed like he hadn't done since I started high school.

"I'm sorry about their boy. About your friend Steven."

"Me, too," I said, and I started to cry. My dad put his hand on my back. I was surprised I had cried. Even though it was terrible, we hadn't known the Carlsons well, and my father was wrong when he said Steve and I were friends. I knew him and we'd palled around some at school. He played football. I preferred baseball and even during baseball season I was more interested in books. But in the months following their murders I would come to learn more about Steve and the Carlsons than I ever imagined. The whole town would, so that by the end of the investigation we would think of them almost as our own family, and mourn them in a way we never would have had they simply died in some accident.

My father gave a big sigh and got up off my bed.

"You should get some sleep now," he said. "Everything is all right tonight, and tomorrow won't be easy."

He put his hat back on.

"You're going back out?"

"Someone's got to stay at the jail, and we need men at the Carlsons'. State's coming in to give us a hand with the extra patrols and the roadblocks. No one's getting to their beds tonight."

"Dad," I said as he turned to go. "What about the girl?" I hadn't stopped thinking of her, of her face and her eyes. Her body soaked with blood.

"Marie Hale. Her name is Marie Catherine Hale."

"Who is she? How did she manage to escape?"

He stopped with his hand on the doorknob.

"I don't think that she did."

CHAPTER FOUR

The Loss of the Carlsons

BEFORE THE MURDERS came to Black Deer Falls there had been twelve known victims.

Peter Knupp, 26, from Loup City, Nebraska. He'd been found on August 3, lying on his front porch with his throat slit.

The student nurses, Angela Hawk and Beverly Nordahl, both aged 22, found sitting upright in their car in Norfolk, Nebraska, on August 6, not far from a roadhouse bar.

The elderly couple were Walter and Evangeline Taylor, found on August 16 but killed on August 8. They were discovered in bed with their wrists cut on the outskirts of Sioux City, Iowa. Some thought their deaths had been a mutual suicide caught up in the sensationalism of the moment.

On August 13, truck driver Merrill "Monty" LeTourneau, 40, along with an unidentified drifter, were found a mile apart on Highway 30 near Grand Junction.

August 18: Jeff Booker, 24, and Stephen Hill, 25, gas station attendants killed in the same attack, their bodies found a day apart, as Stephen Hill's was located across the road in an open field, his pants around his ankles and a deep cut in his inner thigh.

August 24: Cheryl Warrens, 34, a waitress at a truck stop in Mason City, where Monty's rig had been abandoned.

And then the graduate students in Wisconsin on August 29: Richard Covey, 24, and Stacy Lee Brandberg, 23.

No doubt their names are familiar. But perhaps none is more familiar than Marie Catherine Hale. The way it was splashed across the headlines and her photo posted on the nightly news, it would be impossible not to know her or to have formed an opinion one way or the other. Murderess. Accomplice. Hostage. Seductress. Victim. Over the course of the investigation she would be characterized in every one of those ways. But those were only headlines. They were only guesses. Easy labels to fit her into easy boxes.

Marie Hale was a pretty girl, not quite sixteen, more than a full year younger than me, though she often seemed much older. She was pretty but not the beauty the papers said she was beneath the flattering photos they printed. Most days of her incarceration she spent standing beside the window of her cell, wearing borrowed clothing—pants that were too long and had to be rolled to the ankle, a white buttoned shirt—and her brunette hair tied back with a short piece of black ribbon. She wore no makeup and never asked for any, except for a tube of red lipstick my mother gave her, to cheer her up, my mother said, though later she would remark that it looked somehow much darker on Marie than it had on her. She was quiet, and her cell was kept very clean, though I never saw her clean it. She spent most of her time looking out across the parking lot and into the long stretch of trees that separated the jail from the county highway. When she moved, it was to pace, slowly, but with a patient sort of purpose. She reminded me of the large cats I once saw stalking me through their enclosure at the Como Zoo on a family trip to the state capital. Harmless but only for the bars.

It might seem strange that I would think so. I was a young man and an athlete, fit from a summer spent racing after balls in center field and delivering papers. But any man twice my size would have felt the same. She was unsettling. When she paced, and when she sat, very still and so calm, her eyes just like they were the night I saw her slicked and covered in the Carlsons' blood. I tell myself I never really feared her, but at first I would only dare to reach through the bars when she was standing by the window. Only then did she seem as small as she was, only then did she seem as lost—like a girl awaiting a thunderstorm or a strike of lightning.

I told Percy about her the morning after the murders when he picked me up for school. I told him how I'd seen her inside the Carlsons' living room. I guess I shouldn't have, just like I shouldn't have looked. But I'd known Percy since the day he saw me in first grade and decided he would be my best friend. I could trust him.

"How's your dad doing?" I asked as we sat in the school parking lot.

"How's *your* dad doing?" Percy asked back. Then he sighed.

"I wonder if anyone else's dogs turned chicken like ours did. You don't really think it's a Bloodless killing, do you? I mean, that'd be too awful."

"Would it be better if it wasn't?" I asked. "Would it have been kinder to Steve and his mom if it had been Bob who had done it? If he'd just snapped and taken a hatchet to everybody?"

"No," Percy said. "Christ, the things you think of."

But I was wondering, too, whether it was really a Bloodless Murder. It hadn't been exactly the same. There had never been anyone found alive at any of the other crime scenes, for a start. And there'd never been any blood. Or at least not as much as had covered Marie Catherine Hale.

"I don't want to go in there," Percy said, staring at the school. "I feel like as long as I don't go in there, none of it actually happened."

But it had happened. Search parties were still out looking for the killer. The state patrol had come in to set up roadblocks and do door-to-door house checks. There at the school it could have been any other day. But if we looked farther out, we'd have seen cops and men and dogs, combing through the fields. Socking us in. I tapped Percy twice on the arm with my fist, and we got out and went inside.

The Carlsons were a successful family. Not well-to-do but respected. The farm had been in the family for two generations, and people in town knew Mr. Carlson as a good farmer, with either a real knowledge for crop rotation or the inside track on obtaining federal subsidies, depending on who you asked.

Their son, my classmate Steve, was universally liked. Not the best player on the football team but he made first string. He wasn't funny, but he was quick to laugh, which is often just as important.

And the night before, someone went into the Carlson farmhouse and slit each of their throats. It was already being whispered that they were killed close enough together that, had they reached out, they could have held hands.

Percy and I walked through the halls riding the news of the Carlsons' deaths like a strange sort of ripple—it was easy to see the difference between those who knew and those who didn't, and stranger still to watch the news hit: to see Joanie Burke's face go slack and watch her reach out and grab for the arms of the person who told her. I saw Carol coming down the hall and knew that she knew; her eyes were blank and red-rimmed.

"Michael," she said, and then she just stood there hugging her books. A cry rang out from somewhere, and it woke her up, and she shook her head and walked away.

Our class at Black Deer Falls High School is made up of 212 students. The entire school, from freshmen to seniors, amounts to 1,169. Steve's sudden and permanent absence ran through us like a crack through ice. It was something we treaded around lightly until we were sure it would hold. All day long we waited for one of our teachers to receive a slip of paper at the door and announce that it was all a mistake, that Steve was fine, just out with flu. Even I was waiting for that.

By the time the day was over, I was exhausted. People figured I knew what had happened, since Sheriff Jensen was my dad, and

I didn't mind them asking. But there were only so many times I could say that I didn't know.

"You've got to go by the jail," Percy said when we met at my locker.

"I just want to go home."

"No you don't. You've had your nose stuck in the papers all summer and now that the Bloodless Murders are here and the witness is sitting in your dad's jail, you're going to tell me you want to go home?"

I glanced at him. Practically since the moment it happened I'd been thinking of what a story it was. What a headline, dropped so suddenly into middle-of-nowhere Black Deer Falls. I wondered how Matt McBride would write it up for the *Star*. I wished I'd been around at the Carlson house when he'd showed up on the scene. I started to think about asking him if I could help him out. And every time I thought that, I hated myself for it.

"Look," said Percy. "I know it's real now. I know it's Steve. But that makes it more important, doesn't it? For you to find out. For us."

"Don't you think I'll seem like a—" A busybody, a grubbing opportunist. "Like a snoop?" I asked.

"Well, yeah, but," he said, and shrugged. "Come on, I'll drive you."

By the time Percy dropped me off in the parking lot of the sheriff's station, my curiosity had won out. I had to know if the murders of Steve and his parents had really been a Bloodless killing. Part of me even hoped that they were. And it wasn't just me. The whole town was torn between grief and wanting that mark for Black Deer Falls on the map. We didn't know then what it would mean; we were caught up in the story like everyone else.

I went inside, figuring I'd ask around and see if Bert or Charlie needed any help or ask Nancy if she wanted me to run any errands. I half expected it to be empty, for my father and the deputies to be working the scene out at the farm. But when I got there, my dad was standing in the door to his office, surrounded by both of his deputies. Of the three of them, only Charlie looked fresh, but then he always did, with his thick dark eyebrows and slicked-back hair. My dad looked like he might fall asleep standing up with a cup of coffee in his hand.

"Michael," my dad said, and the deputies turned.

"Hi, Michael," said Charlie.

"Hey, Mikey," said Bert, before looking back at my dad and stepping out of his way.

"You shouldn't be here today, son."

"I'm sorry, sir," I said. "I just thought you could use the extra help."

"I don't know that there's much to do." He rubbed his eyes. "I should be getting home myself soon to try and get some sleep. I guess you can clean up around here a little. Give me a half an hour. Then we'll go home together."

I nodded, and my presence was soon forgotten as I busied myself emptying trash bins and pushing in chairs. My dad and the deputies moved into the relative privacy of his office, and I went on down the halls, putting things back in storage closets that had been left out, and noting the peculiar quiet from the holding cells. They could have been empty. They often were on a weekday afternoon. But I had the distinct impression that they were not and the jailed men were simply silent, as if they, too, were intently listening for anything that could explain what had happened.

When I reached the door to our old kitchen and the women's cell, it was almost by accident. It was my old house, after all, and I often wound up there. My feet just carried me in that direction if I wasn't paying much attention. I'd look up, and there would be the door. Brown wood, painted white on the jail-facing side, as if the change of color provided another layer of separation between the two adjoining structures.

I stopped and stared at the white paint. All of a sudden I felt like I was a kid again, that my mother would be inside, standing at the stove or seated at the table. But there was only a girl on the other side, in the cell, and she must have heard me come up the steps. She must have been waiting. Wondering what I was doing there. So I opened the door.

They had cleaned her up. Gone was the blood, soaked and streaked from head to foot, down the bathtub drain. Gone were the blood-drenched clothes, stained so dark that I could barely remember what they were.

Marie Catherine Hale wasn't facing me when I came in, and her hair was dry now, and soft-looking, a deep brown that lightened at the edges. She didn't turn when she heard the door, just kept looking through the window at the parking lot and a sliver of street below, and beyond that the heavy, wide lines of trees that stand between the jail and the highway.

"It will be dark soon," she said. "I was wondering if I would see you. Michael."

"You know my name," I said.

"They talk about you a lot."

She turned. Her eyes were large and hazel, flecked with brown and not the reddish-brown I'd imagined after seeing her so drenched in blood. Her voice was low and calm. Businesslike.

"You shouldn't be here," she said, and then, before I could agree: "Or maybe you're thinking that I shouldn't be here. But you'd be wrong." She smiled a little, just with the corner of her mouth. "I'm—"

"Marie Catherine Hale," I said. "I know."

"I know you know. But that's all you know. All they know." She had her hair down that day. Out of the ribbons she favored later, for court. "You can just call me Marie, you know. You don't need to say the whole thing."

"But that's what they'll call you in the papers, if you make the papers," I said.

"I've already made the papers. The reporters got here this morning. You missed them, I guess, but you won't. I'm about to make your little town briefly, uncomfortably, famous."

Briefly, uncomfortably, famous. I liked her choice of words. "How old are you?" I asked.

"I'll be sixteen in December. You got a smoke?"

I patted my pockets even though I didn't smoke myself. "Sorry."

She turned away from the window in a fast spin and paced the short length of the cell before plunking down on the bed, which was better than what the men's cells provided but still not much more than a cot. "Figures. They wouldn't give me one downstairs either. Said I was too young."

"You seem older."

She frowned slightly. "Yeah. People always think I'm older than I am."

She tapped her fingernails against the bars. When she looked at me again, a thrill went through my whole body—she'd been there; she'd been in that house when it happened—but it was more than that. Marie Hale was not the kind of girl I was used to talking to. She was a fast girl, with her smokes and the way she moved, that direct look in her eyes. She was the kind of girl the sheriff's son is supposed to ignore.

"What happened to you?" I asked. "What were you doing at the Carlsons'?"

"That's a long story."

"I love stories," I said. "Long, short, and in-between."

Her eyes sharpened, focusing in on me like they had through the Carlsons' window. It had been nearly impossible to piece those two images together, the girl covered in blood with this one, until that moment.

"Is that why you're here?" she asked. "To get the story?"

"No," I said. I gestured quickly to the rest of the room, the attached kitchen, the bare dining table with only one chair. "I used to live here. I wasn't even sure that you would be in the cell.

There's got to be someplace more comfortable you could stay until your family can come and get you."

"My family," she said, and laughed.

The words seem foolish to me now, but at the time I didn't know what was so funny. No matter what my dad seemed to think, I couldn't imagine that she was anything other than a lucky girl who had survived a horrible attack.

"No one's coming to get me," she said. "They're charging me downstairs."

"Charging you?"

"As an accomplice."

"But that's crazy."

"Why is it crazy?" she asked.

"Because you're just a girl," I said. And even though I knew she wasn't, she could have been from Black Deer Falls. She was no big-city sophisticate or a tanned blond from California. She talked the same way we did. Walked the same way. Went to our same churches.

"But did you?" I asked. "Are you?"

She shrugged. "Better not say any more." She held up her right hand, as if she were taking an oath. "Anything I say can be held against me in a court of law. And you'd better get out of here. Go back where you came from before you're missed."

I turned to go without another word, thinking she must be lying about her age to be able to order me around like that.

"Michael," she called out. "When you come back: bring some smokes."

CHAPTER FIVE

The Funerals

OVER FIVE HUNDRED people attended the funerals of Robert, Sarah, and Steven Carlson. They spilled out onto the lawn of First United Baptist, which wasn't even the Carlsons' church (they were Methodists) but the only one in town large enough to be up to the task. Folks came from all over the county and even into the Dakotas, people who had never so much as met a one of them. The viewing line before the three ivory caskets stretched far beyond the parking lot and took more than two hours.

It was a hell of a thing, seeing those three caskets draped with roses and daisies and closed so tightly. One of them with Steve inside—Steve, who a week ago had run into me accidentally in the hallway, and those were our last words, our last interaction, an inane cluster of laughter and fake punches.

It didn't make sense that he could be dead. That he could be killed, and be killed in his own house, just lying there without fighting. None of the victims ever seemed to put up a fight.

"I don't understand how it could've happened," I whispered, and my dad squeezed my shoulder.

"I don't either. But we shouldn't talk about it here." My family was already singled out because my father was the sheriff. All eyes were upon us when we approached the caskets.

Except for little Patricia's. The surviving toddler squirmed in her aunt's arms in the front row, chubby fingers reaching for the wide brim of her aunt's black mourning hat. She looked so unknowing. So happy. I wondered what she'd seen in her house that night, what she would remember. If when she grew up she would have her own story to tell.

I looked away to see Matt McBride. He was there covering the funerals, and he'd been watching me as I watched Patricia, so I slipped away from my family and made my way over to him.

"Hello, Mr. McBride."

"Hello, Michael." He shook my hand. "How are you?"

"I'm all right, sir. How are you? Is your wife—?"

"Over there, talking to Bob Carlson's brother, Neil." He smiled. "I think she just doesn't want to be seen with me when I have this camera around my neck." He held it up when he said so. I'd seen him before the service started, taking photos of the caskets draped in flowers. And then again, photographing mourners in the viewing line. Other, out-of-town reporters had been stopped at the door. But Mr. McBride had known the Carlsons, and we were used to seeing him around photographing us at events and at the county fair.

I remember thinking how at ease he looked. How professional. He knew I wanted to be a journalist someday. I'd blurted it out one afternoon that summer when I was delivering papers for him, and he talked with me about it for a long time even though he'd been on his way out the door. We stood in front of the offices of the *Star*, in front of the windows with the title emblazoned across them in flaking gold paint, and he let me ask him about everything I could think of.

"I heard you were at the house that night, in one of the search parties," he said. "I'm sorry; that must have been hard."

I nodded, and he looked at me sympathetically.

"Well, Michael," he said. "I won't keep you. But if you need anything, I'll be around."

After the funerals, Percy and I went to the boat landing on the south end of Eyeglass Lake, a hard-to-find hideaway for upperclassmen and the occasional bunch of kids hunting frogs or turtles. It's not used much anymore for boating or fishing—the water teems with weeds and lily pads. Eyeglass Lake may have been clear as a pair of eyeglasses once, but that was a long time ago, and my dad and his deputies generally consider it too much of a pain to check up on.

Percy backed his car up so that it faced the road and set the parking brake so we wouldn't wind up in the drink. Then we got out and I leaned up against the taillight while he got two beers from the trunk.

"Watch the rust," he said as I popped the top, and I slid over a few inches to keep it from staining my good trousers.

After a few swallows, Percy said, "I've never seen that many peo-ple crammed into a church before. Or that many unfamiliar faces."

"Me neither."

"Did you talk to her?" he asked.

"Who?"

"Don't play dumb."

"Marie Catherine Hale," I said. "Yeah, I saw her."

"So what's she like?"

"I don't know. A girl."

He threw something into the water, a rock maybe or the tab of his beer. "I heard they're charging her with the murders, but that can't be right."

"It isn't right. Not exactly. They want her to give up her accom-plice. The real killer. But she hasn't yet." The real killer. The man who had done it. No one believed that it could have been her. She was a girl, and girls didn't kill. She was small, when Monty LeTourneau had been big. She was weak, when Steve and his father had been strong. But no one had any problem believing that she had helped.

"Your dad must be going apeshit," said Percy. "He talked to Judge Vernon yet?"

"No one knows what to do," I said. The truth was, my dad, our prosecutor, even our judge were out of their depth. The Bloodless Murders had crossed state lines and had multiple seemingly ran-dom victims. They'd never encountered anything like it.

"What does that mean for the girl?" Percy asked. "They won't put her in the chair?"

"Minnesota doesn't have the chair," I said. I knew that because I'd asked my dad the same question. When we had capital punishment, we had preferred hanging. "But Nebraska has the electric chair, and that's where it all started."

Percy stared out at the dark water. "Seems stupid of her not to give him up. Seems worse than stupid, to let him go free, keep on killing."

"They'll get him eventually." There had never been more than one Bloodless Murder in the same town. But just the same, we kept our eyes on the trees. Then Percy took his beer and threw it into the lake.

"What'd you do that for?"

"I don't know." He stuffed his hand into his pocket. "This day makes me not want to drink. Those caskets. And all those people . . ."

All those people. On one hand, it was touching that strangers would come and give our community's loss more significance. On the other, it robbed us of our intimacy. But everyone in attendance had been properly somber and restrained. And if a few had stared a little too long, well, that was to be expected, wasn't it? When something was as horrible as that?

I took a last drink and threw my beer into the lake beside Percy's. The funerals were an event not because so many strangers had come. It was a spectacle because it was a spectacle. The Carlsons' deaths had been a spectacle.

"And that baby," I whispered.

I thought of her cherubic, reaching arms. I imagined her sitting on the floor of the living room in the Carlson farmhouse within a few steps of her dead parents and her dead brother. I imagined Marie Hale standing in the same room, red from head to toe.

Widow Fern Thompson had been the one to telephone Charlie at the sheriff's office. None of us had known her husband; she had moved to Black Deer Falls after he died and bought a small house with their savings and his service pension. She was well into her sixties, with no children, and was a bit of a shut-in, and every now and then the ladies at our church would get together and go to her house to bring her a luncheon.

When she called the sheriff's office, she told Nancy that something was wrong at the Carlson place. The lights were still on and the cat had been meowing to be let in. And she could hear the baby crying. Charlie had been hanging around the station that night, as he liked to do when Nancy was working—everyone knew he was sweet on her, and with her bright blond curls and rose-lipped smile, most of the rest of us were sweet on her, too—so he said he'd go out to the farmhouse and take a look. It was Nancy who urged him to get my dad on the radio and bring him along. Charlie'd tried to refuse; there was no reason to bother my dad with something like that, but Nancy'd insisted. There was a note in Fern Thompson's voice, she said, that she didn't like.

Fern kept a rather constant eye on the Carlsons. She alerted them when the family dog ran out into the marshes or when John P. delivered the mail and failed to close the box properly like he did sometimes at our place and the letters spilled out onto the grass. The investigators latched on to that: that the

Widow Thompson's habits weren't something that any murderer just passing through could have known. It was further evidence, they said, that the killer was not from Black Deer Falls, as if we had had any doubt.

"Let's get out of here," Percy said.

"Where are we going?"

"The park. Everyone's going down there to have a drink for Steve."

"I thought you weren't in the mood to drink," I said. "Who's 'everyone'?"

"Everyone who can slip their parents and make it. And they want you there, Sheriff's kid." He opened his door and leaned through to pop the passenger side open.

"So the girl," he said as we pulled out of the landing, "is she pretty?"

"What?"

"They say she's pretty. Black hair, blue eyes, red, red lips . . ."

"Her hair is brown," I said. "And her eyes are hazel. And she's all of fifteen years old."

"Near sixteen. It's not like she's a freshman."

"Is that all you think about? Typical Valentine."

I laughed, and when he tried to punch me in the ribs the car jerked back toward the reed-filled lake. The things that came out of his mouth sometimes. Percy was a regular in detention and by now was an expert at washing chalkboards and classroom windows. He was always goofing about his romantic future and his many wives. Sometimes it was four. Sometimes it was six, like

Henry VIII. It definitely had to be more than three, so he could best his old man.

It was a short drive to the park, and when we got there the sun had just gone down.

"Michael Jensen," someone said, and tossed me a beer. It happened fast, and I couldn't see who it was. The voice sounded maybe like it was Joe Conley or Morgan Todd, both football players like Steve and to me almost indistinguishable aside from the different numbers on their backs.

I cracked it open. "Thanks for the invite." They'd started a fire but kept it burning low in case one of the deputies rolled through. In the orange glow I could make out faces: everyone gathered around was from the football team. I figured they'd extended my invitation for insurance—if they did get caught, at least they had the sheriff's kid there as a shield. As for Percy, he was an always-welcome addition for his clowning, and since he could usually score the most beer.

We stood around and drank to Steve. One beer disappeared and then two, and three, and Percy played his usual trick of lighting his shoes on fire. Those closest to Steve, the ones he would have called his best friends, weren't there that night and I was glad. It was too soon.

"So have you seen it?" Joe Conley asked. "The house, I mean."

"Why would he have seen it?" Percy asked back. His usually affable voice was sharp with warning, and I realized he'd had less to drink than he'd been putting on.

"I just thought he might. His dad's the sheriff, and he works at the jail. I'm just asking is all. I mean, who are they sending to clean it up?"

"Nobody," I said. "Charlie and Bert have already been through it taking photographs, but my dad says the FBI is sure to want a turn."

"The FBI," Morgan said, and whistled. "In Black Deer Falls. Who'd have thought the biggest murder spree of the century would end up here?"

"Who says it's over?" said someone else. "You think the girl did it by herself?"

"None of this makes sense," Joe said, and wiped his face. "I half don't believe it. I half think those coffins were empty. I wish they were." He looked at me. "If we went to Steve's, who'd be there to stop us?"

"There's a state police car parked there from dawn to dark."

But it was after dark.

CHAPTER SIX

The Carlson Farmhouse

WE KNEW IT was a bad idea. But something had come over us, standing there together with the fire going—the grief and beer had combined with blurry feelings of shock and the pent-up frustration of a long summer of light sleep and locked doors. Not a one of us said we shouldn't go. We just piled into our cars and drove north on the long stretch of County 23.

The drive wasn't more than fifteen minutes, the last stretch of it out on back roads, unpaved. We spotted a line of pheasants crossing in our headlights just before we got to it: a few hens and a rooster, his dark green head feathers flashing—and Percy pulled over well shy of the start of the Carlsons' long gravel driveway. Joe was with us in Percy's car, and the rest of the guys followed in two cars behind.

"No sign of a cruiser," Percy said. "Maybe we should still drive past and take a look?"

Joe exhaled and twisted in his seat to look around. Up the road stood a red mailbox with the Carlsons' name on it printed in white paint. It was a pretty place, I'd always thought, a white gabled house with gray shutters nestled in a copse of maple trees.

"They could've stayed late, parked behind the barns," Percy said, and nodded toward them, two large barns, red with white trim in the daylight but only hulking shadows in the dark.

"Don't be chicken," Joe said, and when I didn't say anything, Percy threw the car into drive.

We pulled right up beside the front porch, like we would have if we were stopping by to see Steve or picking him up to go to the drive-in over in Pelican Rapids, two things we had never actually done. We stared up at the house. Already it seemed haunted, though not by ghosts; I had no notion that we would go inside and discover the specter of Steve and his murdered parents. The house was haunted by the experience. It had been stained by the horror that took place within its walls, and even though it stood empty, it would never quite feel empty again.

"Aw, hell," Percy said suddenly.

"What?"

"Widow Thompson is sure to have seen us. She's probably on the phone to your dad's office right now."

"Maybe not," Joe said. "Maybe she's still out with the rest of them at one of the repasts."

I looked closely at Fern Thompson's place. Someone would have picked her up and taken her to the funeral. But they might have also dropped her off again, tired and with a small casserole to put into her refrigerator. If she was home, of course she had seen us. She was watchful before and would be even more so now, and it made me sad to think how afraid she must be living so close to something like that and how much lonelier she would be without the Carlsons' lives to look in on. I opened the car door and stepped out.

"What are you doing?" Percy exclaimed, and got out after me.

Mrs. Thompson knew who I was. I hoped she would understand that we were there not to gawk but because we needed to see; that she would understand when we didn't quite understand ourselves. "Fern Thompson is a nice lady," I said to Percy. "She took in Steve's cat when none of the relatives seemed to want it. My dad told me."

"Oh," Percy said. "That was good of her. And it's good to think . . . that they both have company still." He turned toward Mrs. Thompson's house and gave a little wave in the headlights, turning on that Valentine charm that I had to admit let him get away with more than he ought.

I turned back to the Carlson house. I wondered how long it would remain the Carlson house. In the memory of Black Deer Falls, probably forever. But it was a nice place, on a nice plat of land. It would be a shame for it to stay vacant, to fall apart slowly, its beams sagging, dust and cobwebs taking over the shelves and corners. They didn't deserve this, I thought, and I meant every one of them: Steve and his family, the house, his cat, and his old hound dog.

"Are you sure you want to do this?" Percy asked as Joe got out and the other cars rolled in and shut off their lights. But nobody answered. We were there already.

We went in through the back door.

"Christ," Percy said, examining it. "It doesn't even have a lock."

"Lots of doors don't have locks," said Joe.

"Maybe they didn't used to," he corrected him. "But after this summer . . ." He trailed off. Lots of locks had been added once the murders started. But no one really imagined we would need them.

We stepped farther into the house and Percy and some of the other guys flicked on their lighters. We let Joe lead the way through the mudroom and then the kitchen, with the pantry off to the right. It was freshly clean—the cupboards shut and the dishes put away, a pair of salt and pepper shakers shaped like little milk bottles rested beside the stove—and I got the sense that someone had tidied it up. Maybe even Bert, after the photos were taken and the room was processed. It was something I could see him doing, going through the kitchen and setting things right that had been knocked over.

"This feels weird," Percy said, "like breaking into somebody's house." He winced. "Well, I know we are, but you know what I mean."

"Yeah. I know what you mean." We were breaking into somebody's house. Except those somebodies were dead. That the house remained filled with so much of their lives—family photos, a stack of clean folded clothes on the bottom step of the staircase—shouldn't have surprised us, I guess, but it did. We were walking through the last echoes of the Carlsons and each new personal thing that rose out of the darkness into the light from our lighters made us jump.

"We shouldn't be in here," one of the others whispered. "It feels wrong."

"Then you shouldn't have come," said Joe.

"No, I mean the house feels wrong," he hissed back.

It was true. The house was beginning to lose its lived-in feel. It had been mostly shut up since the bodies had been moved out and the homey smells of cooking and fresh fabrics and Steve's mother's perfume had begun to settle into the carpets. It was starting to smell like the old farmhouse that it was. I tried not to breathe too deeply, afraid to catch the scent of dried blood or rot. I imagined I could smell it even though I knew the blood at the scene had mostly been on Marie Hale. And even though I knew that Steve's and his parents' bodies hadn't lingered for more than a few hours.

Percy walked into the hallway, footsteps light as a cat's. He reached out and touched a bit of lace beneath a painted vase full of dried flowers, careful to keep the flame of his lighter at safe distance.

"This could be any of our houses," he said.

We looked at each other uncomfortably. Even though the lace and painted vase were nothing like what was inside Mo and Jeannie's place, it really could have been any of our homes. It could have been any of us lying dead that night.

We walked through the hall, and Percy put his hand on the banister, his foot rising to rest on the bottom step beside the pile of folded laundry.

"Well," Percy said as the stair creaked, "no need to go up there, right?"

I looked over his shoulder, through the wide open square that led to the living room. Joe was already there, his lighter tilted toward the floor. It was bare except for chalk marking lines.

I stepped past Percy and went into the room where the Carlsons had died.

Their living room was only a little bigger than the one in our house. A fireplace was set at the south end, and above it was a dark wooden mantel clock. It was no longer running and had stopped at 10:22. The electricity to the house had been shut off but I didn't know when, so there was no way of knowing whether the clock had been stopped intentionally after the murders.

Joe pointed at the floor and asked, "What do you make of that?"

I shrugged. I couldn't make any more sense than anyone else of the marks and numbers the investigators had made in chalk. But staring at it, there was something disturbing about the impermanence—as if the whole of the murders could be blown away by a good wind or rubbed away with our hands.

"There's not much here," Joe said, sounding disappointed. He turned to the couch. It was untouched. Unstained and not the slightest bit askew.

"Hang on," said Percy. "Didn't you say that girl came in covered in blood? Like, covered in it?"

"Yeah."

"So where is it? Where's the rest?"

We looked around. It infuriated me suddenly, to think that Steve and his family had died in this sterile, preserved room. That they had died without a fight, without screaming, with Mrs. Thompson settled into her rocking chair just across the driveway.

"And it's weird that this floor is bare," said Percy. "Was there carpet? Maybe Bert and Charlie tore it up?"

"No, there used to be a rug here," said Morgan. He pushed through us and bent down.

"Under the couch. There's something under the couch."

We dropped to our knees and tugged on it, a large rolled-up rug. Bert, Charlie, or my dad must have rolled it out of the way to mark up the floor. We looked each other in the eye and then unrolled it across the wood.

There was blood on the rug all right, though not three bodies' worth. Instead there were several small pools, close enough together that we could imagine it all: which came from the first body and which from the second and third. We could imagine how they lay, each close enough to the other to touch.

"Christ," Percy said. "We should get out of here."

"Don't get sick," I cautioned. I'd seen him get sick over a deer before. As recently as last season, when he shot one younger than he thought she'd been. A big fawn essentially, barely out of her spots.

"I won't," he said, but he was breathing hard like he was about to. "What the hell's that in the middle?"

I bent to peer at the center of the carpet, where spots of red dotted the rug in an uneven circle. Blood had been smeared and tracked from there in small footprints. And there were smudges near where the bodies bled as well. I swallowed.

"That's the girl."

It was where Marie had stood as all the blood on her hair and clothes dripped down.

"Something's not right," said Joe. "How did she get covered in their blood? It's too clean—" He gestured to the carpet as his voice grew louder, indecently loud in the quiet.

"Take it easy—"

"There must be more! Where is it?"

She had been coated in all of their blood; I'd seen it with my own eyes. I stared at the small sterile spots where Steve and his parents had died—where they fell, where they lay. How did it get from their wounds onto her? Thick and wet and smeared across her face. Soaked into the roots of her hair, red running down to the ends. Enough to saturate her clothes from her shirt to the socks in her shoes. Like it had been poured over her from a bucket.

Walking around on the unrolled carpet, trying to imagine Steve and his parents' final moments, I'd nearly forgotten that anyone else was there, until Percy yelped, "Jesus!"—and grabbed me by the elbow.

"What?" I half shouted.

His arm was stretched out. His lighter was shaking.

"There was a face in the window."

We looked, but whatever he had seen was gone. Nothing there but darkness and the shadows of Mrs. Carlson's lilac bushes.

"I don't see anything," Joe said.

"It was there," Percy said. He said "it" and not "they," and for some reason that made the back of my neck prickle.

"Where there?" I asked.

"Just . . . there!"

"Standing or crouching? A man? A woman? Maybe Fern Thompson?"

"It wasn't Fern Thompson," he said, and gave me a look. But he couldn't explain who it was. The face had simply been there, he was sure of it. Pale and up close and staring. And then it was not. We didn't have much time to ponder it because that's when we heard the distinct sound of tires crunching up the gravel driveway.

"Oh shit," Morgan said.

"Quick, help me roll this up." Joe bent down over the rug. Lighters went out and we hurried to the sides of the carpet, holding our breaths against the faint scent of blood.

"I guess old Widow Thompson wasn't as understanding as you hoped."

We got to our feet in time to hear the back door open, and for Charlie to yell:

"Percy Valentine. Michael Jensen." I couldn't help but notice the way his tone changed between our names—unsurprised for Percy and disappointed for me. We hurried back through the hallway and into the kitchen, and when he saw us, he shook his head, his hands on his hips, feet spread wide like a gunfighter about to draw. "And the rest of you. Let's go, boys."

"Yes, sir," we said, and walked quickly past.

"What the hell were you doing in there? You didn't mess with anything, did you?"

"No, sir."

As we got into Percy's car to follow Charlie to the station, Percy asked, "So how long did Widow Thompson give us before she called you in?"

"Widow Thompson?" Charlie squinted quizzically. "I just saw the backs of your cars when I passed by on the road."

I looked across the yard to Mrs. Thompson's house. She may not have called us in, maybe hadn't seen us drive up at all, but she was watching now. I could see her plainly against the yellowed lace of her curtains. She had Steve's tomcat, who I later learned was called Mr. Stripes, nestled in her arms.

"Is it just you, Charlie?" I asked, even though I saw only the one patrol car. "Bert didn't come?"

"Just me."

"Then who was in the window?" Percy whispered.

CHAPTER SEVEN

At the Station

THE BUNCH OF us being marched into the station was as embarrassing as anything I'd ever experienced. Charlie made me go in first, and I must've been a sorry sight: head hanging, shoes scuffing the floor. He hadn't put cuffs on us or anything, but it felt like he had. I'd never been so ashamed, and I'd never resented anyone so much as I resented Joe Conley and the other guys, though I guess that was kind of unfair.

My dad was standing there; he knew what we'd done. I expected his face to be red to bursting. But he just pulled me aside and whispered, "I expect you know why those boys asked you and Percy along for this." It wasn't a whupping, I suppose. But it was almost worse. He knew we'd been used. And that we should have known better.

"Your parents are coming to get you," my dad said as we stood lined up against the wall and window of his office.

"So, we're not in trouble?" Morgan asked.

"I would guess you'll be in plenty. But not from the law. This was stupid, boys. Stupid and disrespectful. The Federal Bureau is sending out their investigators in the morning, and after that, I'm sending Charlie and Bert out to get rid of everything out there: the rug, the chalk." My dad frowned at me. "Anything that would be worth gawking at."

Down the line, a few of the guys teared up again, and I almost spoke. It hadn't been about that, for them. It had been about Steve.

"Sheriff Jensen, sir," said Joe Conley, "my dad's on shift at the seed factory—"

"Don't worry; we already put a call in. He's on his way."

"He's leaving his shift?"

Percy and I looked at each other. At school we all knew that Joe's father was mean as a snake. That despite Joe's height and athletic build he would sometimes show up in the locker room with bruised ribs and strange marks on his back.

"Can you call and stop him?" Percy asked. "My old man has to come from there, too, and he won't mind. We could bring Joe home, and then I could drive my car and he wouldn't make me leave it—"

"Percy," my dad said. "Shut up."

After that he left us, to stew, I guess, all of us standing there and waiting for the ax to fall. One by one we were taken away, wincing at the storm clouds on our fathers' brows and envious of the ones who were picked up by their mothers, even if Jake Clapper's mom did thump him with her handbag something fierce.

Pretty soon, it was only Joe, Morgan, Percy, and me.

"Hey," Percy hissed to me.

"What?"

"You should tell your dad. About the face."

The face he'd seen in the window out at the Carlson farmhouse.

"You're sure it wasn't Charlie?" I asked.

He shook his head. "Couldn't have been. It was already gone when we heard Charlie pull up. And it didn't look like him. No hat."

"Well, who did it look like?"

But he couldn't say. I asked him about it often over the coming weeks, but in the end he couldn't even be sure if what he saw was a person.

I took a deep breath and went over to my dad.

"What is it, Michael?"

"I don't think we were the only ones at the Carlsons' tonight. Percy says he saw someone else. Standing outside looking in through the living room window."

He reached up and rubbed his eyes and forehead. He was still exhausted, and I felt guiltier than ever.

"But no one else in the house?" he asked.

"Not that we saw."

"All right. I'll send Charlie back out to take a look around, and Nancy," he called across the room to her, "will you call out to State Patrol and see if they'll give us a hand with a twenty-four-hour watch on the Carlson house?"

"Will do."

He turned back to me. "Anything else?"

"No, sir," I said, and returned to my place against the wall.

"I'm sorry we got you into this, Jensen," Joe said.

"You didn't get me into anything," I said. And it was going to be worse for him anyway.

It was another hour before Joe's dad showed up. He walked in looking irritated, but as soon as he saw my father, he shook his hand and apologized for the whole mess. Even thanked him for being so understanding about it since Joe was so broken up about Steve. They made small talk for a few minutes, chuckling about their delinquent sons, Joe's father shaking his head amiably, his big broad shoulders still built like he played football. That niceness was what made him dangerous. If he'd have been a drunk and a screwup like Mo, none of us would have been afraid to talk. But to say Joe's father was cruel? Who would have believed us?

As he and my dad were talking, the door to the interrogation room across the station opened and Marie Hale stepped out with Edwin Porter, our public defender. We all stared, and Mr. Porter tried to hurry her along, but she put her hand on his arm. I didn't know what was going to happen as she stood there, facing us. I was afraid that Joe and Morgan and maybe even Mr. Conley would start shouting at her, demanding to know what she knew. Maybe that's what would have happened, if there hadn't been so few of us left by then. Instead, Mr. Conley broke the stillness by walking to his son and taking him by the collar.

Marie's eyes narrowed as the Conleys left the station, like she sensed that something wasn't right. I wondered what else she'd heard, how much she knew about why we were there and what we'd done. We hadn't heard any sound from inside the interrogation room, but I'd been in there and I knew it wasn't soundproof.

Mr. Porter tried to guide Marie back toward the stairs that led to her cell, but she tugged a little against him and stared through the windows that faced the parking lot. Then her eyes narrowed again, and she looked at me and motioned with her chin. I knew immediately what she meant. Joe's dad hadn't bothered to wait until they got home. He'd pulled him into a dark spot beside the building.

I pushed off the wall and went to the window. I could see them. Just the shapes of them pressed against the wall.

"Dad!"

I called him over and he looked. Then he pushed through the door with Charlie not far behind.

"Stay inside, the rest of you," Charlie ordered. He pointed to Mr. Porter and Marie. "And get her back up to her cell!"

Nancy got to her feet behind the receptionist desk and hurried to help, a set of keys jangling in her hands.

"Come on, dear," she said, and I couldn't tell whether she was speaking to Marie or Mr. Porter, a small man with a bald pate and wisps of dark hair. She ushered them through the station toward the stairs, and Marie looked over her shoulder at me.

"What do you think's happening out there?" Percy asked. It had gone quiet after my dad's initial shouts. Then it started again, and we heard a new voice join in.

"Oh Christ, it's Mo," Percy groaned. "He's bound to make things worse."

But he didn't. Though Mo can sometimes complicate things, he also has a knack for speeding things up, and within two minutes he and my dad came back inside the station with Joe walking between them. Joe was crying, and his nose and lips were bloody. In the parking lot, Mr. Conley started his car and drove away.

"Should have dragged him in here and thrown him in a cell," Mo said angrily.

"Next time," my dad said. "If there is a next time. For now . . ."

"He can stay with us," Morgan said. "We're used to it."

"Is that all right with you, son?" my dad asked, and Joe nodded.

"I don't know what's keeping my mom," said Morgan. "My dad has the car, but she can usually ask our neighbor. . . ."

"Percy and I'll take them," Mo said. "You boys ride with me in the truck and Percy can follow behind in that rust-bucket car of his."

"All right," my dad said. "I'll call Mrs. Todd and tell her to expect you."

It wasn't long after they left that my dad gave up his silent treatment and led me out to the cruiser to go home.

"Thanks for doing that, Dad," I said as we drove. "It was . . ." I searched for the right word. Brave. Heroic. Good.

"It was nothing," he said softly. Then he shook his head and patted my knee. "I didn't mean that. It wasn't nothing. It was just another bad, bad thing."

"But Dad—"

"It's all right. I know we can't fix all of it. But it would be nice, right now, to fix just one."

That night, long after the rest of my family was asleep, I sat awake in my bedroom thinking about the Carlson place. The empty rooms like time had stopped. The dark pools of blood soaked into the carpet. And that strange red circle the size of a girl. Every Bloodless Murder had more questions than answers. But these were questions about people we knew. I imagined Steve, lying with his throat cut across from his mother and his expression of disbelief as they both died. I imagined his father, trying to protect everyone. Except that it didn't seem he had. He had lain down right beside them, and his blood had formed a similar, quiet stain.

When I finally slept, in my dreams I was inside that house. Only Steve's father was my father. And my mother and Dawn were standing in the Carlson living room on top of that stained carpet. In the dream I couldn't save them. In the dream, they were standing there but they were already dead.

CHAPTER EIGHT

Monsters

AS PENANCE FOR what I'd done and not at all to eavesdrop, I spent a lot of time that weekend sweeping up and doing chores around the jail. And after a little while, Bert and Charlie stopped treating me like I was in trouble and things went back to normal. Normal enough that Nancy, our receptionist, didn't think it strange to ask me to go upstairs and see Marie.

"What for?" I asked.

Nancy shrugged. "She heard you were here and asked for you. I don't see much harm in it as long as you don't stay too long." She glanced out the windows. It would be growing dark soon. Everyone's mother wanted them home before dark those days.

I made my way through the building, past the empty offices and the corridor that led to the men's cells—also empty, as if even the drunks were respectfully restraining themselves on account of the murders. I mounted the steps to the women's cell and my old house with its white-painted door. It occurred to me that Marie and I were nearly the only two people inside the whole place.

It was irresponsible of Nancy to let me go. She hadn't even asked Charlie for the okay. But Nancy was beautiful enough to be famous and, as such, she pretty much had her run of things. Not to mention, after her personal tragedy—Nancy had lost her little girl in a house fire some years back, along with her husband—not even my dad had the heart to scold her.

I knocked on the door to the women's cell. When I got no reply, I opened it a fraction and said, "Marie?"

"Yes?"

"May I come in?" I pushed the door a little farther, wide enough to see a sliver of her back. She was seated on her bed in another pair of blue jeans and possibly the same white shirt.

"This isn't my room, Michael," she said. "It's a jail. You don't need to ask permission."

I hesitated. When it became clear that I was unable to move without say-so, she said, "And I did ask you to come. So come in."

She had her hair down again, brushed back from her face. One knee was drawn up, hands folded in front of it with her fingers intertwined. She was staring out the window, though from that angle she wouldn't have been able to see much but a few treetops and some sky. I stepped into the room and awkwardly shuffled about, trying to decide whether to stand or to pull a chair over from the kitchen.

"You don't smell like beer anymore," she said. "Like you did the other night."

"Oh," I said, and wiped at my chest like the scent was still there and would come off. "I'm sorry."

She shrugged. "I'm used to it. Maybe it even reminds me of home."

"Where is home?"

"Nebraska," she said. "You know that."

But by then Nebraska was only a guess. No one had been able to locate a girl by the name of Marie Catherine Hale and there were no girls reported missing who matched her description, aside from a few runaways whose families would later shake their heads when they were shown Marie's picture, disappointed and also relieved.

She turned on her bed, and the movement barely caused a shift in the thin mattress, the edges of which were carefully made with what my mother called "hospital corners." She looked me up and down.

"Though none of the fellas I knew walked around smelling like beer in a necktie."

I remembered what we were wearing that night—our church clothes from attending the funerals.

"The funerals were that day."

"Oh," she said.

She didn't ask about the Carlsons' funerals, not the whole time she was with us. It might have seemed macabre if she had. Perverse. At times during our conversations I wondered whether she realized that and the omission was deliberate.

She did, however, ask if I knew them.

"You must have," she said. "In a small, kind town like this."

"I did. Steve was in my year at school."

"What was he like?"

"Steve? He was nice. He played football . . . tight end, I think."

"And you knew him a long time?"

"Since first grade at least."

"What else?"

"What do you mean?"

"What else can you tell me about him?"

"I don't know if I should." And at that point there wasn't much more to tell. It was still too soon for the folks of Black Deer Falls to have mined each other's memories, to revisit our every interaction with the Carlsons and go through their belongings until we all felt like better friends. And being there with Marie felt wrong. Talking about his life with the girl who had been found slicked with his and his parents' blood. Even though it was hard to believe that she had anything to do with it. Every time I looked at her my brain wrestled with the sight of her the same way any jury would have: she couldn't have done it. She wouldn't. She was too small. Too young. Too pretty. And she was a girl. Only her accomplice could make it make sense. After we had him, then we could look on her as we pleased, casting her as the frightened hostage or the present-day Bonnie Parker who seduced him into it and egged him on.

Marie sighed. She stretched her arms up over her shoulders and something in the stretch made me look away, as if it was too intimate. I thought again that we were alone and I had rarely been alone with a girl except on dates to the drive-in or the café.

"You didn't bring any smokes, did you?"

"I forgot. Next time, I promise."

"Next time," she said quietly. "Well then, what did I ask you here for?"

I watched her as she tucked her knees up under her chin and hugged her legs. How many times had I seen my little sister, Dawn, sitting on the porch swing just the same way, her little brow furrowed, eyes narrowed to slits and hard as marbles, thinking unknowable young girls' thoughts? But Marie Hale had far more secrets than Dawn. There were so many things I wanted to ask. How did the murders happen? Why were there no signs of a struggle? Why were they chosen? *Where was the blood?*

Always, always, where was the blood.

It seemed impossible that she could know.

"Do you believe in monsters, Michael?"

"Monsters? Not since I was seven."

"Seven. That's pretty old to, I guess. But it's not right either. Deep down we all believe in monsters."

Her gaze drifted back to the window.

"Before this is over, you won't believe the kinds of things you'll hear about me. Maybe even about your friend Steven. He'll be the one they focus on, you know. Not his old father or his adult mother. Just him. So young and handsome. And that little baby, so tragically left behind." She snorted. "Like it'd been better if . . ." Marie stopped. She didn't like talking about that baby. She never wanted to hear about Patricia, except for once weeks later when she asked if the aunt who took her in had really wanted her.

"Did your friend Steven date a lot? Did he get around?"

I thought it was an odd way to phrase it; boys didn't "get around."

"He dated some. Nice girls, mostly."

"Mostly?" she asked. "Isn't that the only kind you have here?" She slid her hands down her legs and fiddled with the rolled cuffs of the jeans she wore. She looked nervous—no, not nervous. Restless. Like it was taking all of her restraint to stay on that cot. I wished I smoked; I'd have given her one just to calm her down.

"It won't matter anyway," she said. "Who he dated. They'll find everything out. Where they went. What they did in the backs of cars, because even the nice girls do *something*. Maybe they'll keep the details out of the papers. But they'll hint. Like they did with those two nurses. Just a small note that they were regulars at the roadhouse and had many acquaintances there. *Acquaintances.* Damn reporters." Shockingly, she spit on the floor.

"You've been following the papers."

"Of course we were. But it isn't just the reporters. It's everyone. If the victim is young or beautiful, such a tragedy, they say. Such a loss. That's how it starts." She cocked her head, coquettish. "Then they change their tune. Not enough to be . . . defamatory. Just enough to make folks wonder: What could something so beautiful have done to deserve it?"

"No one could deserve that," I said quietly.

"I know." She sighed and put her feet down. "But it doesn't stop them from wondering. Have you ever heard of Mercy Lena Brown?"

I shook my head.

"She was a girl from Exeter, Rhode Island, who lived in the 1800s. She died when she was nineteen, and shortly after, her neighbors became convinced that she was returning from the grave and draining the life from her brother. So they dug her back up and cut her apart—they cut off her head so she wouldn't rise again; they burned her heart in the town square and fed her poor brother the ashes."

"That's—" I said as my mind struggled to recall what little I knew of New England. Hadn't the Salem witch trials been not long before that? Wasn't the whole region prone to fits of hysteria, with each citizen granted a torch and pitchfork upon reaching majority age? "That's ghoulish. And ridiculous."

"I suppose it was," said Marie. "But it wasn't to them." At the time, I had never heard of Mercy Brown. It sounded made-up. A folk-legend. But it wasn't. It was one of many fear-induced exhumations peppered throughout New England and even stretching into the Midwest. When I was researching it, I actually found some references to exhumations in Minnesota.

"Tuberculosis is what she died of," Marie said. "A doctor said that when they cut her open, but no one cared. They fed her tubercular heart to her brother anyway, and they did it with their father's permission."

She smiled a little at those final words.

"Did it save him?" I asked. "The brother?"

"No, it didn't save him! Michael." She shook her head at me. "He joined her in the cemetery, not six months later. Of course, they left *him* whole." We both laughed a little. I was embarrassed to have asked.

"You know," I said, "Steve wasn't really my friend."

"I figured. You two . . . didn't seem a matched type." She leaned back and stretched her neck. "The prosecutor from Nebraska's on his way," she said, and raised her nose like she could catch his scent. "I guess they're going to charge me there, too. They must be finding my footprints and fingerprints everywhere. Putting it all together."

"Why don't you just tell them who was with you?" I asked. "Why don't you just give him up?"

"Because," she said simply, "it wouldn't do any good."

After that I went back downstairs. Nobody saw me coming back from the women's cell, or if they did they didn't say anything, maybe to save themselves the headache of telling my dad.

I walked over to Charlie as he sat at his desk doing paperwork and pretending not to steal glances at Nancy.

"Charlie?"

"Yeah, Michael?"

"Did you go back out to the Carlson farm last night to have a look around?"

"Right after you and your dad left for home. Didn't find anything—no other tire tracks, no evidence that anyone had been messing with the doors."

"No footprints in the flower beds?"

"Not a one. And I checked all around the house, not just where you said by the living room window. I even woke poor Fern

Thompson to ask if she'd heard anything, so she won't thank you for that."

"Okay. Thanks anyway," I said softly.

I went home that night, and didn't think anything more of Percy's "face in the window." At the time, it was easy enough to believe it had all been in his imagination.

CHAPTER NINE

The Prosecutor from Nebraska

DISTRICT ATTORNEY BENJAMIN Pilson arrived in Black Deer Falls on September 24, six days after the killings of Steve and his parents. He was six-foot-two, with a straight back and a fine haircut, and he blew into town with a mind to take charge of an investigation he viewed as having been poorly handled by the small-town local authorities. He wasn't wrong about that exactly—my dad and the deputies had made no headway with Marie, and evidence from the Carlson house hadn't yielded any new clues about the killer or his methods, but you would have thought Pilson was the lead federal investigator from the way he burst into my dad's station, all necktie and stiff handshakes. He didn't pay much attention to Bert, but he was downright charming to Nancy, leaning over her desk and complimenting the big gold brooch she wore every Wednesday. As for me, sweeping quietly in the back, I might as well have been invisible. Until later, when he had a use for me, which told me everything I needed to know about the kind of man Benjamin Pilson really was.

My dad took Pilson into his office, but he didn't close the door. It wasn't hard to slide up with my broom and overhear what they were saying.

Turns out, he had come to try and take Marie.

"We'd like to get her down to trial in Nebraska," he said.

"I'm sure you would," my dad replied. "And I'm sure you will, eventually. But from what I understand we have the best shot right here: a suspect found at the scene of the crime, covered in blood, and a room full of finger- and shoe prints."

"That is true. You and your deputies are owed more than a cold beer. I hope you'll let me buy you one on behalf of the citizens of Nebraska."

"Thank you," my dad said. "I'm sure Charlie and Bert won't say no to that."

"Were they the first on the scene?" Pilson asked.

"Charlie and myself. We secured Miss Hale and the surviving minor child and conducted an initial search of the premises."

"That must have been harrowing. I've heard you were acquainted with the victims?"

"I was. And I don't mind telling you it was the hardest thing I've ever had to do."

Pilson paused. "So it was just you and . . ."

"Deputy Charles Morris," my dad supplied. "Joined shortly by Minnesota State Police."

There was a beat of silence. My dad's tone was losing its ease.

"I wish you'd found a murder weapon," Pilson said finally.

"So do I," my dad said. "But no one has that I've heard of."

"I heard you had some trouble out there the other night. Some local boys, compromising the scene."

My broom froze in my hands.

"I don't know how you heard that, Mr. Pilson, but the scene had already been processed. And I don't know what your hurry is. Nebraska will have its turn, just like Wisconsin and Iowa."

"Wisconsin can't place her at the scene. Not so much as a footprint. And I spoke to the Iowa prosecutor this morning and he's happy to continue their investigation while I take a run at it first. I'm not trying to take anything away from you; I want to work in conjunction with you—"

"From Lincoln."

"Yes, from Lincoln."

I heard the creak of my dad's chair as he leaned back. "I think we'd like to keep her here."

There was a pause, and Pilson asked, "What have you gotten out of her? A name? A motive?"

"As for a name, only her own."

"Marie Catherine Hale," said Pilson. "We had no luck tracking down anyone with that name either. But we're working on it. She's probably from Nebraska, after all, since Nebraska is where this all started."

He'd been right about that, even if he didn't truly know it then. He was thinking of the first known victim at that time: Peter Knupp from Loup City.

"I'd like to meet with the prisoner," Pilson said.

"Of course."

I quickly moved away as my dad got up to show Mr. Pilson to the interrogation room. This time Pilson noticed me, and after an appraising glance he shot me a fast hard wink.

"Bert," my dad said, "will you please bring Miss Hale to speak with the Nebraska District Attorney?"

Bert went up and got her, and on her way through the station she looked at me. Then he escorted her inside.

"Kind of a pretty thing, isn't she?" Pilson said.

"Barely more than a child," said my dad.

"Has she seemed traumatized? Frightened? Has she given any explanation for her involvement?"

"She hasn't said much of anything."

Pilson walked in and closed the door.

I wish I could have listened, but every eye in the station was on the interrogation room. And anyway, it wasn't long before Marie started to shout.

"You can't do that, you dirty bastard! I didn't do anything! I didn't do it!"

Nancy and I looked at each other; Nancy had her hand to her mouth. Marie had been so calm and quiet since the night of the murders. After another minute, Pilson came out and straightened his tie while Marie continued to wail and curse.

"What on earth did you do?" my dad asked.

"She'll calm down," Pilson replied. He held out his hand, and my dad, ever polite, shook it. "I'll see you in St. Paul in a few days, Sheriff Jensen. I've arranged a special hearing with the district court." He glanced back at the interrogation room, and the screaming girl inside. "You'll get some peace and quiet again after I take her with me to Lincoln." And then he strode out of the building, leaving my dad to clean up the mess.

"She won't quit," Bert called as he tried to calm Marie. "Sheriff!"

My dad reached for his handcuffs.

"Not the cuffs, Rick," Nancy objected.

"It's only for a minute. We can't have her injuring herself."

He went in and we listened to them wrestle—to Marie screeching and to my dad's voice, always steady, telling her he wasn't going to hurt her. Pretty soon it was quiet except for her breathing (and Bert's).

"What did he say to you," my dad asked, "that upset you so?"

I crept closer until I could see her, hands cuffed to the table, half standing and arms taut against the bonds like a horse trying to pull free. She looked right at me.

"He wants to try me for felony murder!"

"But you didn't kill anyone," I said. "Did you?"

"No!"

At the time we didn't know that in Nebraska, a person could be convicted of felony murder even if they were not the one with their hand on the knife or their finger on the trigger. Nor did we know that such a conviction could result in a penalty of death. We thought that Pilson was just blowing smoke.

"If you're innocent, it would go easier if you'd tell us what happened," my dad said. "Just explain it to us, piece by piece. Even if you can't give us his name."

Marie closed her eyes and shook her head fiercely. "He wants to kill me," she kept saying. "He wants to kill me."

"You have to defend yourself, Miss Hale. Or we can't help you."

She opened her eyes.

"I'll tell *him*," she said, and nodded to me.

"What, you mean Michael?"

"Yes. Michael. I'll tell him everything. But only Michael."

CHAPTER TEN

The District Courthouse

I THOUGHT I'D misheard. Marie Catherine Hale, the only witness and presumed accomplice to the killing spree that had frozen the entire country, chose me to hear her story.

"Absolutely not," my dad said to me when we got home.

"But why not?" my mom asked.

My dad and I turned. We hadn't seen her standing in the kitchen, the glasses that usually hung around her neck perched on the end of her nose, using her thumb to hold her place in a novel.

"What?" my dad asked. "And how do you know about it already?"

"Nancy called me from the station. She said that Michael is the only one the girl's been willing to talk to."

"Nancy." My dad put his hands on his hips and shook his head like he was going to give her an earful, but we knew he would do no such thing. He looked at my mom. "You can't want him to do this."

"Didn't you tell me last night that you weren't getting anywhere?"

"That's not the point." He glanced at me and spoke in a low whisper. "The things he would have to hear—he's just a boy."

"I'm seventeen," I said. Then they looked at me and I looked at the floor.

"You weren't inside that house," my dad said. "You didn't see those bodies."

"He won't have to see, though, will he? Just to hear."

"If we agree to this, it'll amount to a confession, and he'll be privy to the entire investigation. Blood evidence. Autopsy reports. The photographs of the Carlsons and the rest of the murders, too."

My mom paled. She hadn't thought of that. Honestly I hadn't either. But I would be lying if I said I didn't want to do it. I wanted to see and I wanted to hear and I wanted to be the first to know. Even then I knew that Marie's confession was the story of a lifetime, the interview any reporter in the country would have killed for.

"Linda," my dad said. "You don't want him to see all that, do you?"

I didn't dare move a muscle while she thought about it, afraid to look too young and make her say no. Afraid to seem too eager and make her say no for a different reason.

"If that's what she wants," my mom said, "and the judge says it's all right, then who are we to say he can't? She deserves to confess, doesn't she, if she played a part in it? And Bob and Sarah and Steven . . . don't they deserve it, too?"

My dad's shoulders slumped.

After that, getting the other officials to sign on was easy. Mr.
Porter reviewed the request, and after determining that it didn't
violate any of Marie's rights, he agreed to advocate for her at the
district court hearing that Nebraska DA Pilson had set up. Our
prosecutor also gave the okay, and—a little surprisingly—so did
the DAs from Wisconsin and Iowa. I didn't know them and have
never seen their pictures, but in my imagination they look a lot like
Mr. Porter: balding and tired around the eyes, long past dreams
of courtroom glory.

But what it really was, was that none of them really wanted
Marie. They wanted him. The one who the search teams and state
patrol were still looking for. The one who might kill still more.

When Mr. Pilson heard about the confession, he dismissed it as
a joke, though it was later heard from a woman who worked at the
St. Paul hotel where he was staying that he smashed the telephone
down so hard he cracked it.

Benjamin Pilson was not about to let a girl's whims derail his
plans. He was of the fire-and-brimstone sort, firmly on the punishment side of the punishment versus rehabilitation argument.
He was not swayed by Marie's youth nor by her sex nor by the
incredulity that she would be capable of committing such heinous murders. He wanted her brought to Nebraska in chains. He
wanted her dragged before a jury. He may have also been coming
up for reelection.

The day of Marie's hearing, I rode with my dad in his cruiser
while Marie rode in a separate transport driven by Charlie and

accompanied by Mr. Porter and my mom. The drive to St. Paul took several hours, and by the time we arrived I was already sweating through my good church shirt. One hearing would decide whether Marie would stay in Minnesota or be transported back to Nebraska. It would decide whether my part in the story was just beginning or whether Marie and the Bloodless Murders would vanish from Black Deer Falls as abruptly as they came.

My dad found a parking space down the street, and I got out and looked up at the Ramsey County Courthouse, a tower of golden limestone with rows of windows running down it like silver ribbons. There was a flurry of black cars and reporters between us and the entrance.

"What am I doing here, Dad?" I asked. I had no experience in interrogation; I had never taken a confession. I was a would-be journalist who had delivered papers and chatted with a local editor.

"You don't have to do this, Michael," my dad said. "Not any of it."

But I did, didn't I? For Steve and his family, and for the other victims we hadn't known. Marie Catherine Hale had to talk. Whoever had cut that bloody trail through four states was still out there, and she was the only person alive who knew who he was.

I took a breath and walked toward the crowd of people that stretched down the street and even across it, flooding the sidewalk that looked across the Mississippi River to Harriet Island. The city smelled like exhaust and, from farther away, of something fried in butter and the meaty whiff of a hamburger. My stomach rumbled, but I couldn't have eaten a bite. There were so many reporters. When we reached them their car doors cracked open and they spilled out around us like eager insects. Pilson had said it would be a quiet hearing. But I would come to learn that Benjamin Pilson loved the press.

"Is it true she was found alone and covered in blood?"

"Were the bodies bled like those kids in Wisconsin?"

"Had they been bound? What about the baby?"

Cameras flashed right after the questions, as if the questions weren't important and were only meant to rattle us, to coax out the perfect expressions of horror. Then, just as quickly as they'd come, they disappeared, pushing and shoving back toward the street.

Marie had arrived.

The papers hadn't published any photos of her yet—they couldn't, as no one had been able to verify her identity—so the country hadn't been able to paint any kind of picture. Was she pretty? Ugly? Poor? No one could say. But that would change. The photo that everyone came to associate with Marie Catherine Hale was taken as she walked into the courthouse.

She looked different in her court clothes: a mid-length black skirt belted at the waist, a white blouse with long sleeves, and a dark green sweater draped over her shoulders. Her hair was tied back with what would become her signature black ribbon, and she was helped along by an escort of Edwin Porter on one side and my mother on the other. My mom was well-prepared for the task; she used one hand to fend off reporters and kept the other clamped onto Marie's thin elbow. Marie flinched and pulled a little in her grip as she shied away from the flashbulbs. Later, the photos would show a very pretty, somewhat reluctant girl with a fashionable hairstyle and carefully done makeup. A few caught her gazing wistfully away, toward the river. Toward better days, thought some. Toward escape, thought others. But the photograph that stuck was one of her smiling—just with one side of her mouth. It had only been a moment—a reporter had called out some silly thing, and she had smiled. But that instant would damn her in so many minds as the murderess who smiled while people lay dead. In the photos her lips appeared dark. They were often called crimson.

"Where'd she get the lipstick?" I asked.

"Your mother gave it to her," my father said, a bit dazedly. "She got her ready for the trip. I didn't know your mother owned a lipstick like that."

Inside the courthouse, the frenzy of reporters was worse. A regular circus, my dad said.

"They're only doing their jobs," I replied. But the looks in their eyes were as quick and blank as a bird's hunting for bugs in the grass.

Inside the courtroom we took seats behind our prosecutor, Mr. Norquist, who had come to represent the interests of the people of Minnesota—a formality since he had already agreed to Marie's request. Marie's lawyer, Mr. Porter, was beside him. And Marie would have the final chair.

"You doing all right, Michael?" Mr. Norquist asked me.

"Yes, sir."

"Good. You shouldn't need to say anything more than, 'yes, your honor,' should the judge ask you anything." He nodded to Benjamin Pilson when he came in and took his seat on the opposite side. Pilson just smiled, lines going deep into the sides of his mouth.

It was a closed hearing—cobbled together and as informal as could be wrangled. But it felt plenty formal to me. And after the buzzing crush of the street and the interior of Memorial Hall, my fingers twitched to loosen my tie.

"So," the judge said, and folded his hands together. "All of you are here to fight over who gets to prosecute this little girl first."

"That's . . . a bit of a mischaracterization, your honor," Mr. Norquist said. "We all of us in every state wish to get to the bottom of this."

"All right." The judge studied some papers. "And Wisconsin and Iowa agree that Minnesota can take the first crack at it. But not you, Mr. Pilson?"

"That's correct, your honor," Pilson said.

"And why is that? Nebraska isn't even the state where the most murders occurred"—that dubious honor went to Iowa—"so why take her back there? Simply because it's where it all began?"

"Yes, your honor. And because, since Nebraska is where it all began, we feel certain that Marie Catherine Hale is from our state. That she is a daughter of Nebraska."

"A Nebraska daughter," the judge mused, "subject first to Nebraska discipline."

Pilson handed a sheaf of photographs to the bailiff. The judge looked through them as Pilson described them at length.

"Peter Knupp. A lifelong resident of Loup City, Nebraska. Only twenty-six years old. He worked night shifts as a machinist and had recently purchased his first home. On the morning of August third he was found on the front porch of that home, laid out and bled like a hog. Cuts at his throat, and the interior of the thigh. Angela Hawk. Twenty-two. Found beside her good friend Beverly Nordahl, also aged twenty-two. They were discovered sitting upright in the driver's and passenger seats of Miss Hawk's car with their throats slit."

The judge pursed his lips and set down the photos. "We've all heard these facts before. We've read about these heinous and vicious acts and agree that they were heinous and vicious. Is that the only point you're trying to make?"

Our prosecutor, Mr. Norquist, stood.

"Your honor. The fact is Marie Catherine Hale was apprehended in Minnesota. Covered in the victims' blood. And it is in Minnesota that she has agreed to confess her level of involvement. To give these families the comfort of the truth and provide the country with answers regarding the—impossible nature—of these crimes!"

The judge paused. Mr. Norquist had said the magic word. *Answers.* Answers were what we craved, even more than justice. Why hadn't they struggled? How had he done it? And where, where was all the blood?

"I've been informed there is ample evidence tying these new

killings to the others," the judge said. "We do know they're connected? More blood was found on this young lady, after all, than at all of the other crime scenes combined."

"Her fingerprints and some footprints have now been identified at other scenes," Pilson affirmed.

"But no evidence of anyone else? A larger, stronger perpetrator?"

"No, your honor."

"And now she wishes to recount the events of the killings to one young"—he looked down at his papers—"Michael Jensen?"

"Which is a ridiculous notion," Pilson began. But the judge silenced him.

"I think it's time to hear from the girl in question. Miss Hale?"

Marie looked up. "Yes, sir?"

"Why would you want to give your statement in this way?"

She looked at Mr. Pilson. "He wants to say I killed them when I didn't."

"And do you understand that anything you say during the investigation can be used against you in a court of law?"

"Yes, sir."

"And do you understand that under this agreement you have been offered no protections against further prosecution—no deals—and may become subject to punishment depending upon what is discovered through your statements?"

Marie hesitated again, this time for much longer. "I just want to tell my story. And for him not to be able to kill me for something I didn't do!"

"Kill you?" the judge asked, and looked to Pilson.

"Your honor, in the State of Nebraska one does not need to be the perpetrator of a murder in order to be convicted of felony murder," Mr. Pilson said. "And the conviction may constitute a sentence of capital punishment."

The judge blinked. "The death penalty?"

We were all silent. Marie was so young. And a girl.

"Yes, your honor," said Pilson. "And just so there is no future confusion on the part of Miss Hale, I want it known that I believe the State of Nebraska has a right to justice on behalf of these young people whose lives have been cruelly taken."

Marie's attorney, Mr. Porter, stood quickly, skidding his chair slightly across the marble floor.

"Your honor, are we discussing execution for a girl who is willing to fully cooperate—?"

"As she sees fit," Pilson said. "She's only cooperating as she sees fit."

"She is fifteen years old," Mr. Porter said.

"Nearly sixteen. Based on the birth date she has provided. Not that we've been able to verify it or to find record in any state of a person by the name of Marie Catherine Hale. . . ." He leafed through his papers as if he might suddenly find some. "Yet the State of Minnesota is ready to accept whatever tale this alleged murderess wants to tell, when she stands accused of participating in the willful slaughter of fifteen individuals, including a father, mother, and son killed with their youngest daughter watching.

"I had heard that Minnesota was a kind part of the country,

but perhaps 'kind' was the wrong word. Perhaps the word is 'fool-hardy.'"

My dad gave a soft, annoyed snort. I expected that the judge would remind Mr. Pilson that he was standing before a Minnesota court. But he turned his attention to Marie.

"Miss Hale."

"Yes, your honor?"

"Do you understand that you are entitled to a defense and are in no way obligated to admit to any involvement or wrongdoing prior to your trial?"

"I don't want there to be a trial."

"Do you mean then to enter a plea of guilty and waive your right to a trial by a jury of your peers?"

"No, sir. I only want to tell Michael what happened."

"Miss Hale, how exactly are you acquainted with Michael Jensen?"

"He's the sheriff's son. He was there when I was brought in. And he's visited me a couple of times."

"Has he made you any promises? Coerced you in any way?"

"No, sir."

"And you," he said to me, "Mr. Jensen. Are you willing to undertake the recording of Miss Hale's accounting, knowing the grievous responsibility it entails?"

"I am, your honor."

"Your honor," said Marie, "all I ask is to stay at the jail in Black Deer Falls and tell my story to who I choose. I don't want anything else."

The judge looked at Marie, sadly, like he thought she was making a mistake.

"Why not tell an adult?" he asked. "Mr. Porter, or even that nice lady behind you?" He gestured to my mother.

"Because, sir," she replied, "I know I'm young but I've been around long enough to know that you can't really trust adults."

"Sweetheart, that's not true."

"I only want to tell Michael."

"But why?"

"Because he's the only one who'll believe me."

The judge waited a long time, until he was sure she wouldn't be moved.

"Counselors, approach."

Pilson and Mr. Norquist went, with poor Mr. Porter hurrying behind. Mr. Porter would tell me later that he had bargained for all he was worth. That nothing swayed the Nebraska DA except the dangling of the bigger fish: if Marie gave up her accomplice and he was subsequently convicted, Mr. Pilson would lobby his governor to spare Marie's life.

"Marie Catherine Hale," the judge said. "It is the decision of this court that you be granted your request. In Minnesota you were arrested and in Minnesota you will stay."

Pilson scowled. "The State of Nebraska would ask that it be allowed to appoint its own investigators to verify whatever claims are made by the accused."

"You spend your taxpayers' money however you see fit, Mr. Pilson."

Mr. Porter cleared his throat. "And should Miss Hale's confession lead to the capture or arrest of the primary perpetrator, we would argue for leniency in sentencing."

"Mr. Porter, that is an argument for another day." The judge banged his gavel, and Mr. Porter shrank. Over the years that he had been our prosecutor, I'd seen him go before Judge Vernon lots of times. But that day he seemed rattled, like he had never pled a case.

As we walked out of the building, well behind Marie and the throng of reporters, I heard Pilson call my name.

"Young Michael Jensen," he said, and shook my hand.

"Yes, sir."

"Thank you for coming here today, son." He smiled. It was all ease and no hard feelings. "I guess I'll see you back in Black Deer Falls." He walked away. We'd pass him again in front of the courthouse, surrounded by reporters.

"He's coming back to Black Deer Falls?" I asked.

"By the time all this is over, I expect he'll nearly be a legal resident," quipped Mr. Porter, and my dad chuckled. Mr. Porter looked at me regretfully. "Kidding aside," he said, "you know this is only just beginning. It isn't just justice that hangs in the balance. It's Marie Hale's life. None of this is going to be easy. Or fast."

He was right about that. Marie Catherine Hale would be with us into the winter, until she was transferred to Lincoln for her trial, and execution.

"Something else on your mind, Ed?" my dad asked. "You seem uneasy."

"I suppose I am. There's something about Marie. Something that hasn't sat quite right."

"What's that?" my dad asked.

"She has never once indicated that she's sorry."

CHAPTER ELEVEN

An Unqualified Interviewer

BY THE TIME I returned to school the next day, word about the confession had already spread throughout Black Deer Falls. Ever since the funerals and our ill-advised break-in of the Carlsons' home, my name had been passed around in frantic whispers, and I kept thinking of what Marie had said, how she figured that Steve and I hadn't been friends. How we weren't a matched type: Steve the all-American athlete and me the by-the-book sheriff's kid who read too much and didn't care if his baseball team made the playoffs.

Before Marie, people had known who I was, but I'd still been invisible. After the court decided I could interview her, it was like I'd been painted red. My English teacher, Mr. Janek, watched me from behind his desk for the first five minutes of class as if he expected me to present a note asking to be excused. When I didn't, he got up and stumbled through his lesson, making the chalk cry against the board and looking at me every time he did it, like it was my fault.

In the halls between classes, I existed in a bubble of quiet. Except for Percy.

"So," he said, and leaned against my locker. "When do you start?"

"I'm going to see her after school. But I don't know if she'll say anything important, or if I'm supposed to—" I stopped. It occurred to me for the millionth time that I had no idea what I was doing.

"You nervous?"

"Yeah. Really nervous."

My dad had coached me a little, running me through the facts of the case, cautioning me against leading her in one direction or another. "Don't put any ideas into her head," he'd said. "Just let her talk." He'd brought out a map of the United States and marked the locations of the murders with a red pen, writing the dates beside them and tracing the likely trail of the killers along the highways through Nebraska to Iowa, to Wisconsin and back to us. "If there are any inconsistencies, don't call her out. Don't be confrontational. We can go through it all together, after you're finished."

"What have you heard," I asked Percy, "around town?"

Percy shrugged. "Jeannie says there's a women's coalition forming at church, but they can't decide whether it's a coalition to run her out of town or to protest her being locked up in the first place."

"Is Jeannie still keeping that shotgun by the door?"

He nodded. My parents were still locking the extra locks, too, and keeping Dawn's curfew well before dark. It wasn't over for us. The eyes on me weren't just curious; they wanted me to do something. I was used to them looking at my dad that way. I never realized how heavy it would feel.

"The Nebraska DA wants to kill her, Percy."

He blinked.

"But he won't," he said. "I mean, lock her up forever, sure. But she's a girl. Nobody's going to execute a girl, no matter what she did."

"Maybe." I looked at the clock on the wall above our lockers. "I don't know how to talk to her. I don't know what to say."

"What do you mean?" he asked.

"I mean she's gone through something." But I couldn't figure out how to tell him what I meant. That something had happened to Marie Hale in a way that nothing had ever happened to us. Guilty or innocent, she'd traveled through something terrible. That made her different, and it made her intimidating, no matter whether she was younger than I was or if she was a girl.

"Maybe I should talk to Mr. McBride," I said. "Do you think he would mind?"

"Do I think he would mind," Percy said, and made a face. "I think he'll jump all over it. Go over at lunch and I'll cover for you in history."

By covering for me, he meant clowning so hard that Miss Murray couldn't think of anything besides rapping him across the knuckles. Good old Percy.

So at lunch, I made my way across town to the *Star*, where Mr. McBride welcomed me despite it being during school hours.

"Michael," he said when I poked my head into his office. He stood up and came over to shake my hand. He never treated me like a kid—not since I had told him I wanted to become a journalist. He treated me like I already was one, even though I was really just another of his delivery boys. "What brings you by?" I stood there for a moment, dumbfounded, but he just smiled, a thin man with dark brown hair that my mother judged as "a little too long but becoming for his profession." He wore a gray button-up shirt and a tie, like he did most days. He almost never wore a jacket. He had glasses with black frames over blue eyes, and they made him look sharp. Clever. I used to wish my own eyes were no good so I would need a pair.

"You don't need to tell me why you're here," he said. "I heard about the Hale confession." He walked back around his desk and sat down, an invitation to sit across from him.

"It's really more of an interview," I said. And what an interview it was. After it was over I could attend any journalism program that I wanted, and the college would probably pay for it. Not bad for a kid from Nowhere, Minnesota.

Mr. McBride knew that, too, but he just smiled, happy to wait in the silence. He was a good interviewer.

"It shouldn't be me," I blurted finally. "It should be you. Or Walter Cronkite."

"My name in the same breath as Walter Cronkite's." He grinned. "I appreciate that. But there's really no way of knowing whether

I, or Walter, would fare any better than you. She requested you, Michael. And she could have requested anyone."

I managed a laugh. "I guess I would just . . . I could use some advice. My dad's coached me on procedure, but that's not the same."

"I suppose you try to find common ground."

I looked at him and thought of Marie the night of the murders. Her eyes, staring out from behind a mask of blood.

"I don't know if I want to find common ground."

Mr. McBride sighed. "I knew the Carlsons, too, Michael. But Marie Catherine Hale is still a person. Still a human being. Any commonalities you come across are normal, and nothing to feel guilty about."

"Maybe I'm worried that I won't remain . . . objective."

He watched me for a long time. He probably figured that I was going to make a mess of things for everyone involved. I'd always thought of him as a sort of outsider in his small neatly kept house on the west end of Main Street. Friendly, but distant, as if as our designated recorder, he needed to reserve room for judgment. Some thought of him as strange or snobbish. Some pitied him for his wife, Maggie, who was also a bit of an oddity: she wore her hair in pretty braided buns and mumbled my name every time we met so I wondered if she actually knew it. They had no children, which some would say was another mark against them, and my mother noted that the couple did not speak to each other much at parties.

But there was a photograph of them on his desk, taken on their wedding day. In it, they looked happy, but I couldn't really say.

They kept to themselves, and it was that more than anything that separated them from us, in this town that seeks to know everything for the good of all.

"What do you want, Michael?" he asked. "What are you after? And think very hard before you answer."

"I'm after the truth," I said finally.

"That's what all good journalists are after. That's all you're looking for."

CHAPTER TWELVE

Interview Begins, September 1958

BEFORE I LEFT Mr. McBride's office to go to the jail and see Marie, he'd said one more thing: "Michael, know your stuff.

"It isn't for you to judge her guilt or innocence. It's only for you to uncover the facts. And being armed with all the information will only help with that."

Maybe I should have taken that advice. My dad had already given me the file on the Carlsons, and letters had been sent to the Wisconsin and Iowa DAs requesting their case files. But I hadn't had the nerve to look. I'd tried—I must've opened it ten times. But I wasn't ready to see those photographs. I wasn't ready to see Steve like that. I knew that once I had, that would be the only way I could ever think of him: dead, and with his throat cut.

And besides, if I'm honest, I already felt like an expert in the Bloodless Murders, just from reading the papers.

When I got to the station, Bert went to fetch Marie down to the interrogation room. While I waited, I poked my head into my dad's office.

"Hi, Dad."

"Hi, son. Shouldn't you be in school?"

"Maybe?" I suggested.

"Well. I'm sure Principal Wilkens will understand. But if he wants to set you to washing blackboards beside Percy for a week, I'm not going to argue."

"Wouldn't that cut into my time with Miss Hale?" I asked, and he narrowed his eyes like I was too smart for my own good. But before he could say anything more, Bert walked Marie through the station. She seemed listless; her arms hung at her sides and her shoes scuffed against the floor.

"Go on," my dad said.

I went into the interrogation room.

"You let me know if you need anything, Mikey," Bert said. Then he tipped his hat to Marie and hurried out. He stood right outside for the duration of the interview.

Marie turned her head toward me. She had her hair held back like she had at the courthouse, tied with a long black ribbon.

"Mikey? Is that what you like to be called?"

"No. Definitely not Mikey." I hate when Bert calls me that. But he'd been doing it since I was eight and I can't break him of it now.

"Shouldn't you be in school?"

"I guess so."

She gave a sort of smirk. "Special privileges. You're welcome."

"When's the last time you were in school, Marie?"

"I never did any high school. Had to stop. Get a job."

I knew lots of kids who stopped coming to school, but only after their sophomore year—farm kids who were needed at home. And they were mostly boys.

"How . . . how have you been in here?"

"I'd be better if you brought me those smokes," she said. "Why?"

"When I was younger and we lived upstairs, I used to have a hard time sleeping. I could hear the echoes from the jail downstairs or the cars starting in the parking lot."

Marie shrugged. "I like it fine. It's nice, actually, to know that there's always someone awake and paying attention." She stretched her shoulders and rolled her head a little on her neck. She said she slept fine but she seemed tired. "When *I* was younger, I used to have a hard time sleeping, too. But only because of the kind of kid I was."

"What kind of kid was that?"

"The kind who knew even back then that the dark was a whole other world. That it soaked up the daylight one like a biscuit dipped in coffee."

I sat down across from her. Her large hazel eyes were too old for her face. It might seem like I'm lying about that—inserting it after the fact. But I always thought that about Marie. That the trauma had aged her. Took the life out and left something else behind.

On the table between us, I laid out sheets of paper. Clutched in my fingers was my most reliable ink pen.

"Well," she said. "Aren't you eager."

I started to put them away but she shook her head. I'd imagined things going differently. I'd imagined myself shouting questions and her breaking down and confessing in tears. But confess to what? Anyone looking could see she wasn't a killer. Anyone except for Pilson, and he only wanted someone to pay—not for justice, but for the headlines and his picture in the papers.

"How did you get mixed up in all this, Marie?"

She shrugged and looked past me. "Same way every girl gets into this much trouble." She looked back. "A boy."

"A boy? What boy?"

My pen hovered in midair.

"What happened to that one you came in here with the other night?" she asked. "The one who got beat up in the parking lot."

"Joe? He's staying with friends. He's safe."

Marie snorted.

"He's not safe."

"Maybe his dad will finally straighten up, now that my dad's involved." But even when I said it, I knew it wasn't true. Marie sighed.

"Well, where do you want to start?" she asked.

"How about with the boy's name?"

She shook her head.

"Then how about some confirmation? That the person who killed the Carlsons and those graduate students, Stacy Lee Brandberg and Richard Covey, Cheryl Warrens"—I threw in the name of the murdered truck stop waitress, a victim who was rarely mentioned—"was the same person."

Marie sat quietly, fingernails scratching at the top of the table. She seemed almost annoyed.

"Was he the same person?"

"Yes," she said finally.

"And who was it?"

"A man."

"A man? You said it was a boy earlier."

She shrugged like there wasn't any difference.

"Will you tell me his name?"

"Nope."

"Why not?"

"Because it wouldn't matter. It was just something he went by."

"So you didn't know his real name?" No one was going to be happy about that. It was the piece of information they most wanted. But she could still tell us enough to find him.

"What else can you tell me about him?"

"Not much. He was handsome."

"Handsome how?"

"Like a film star."

"Was he tall?" I asked. "Dark- or fair-haired?"

"Not tall," she said. "But he could be seen when he wanted to be. You know that kind of person? Presence." She snapped her fingers. "Just like that. And gone just as fast."

"You knew him well?"

"I came to."

"Had you known him all your life?"

Marie sighed again, and I started to panic. Maybe it wasn't going the way she'd imagined either. Maybe she'd change her mind about the whole thing.

"What about the blood?" I asked. "How did the blood get onto you like that?"

Marie frowned. "I don't want to start like this."

"Okay. That's okay. We can start wherever you want."

"I don't know where I want to start."

But we had to start somewhere. I tried to be patient. After all, what were only words to me were much more to her—they were images and sounds, screams and bright red splashes. They were memories.

Then I thought of the Carlson farmhouse. The pile of folded laundry. The rolled-up rug stained by dripped and pooled blood. I thought about the strange red circle that she had left on it. I really hadn't stopped thinking about that, or about her, sticky and soaked from head to toe. She'd looked like she'd walked through a fountain, like the blood had sprayed everywhere. But I'd been inside that house. I'd seen the spotless walls.

"I'll have to know about the blood eventually," I said.

"Just not yet."

"Why? I'm not here to judge you, Marie."

"Maybe not, but you will."

Despite her tough-cookie routine and the scowl on her face, she was scared. I was scared, too. She had seen things that I couldn't imagine. She had done things. Horrible things, yes, but I had never done anything. I'd never even ventured outside of Minnesota except for family vacations.

I reached across the table and laid my hand over hers. It wasn't something I would normally do; it had taken me three dates with Carol to do as much last winter. Marie looked at me curiously. She was a pretty girl, and she knew that. She turned her palm over and curled her fingers around mine. They were small and cold.

"The weapon," she said. "Everyone's wondering about that, aren't they? It was a straight razor."

I took my hand back and wrote. The surety of my penmanship was a comfort. I'd taken shorthand courses at school for the last two years. So had Percy, actually, though he only enrolled to be nearer to all the girls learning for secretarial work.

"The same straight razor every time?" I asked. I've always thought of a straight razor as dangerous, less a tool than a wild animal—something to handle with constant care, same as a scalpel or a hunting rifle. Things like that have a will of their own; they're designed to cut, to injure, and they carry that purpose inside them like a frequency on the radio. Having read about the state of the victims in the papers that summer—deep cuts to the neck, the wrists, the inner thighs—I had already figured that the weapon was something of that sort. But when Marie confirmed it, the image of the straight razor loomed in my mind: real and dangerously light. I could practically hear the sound of it sliding open.

"Almost always the same," Marie replied quietly.

"But what happened to the blood?" I'd seen my dad cut once at the barber, just a nick. It took a moment to start bleeding, like the cut was so fast that it surprised the skin. But these went straight to the vein. There must have been so much. There should have been a mess.

"He drank it."

I stopped writing.

"What do you mean, 'He drank it'?"

But before she could respond, all hell broke loose. Mr. Pilson burst into the station and started to complain loudly about some kind of writ or motion. Both his and my father's voices raised; he actually tried to get into the interrogation room but Bert's big body blocked the door.

"What's he doing here?" Marie cried.

"It's all right, Marie." I stood up. I don't know who I was trying to comfort. Then the voices softened, and Bert let Pilson in.

He stalked in angrily and my dad came in and put his arm across Pilson's chest, as near as he could manage without touching. I'd seen him employ that move before when he was trying to corral Fred Meeks, the farmer, when he was on one of his more belligerent benders.

"Why is he in here alone, without counsel?"

"That's what she requested," my dad said, and Pilson cast him a rude look.

"I want to be here for every interview."

"Then I don't want to talk," said Marie.

"Mr. Pilson, let's step into my office. I'm sure Michael's been making good progress."

"Good progress," he sneered. Truthfully I thought I was until she said the part about the killer drinking the blood.

"What's our killer's name, then, Michael?" he asked.

I thought of a tongue cleaning the edge of a blade. Cleaning it like a cat, over and over, until every drop was gone. But it couldn't have been that way. It would have had to be collected and drunk as from a bowl or a glass, like red milk, and the idea of that made my stomach flip.

"Well?"

"She hasn't told me."

"And I won't," Marie added, and I wished she'd be quiet. If she mentioned the blood drinking we were as good as through. Pilson would go back to the judge and they'd laugh us out of the room.

"Then what good is this?" Pilson asked.

"What good is a name?" Marie responded.

"So we can find him. So we can catch him."

"You haven't even found me, and I'm sitting right in front of you."

"That's because I suspect you've given us a fake name. Miss Hale."

Marie swallowed, and her eyes narrowed angrily. For how much of a liar they took her for, she didn't seem to be very good at it. She had no poker face.

"Bert," my dad said, "please escort Miss Hale back up to her cell."

"Yes, sure, Rick." He slid through us and got her up. The look Marie gave Pilson as she left—I wouldn't have been surprised if she had stuck out her tongue.

"You know she can't be trusted, don't you, son?" Pilson said after she was gone. "You know she's just buying time."

"I don't know that," I said. "Not yet."

He turned to me and his face transformed, all the anger gone. "I know she might not look like much more than a girl, but Marie Catherine Hale is a young woman. A conniver. She'll say anything to gain your sympathy. She'll cry. She'll bat her eyes. A girl like that is prone to lies by her very nature. She's not to be believed."

"Yes, sir," I said. And quick as that, he walked right out of the station.

Bert came down the stairs.

"Well?" he asked. "What'd he want? How'd you get him to leave?"

"We haven't seen the last of him," my dad said. And we hadn't. Benjamin Pilson took a room at Mrs. B.'s boardinghouse over on the corner of 9th and Pine. It's nicer than the motel out by the highway, where visiting patrolmen often stay over. Mrs. B.'s serves a fine breakfast every morning and brunch on Saturdays, open to the public. The other four rooms are most often uninhabited, and several of the ladies' church groups use the parlor to host events and socials. I like to think of Mr. Pilson hunched over the desk in his lace-furnished room, poring over his notes and case files while the Lutheran knitting circle laughs and gossips on the floor below. He stayed with us for weeks on end—God knows what was happening in Nebraska while he was away. I heard my parents talking about him a few times, saying how the case had become an obsession, how he'd hung his whole career on it.

"Michael."

I pushed away from the wall and turned to my dad. "Yes, sir?"

"Take Mr. Pilson with a grain of salt."

"Yes, sir."

"He's had his career but I've also had mine. I've interrogated a lot of people. Only a few have been true liars. The others . . ." He rubbed his eyes. It had been another long day for him, in a long line of long days. "I just mean that lots of people think they know what they know, or know what they saw. They're not liars. They're just wrong."

CHAPTER THIRTEEN

An Impossible Story

I GAVE MARIE a few days to cool off after that initial interview. And so I could, too. My dad's words ran through my head beside Pilson's warning. *She's not to be trusted. She's a liar by nature. She's not a liar. She's just wrong.*

But how wrong could she have gotten it? How could she be mistaken when she said he drank the blood?

I couldn't tell my dad about that part. If I had told him so soon, he would have called the whole thing off. But I did tell him about the razor. He passed that detail on to Pilson, but neither of them seemed impressed. What good was a murder weapon without the actual weapon? It was just another phantom, and one we could have guessed.

I replayed that first interview in my head so many times. Too many times, and now the real memory is lost. I can't remember how she looked when she told me what the murder weapon was, if her lips curled around the words *straight razor* or if she spat them like a bad taste. I don't remember the tone of her voice when she said, "He drank it," or if there was any hesitation before she replied. I don't remember if it sounded like she was making it up as she went.

Of course, I knew she had to be. Because what she was saying— what she was saying it was that had killed all those people and that had killed Steve and his family . . . was a vampire.

A vampire. Like capes and bats and Bela Lugosi.

When I finally went back to the station, I managed to get in without anyone seeing me. My dad was out, Charlie was nowhere to be seen, and the reception desk was empty. I didn't feel like waiting, so I went up to Marie's cell, hoping with every step that she'd take that one part back. Recant it or even ignore it completely. Had I opened the door and found her sitting there smiling, seemingly without any memory of what she'd said, I would've gone along with it.

"Where you been?" she asked when I opened the door. She seemed excitable, and relieved to see me.

"My dad wanted me to stay away until everything got sorted with Mr. Pilson."

"And now it has?"

"Not exactly. This is just a visit, not an interview."

She glanced at my hands, which were empty. I'd brought no paper, no pen. And we were upstairs, alone except for the bars. All of a sudden the cell felt less like a cell and more like a girl's bedroom where I wasn't allowed.

"Why did you say what you did?" I asked.

"Which part?"

I scowled, and she started to laugh.

"I'm sorry," she said. "I didn't mean to just tell you like that. I didn't know I was even *going* to tell you. But the look on your face!"

"So it was a joke? It was supposed to be funny?"

"No." Her laughter died off and she cocked her head, pouting like I was kind of a drag. "This isn't funny. But some things *are* funny no matter how not funny something is."

What about those student nurses? I wanted to say. What about those kids in Wisconsin, lying dead on the ground? Were they funny, too?

But that would've stopped Marie cold.

"I didn't expect you to believe it right away," she said, and shrugged. "I know how it sounds."

Like you've been watching too many movies, I wanted to say. Like you're crazy. But instead I asked, "Can you prove it?"

"Seeing is believing." She sighed. "And I can't exactly show you. But yes, I think I can. After I tell you everything. I mean, the truth is the truth."

The truth is the truth. But what's the truth about vampires? What are the facts about fiction? There didn't seem to be much point in going on if this was the story she was set on telling. But just the same, I didn't want to stop. So I thought about what Mr. McBride had told me, about what my job was. There was still a killer on the loose, and Marie's story was the only one we had.

"Okay," I said.

"Okay," she said, and smiled.

"They're going to lock you in a hospital somewhere, you know. Maybe they'll lock me in, too."

"You'll be fine," she said. "Sheriff's son."

"Is that why you picked me? That's why lots of people pick me."

"For your clean ironed shirt and your handsome face? Sure. And because of how you helped your friend that night when his father got out of line. And because you just happened to be there." She shrugged. "It's like you said: they'd have thrown me in a loony bin. Anyone else wouldn't have given me a chance."

We watched each other for a long time, her seated on her bed and me standing near the door. I didn't know what we would be when the interview was over: enemies or allies. I didn't know if Marie would be alive. If she would be in prison or free. I turned to go.

"You'll come back, though?" she asked.

"Yeah. I'll come back."

By the following Monday, my dad and the attorneys reached a compromise with Pilson, so the interviews could continue. When I found out I was relieved, but mostly excited. It was becoming nearly impossible to pay attention in class, but none of my teachers expressed concern, as if the importance of the investigation outweighed the importance of my education. Only one teacher spoke up: Miss Murray. People noted that of all the faculty she was the least affected by the Bloodless Murders and had been heard more than once criticizing folks for gossiping about the Carlsons' deaths. People around town started calling her "high and mighty" and said she had a lot of nerve looking down on us in the wake of a tragedy.

The other teachers let me go. I was never penalized for late work. No one called on me in class. Even Coach Harvey, my baseball coach and the tenth-grade physical education teacher, had only good things to say when the interviews started. Of course, that's before he knew I would be quitting the team. When I finally did, he got so mad he almost punched a wall, though I don't know why. I'd never been a standout player, and he must've known that I only joined because Percy was on the team already.

I think he sensed that Marie would pull me away. From the start, folks in Black Deer Falls resented her for the brutal change she had brought, and they were unwilling to give anything else up to her, least of all the steady son of their admired sheriff.

I went back to the jail to continue the interviews on Monday afternoon and Marie was already there, hands folded in her lap uncuffed while my father bent over a tape recorder, boxy and gray. It took up most of the space on one end of the table.

"What's that?" I asked.

"Mr. Pilson's compromise," he replied. "If he can't be in the room, he wants everything on tape. This contraption will record your conversations, and I'll deliver the tape to him every night."

"Every night?"

"Or every week. Whatever I can reasonably fit into my schedule," my dad said, and smirked. He punched a button with his index finger, bent over the tape recorder and said, "October sixth, 1958, four oh seven p.m. Interview of Marie Catherine Hale. Recording taken by Sheriff Richard Jensen, now leaving the room. Interview conducted by Michael Jensen." He straightened, and nodded to me before exiting and closing the door behind him.

"You agreed to this?" I asked Marie. She had her hair tied back with the black ribbon again, and the white blouse was tied at her waist and rolled to her elbows over the sleeves of a dark green sweater.

"He'll hear it anyway," Marie said. "Sooner or later, everyone will hear it." Then her expression turned impish, and she reached up and hit a button to stop the tape.

I jumped. "I don't think you can do that."

"Will they know? Is it wrong that part of me wants to tell you lies and boring things just so Mr. Pilson will have to listen to them for hours and hours?"

I smiled. "Maybe he'll fall asleep and have to start all over again when he wakes up."

Marie laughed. Then she reached back to the tape recorder and switched it on again.

"Should we continue where we left off?" I cleared my throat. The recording bothered me more than it seemed to bother Marie. It made me self-conscious, and a little suspicious—tape recordings were a tactic used by insidious foreign governments. But, I supposed, it was only insidious if you didn't know that you were being taped.

"I guess."

I set out my paper and pen. Even though the conversations were being recorded I wanted my own notes, and the recorder couldn't capture everything: Marie's demeanor, her nervous tics and gestures, whether she seemed sad or bored or conflicted.

"Where we left off," I muttered. But I didn't even know where that was. Or rather, I knew, but the phrase, "Tell me more about this vampire fellow" wouldn't come out of my mouth.

"Does your mother iron your shirts so neatly?" Marie asked. "Or do you do it?"

"My mother does."

"I like your mother. She found me those clothes for court and gave me her lipstick. You have a little sister?"

"I do," I said. "Her name is Dawn."

"That's a nice name."

"Do you have any sisters, Marie? Any brothers?"

She shook her head. "It was just my mother and me. Until he came along."

"He? You mean the killer?"

"No," Marie said, and rolled her eyes. "I mean, him. My step-father." That word she did say like a bad taste.

"You didn't like him?"

"No."

"Why not?"

"Because he was terrible."

"How was he terrible?"

She shifted around in her seat. "You know it'd be nice if we could do these in my cell instead of this little room."

"Maybe," I said. "We could move the tape recorder onto the kitchen table. I'd have to stay outside the bars."

"But you could sit close, if you wanted."

She was toying with me, flirting. Batting her eyelashes, like Pilson warned me she would.

"How was your stepfather terrible?" I asked again. "In what way?"

She exhaled sharply.

"In the same way that lots of men are terrible."

"Like in the way that my friend Joe's father is?" I asked, but Marie looked into the corner and refused to answer.

"All right, then, what can you tell me about the first murder? The murder of Peter Knupp." When I said his name, she glanced at me and then away as if he was of no interest. "Did you know him before the murder?" No response. "Was he chosen at random? A robbery, maybe? He was alone in his home—"

Marie sighed but otherwise remained silent.

"He was cut at the neck, and the inner thigh. Bled out."

"Yes, Michael," she said finally. "We were just reminded of this by Mr. Pilson at the hearing."

"Well, do you have any feelings about it? Did you see it happen? He was the first victim; it can't have been easy—"

"He wasn't the first victim."

I stared into her steady hazel eyes.

"The first victim hasn't been found."

My pulse pounded. Another body, another Bloodless Murder. One that no one had discovered or simply not connected to the case? A dozen questions hurtled through my head, crowding it so I couldn't think straight. "Who?"

"I don't want to talk about this."

"But this is what we're here to talk about."

"Not like this."

"Marie, they want to execute you."

"Well, they can't, all right? Because I didn't know! I didn't know what he was and what he was going to do. I thought he was just going to take me away. I didn't know he was going to kill her!"

"Kill who?"

"My mother."

My eyes flickered to the tape recorder. "He killed your mother," I said. Killed her, perhaps right before Marie's eyes.

"And my stepfather. The first murders were my mother and my stepfather. There were two."

"When did the murders occur?" I reached for my pen.

"June," she said, her voice toneless. "Early June. The second, maybe. Or the third."

Early June. Peter Knupp hadn't been discovered until August 3. It had been supposed that he had been dead for several days, but that was still a long time between killings.

"What were their names?" I asked.

"I'm not giving you their names," she said. "I gave you mine."

I wanted to press for more, but I didn't have the heart. Marie's eyes were shiny. She was trying not to cry.

"Do you want to stop for now?"

"Yes," she said. "I'd like to stop."

The minute I offered I wondered if maybe I should have pushed harder. I wondered what Matt McBride would do. He would never shy away from the hard questions.

"All right," I said. "But next time we'll talk more, about the blood drinker."

Marie chuckled a little as she wiped her face. "The blood drinker. That's a good name. He'd like that."

CHAPTER FOURTEEN

A Surprising Discovery

AS MY DAD and the investigators reeled at the news of the murders of Marie's mother and stepfather, my mind kept returning to Marie's story. As they searched for the murdered couple—running down lead after lead of bodies found alone or separately, whether they had died from blood loss or not—I walked around in a haze, trying to think of what could make Marie tell me the things she had. A vampire. The pale, waxy-skinned, walking undead. She was pulling my leg. Except she didn't seem to think it was a joke.

I considered that she could have been fooled. That the killer had pulled off that much of a trick through sleight of hand and props. People had been fooled into things before. All those people in Exeter, Rhode Island, who dug up and cut apart Mercy Brown. In the early 1700s, in Southeastern Europe, a rural town had been so convinced of a vampire in their midst that the government had to install official investigators, and all talk of blood drinking was grounds for imprisonment. That was a long time ago—but not so long ago, people were convinced that a glug of snake oil could cure whatever ailed you.

I'd always thought of those people as gullible.

Marie did not seem gullible.

The Nebraska authorities couldn't find the bodies of Marie's mother and stepfather. Not for all their searching. After a while they figured she'd just been lying again, another lie piled on top of the rest.

"Let them think so," Marie said as the days ticked by. "Let them keep looking."

"You don't want them found," I said one afternoon in the interrogation room. "Your parents?"

"My stepfather wasn't my parent," she said.

"Then why tell us about them at all?"

She shrugged and gestured to the space around and behind her. "Gives them something to do." And by *them* I took her to mean the investigators.

"You never ask me if we've caught him," I said.

"Well, I figure I'd have heard if you did," she said. "And besides. I know that you won't."

"We will," I said, "if you help us."

She shook her head.

"What can I tell you anyway, stuck in here? Any plans he had could have changed. All those men out combing through fields should go home and go to bed. Give their poor dogs a rest." Then she cocked her head at me and asked about Percy's Labradors.

About how the other dogs were that she'd seen through the crack in the drapes at the Carlson farm. She seemed more interested in talking about them, and we talked about dogs for the rest of the session, and how she'd never had one of her own.

That's how it went with Marie sometimes. If I kept at her, there were days I was able to turn the conversation back around, but usually not.

"Don't be rattled," Mr. McBride said when I stopped by his office in early October. "But don't be deterred. Right now she has the luxury of the court's patience. When they catch him, that will all change."

"When we catch him, they'll force her to talk?" I asked.

"Just the opposite," he said. "After he's caught, what she has to say will hardly matter at all."

"Want to come to my place this weekend?" Percy asked me as we walked through the parking lot to his car one day after school. I hadn't seen him much. I'd been at the jail with Marie almost every day after class.

"Huh?" I said.

"Mo got new hunting gear. We can try it on, scout the places for the stand." Percy had been going on about a new hunting stand for weeks. He'd had his eye on a good-looking buck. He'd seen it close to a dozen times that summer, and knowing Percy, that meant he'd become far too attached to the animal to ever be able to shoot it.

"Sounds good," I said.

"You planning on asking Carol to Sadie Hawkins?" he asked.

"Isn't the point of a Sadie Hawkins for the girls to ask us?" Percy knew this perfectly well; he'd spent the better part of the week avoiding speaking with Sandy Millpoint just to give Rebecca Knox a chance to work up the nerve.

"I've seen Carol looking your way, that's all." We got to Percy's car and I set my books on top while he lit a quick smoke. Carol was across the parking lot, standing with some friends around her green four-door Ford. She had the sides of her bright blond hair pinned back with little pearl clips and she looked fantastic: peach lipstick and blue eyes—she was nearly as tall as I was when she wore high heels. But looking at her that day, I found myself comparing her to Marie—her light hair to Marie's dark; her tall, long-legged grace with Marie's smaller, sharper quickness. I knew it was wrong to think of Marie in the same way that I thought about Carol. I knew that from the start.

"I guess I'll go if she asks me."

We got into Percy's car and he tapped the dash, then the steering wheel, and pumped the brakes twice, a ritual that he insisted had kept the car going all these years. I shoved my books against a burlap sack in the middle of the bench seat and rested my arm atop them.

Percy glanced at me as he backed the car out. Normally this kind of news about Carol would have dominated the conversation for the rest of the night. We were both a little surprised to find that I didn't care. I looked at her again and still felt a small familiar tug inside when she smiled. They'd be going to the café after school for fries and shakes. But not me. I would be going to the jail. I wondered how Percy fared, going without me. Being a clown, he could fit in anywhere, with anyone. I envied him that sometimes.

"It's strange to think about dances after all this," I said. "After Steve and his parents." I looked out the window and thought I felt Percy give me a nudge through the burlap sack, almost like a caress.

"Life," Percy said. "It goes on."

That it did. Unfair as it was, we couldn't huddle around Steve's grave forever. I looked across the sports fields, where the school grounds abutted the Lutheran cemetery—pretty, groomed hills lined with headstones and small granite monuments, a few angel statuettes that I'd heard some folks call very nice but a tad grandiose. It wasn't the same cemetery where the Carlsons were buried, but I felt like they were there all the same.

Again Percy nudged my arm through the sack. Only both of Percy's hands were on the wheel.

"Percy, what do you have in this sack?"

"I thought that was your sack," he said as I lifted it up and a fat three-foot-long snake fell out across the bench seat.

Percy screamed. He jerked the wheel and sent the car onto the curb, nearly taking out the tailgate of a parked brown pickup truck. Then he threw the car into park and we both leaped out.

"What in the jumping hells is that?"

The snake's gray-and-black body—if you could call it a body— writhed sluggishly across the worn leather into the space where I'd just been sitting. I darted forward and shut the door. So did Percy, on the other side.

"Shoot! We should have waited until it tried to crawl out and then slammed it in between! How did it get in there?"

By then, our shouting had attracted a small crowd, and someone went running back into the school. It wasn't five minutes later that Bert arrived in a police car and found us all standing around looking useless. He got out with his hand on his service pistol, his eyes wild like he would need to fire at someone at any moment.

"What's going on here?"

Percy and I pointed into the car. The snake was still sprawled inside. Bert approached the window. Then he dropped his hand from his revolver and opened the door.

"What are you doing?" Percy shouted.

Bert leaned into the front seat just as Principal Wilkens arrived, jogging through the parking lot with a shotgun.

Bert pointed at him, as stern as I'd ever seen. "You put that away." Then he bent back into the car and took hold of the snake, crooning to it as sweetly as if it were a baby. "She's only a python," he said when he emerged with the snake curling eagerly around his hands and forearms. "She's not going to hurt anybody. How'd she get into your car, Percy?"

"Hell if I know," Percy exclaimed. "It was rolling around in a burlap sack. Someone must have thrown it in there."

"Who?" I asked.

He shrugged. "Everybody knows that my doors don't lock."

Bert was barely listening. He held the snake up in front of his face and looked into its eyes. "Lucky she didn't die. She was moving closer to you because she was cold. Not enough sun today to heat the car up, and reptiles are cold-blooded. They can't produce their own heat."

"How do you know so much about herpetology?" Principal Wilkens asked, and I was impressed that he knew the word; I had to look it up later in my dad's encyclopedias. Herpetology: the study of reptiles and amphibians.

Bert shrugged. "I've liked them since I was a kid. If she doesn't belong to anybody, I'll take her home. I have an empty fish tank that should do just right."

Percy glanced at me. I'd never actually been inside Bert's house, and just then I didn't particularly regret that. Bert reached into the car for the burlap sack and placed the snake tenderly inside. Then he got into his car and drove away with his new pet.

All of us kids sort of turned to Principal Wilkens, still standing there with his shotgun.

"These kinds of pranks are dangerous," he said loudly. "If anyone knows who did this to Mr. Valentine's automobile, I encourage you to speak with me in my office."

CHAPTER FIFTEEN

Good Cops

THE INCIDENT WITH the snake. I hardly gave it a thought at first. There were so many other things on my mind and nothing had come of it: we hadn't been hurt—even the snake was safe as Bert's new pet. It was a strange prank to pull but that's all I thought it was. I'd even considered it hadn't been left for me at all but for Percy. There was no reason yet to think otherwise.

The fruitless search for the bodies of Marie's mother and stepfather had distracted Pilson for a short time, but it wasn't long before he listened to the interview tapes and heard me say the words *blood drinker*. I had to come clean after that. I expected to be pulled off the case immediately. But when I told my dad he just nodded quietly, like he'd expected she would say something like that.

Pilson, on the other hand, came down like a thunderstorm—I was there when he questioned her and I've never heard such shouting from inside the interrogation room, from him and Marie alike.

"If you don't stop with these wild stories, I'll drag you back in front of a judge!"

"Go ahead and do it, then! Because this is the only story I have to tell!"

I felt for Pilson at first. I really did. Even if he went about it poorly and even if his motivation wasn't exactly pure, he was still after the truth just like the rest of us. If only there'd been an easier way to get it. In the old days, people used to believe that the corpses of murder victims would bleed if brought into the presence of their killers. But not even that would have worked in the case of Marie Hale, as those bodies had not a drop left.

I hung back with my dad near his office while Pilson had his go at Marie, and I remember how intently he listened to what was going on inside the interrogation room. How he seemed poised on the balls of his feet, ready to intervene if it went too far.

I told him that maybe the interviews were a mistake. "Maybe she really is just stalling. Maybe the only reason she chose me was because she thought she could get one over on someone her own age."

"Does Marie strike you as a liar?" he asked, and I thought about it hard, for the hundredth time.

"No, sir."

"She doesn't strike me as one either. We don't know what she went through. If she's hiding something, she's not hiding it from you so much as herself."

He stared at the interrogation room door.

"Keep going for as long as she wants to," he said. "For as long as they'll let us."

When Pilson came out, he snapped his fingers at my dad and directed us into his office. That raised my eyebrows, but my dad took a deep breath and patted me on the shoulder, his way of saying it was fine, that Mr. Pilson was upset, and we should let that one pass. We joined him in my dad's office and shut the door; he had his hands on his hips and was staring at the wall, brow creased deep.

"Look at this." He pointed to my father's calendar, a monthly of paintings of white-tailed deer. The month of October was blank except for a few scribbled appointments, and large black X's crossing off the days.

"You've had her in your custody for weeks. Weeks. And all you have is a made-up story about a dead mother and a lot of rambling about a movie monster in a cape and fake teeth. No new leads. Nothing. Nothing! Look at these—" He slapped his palm against the marked dates. "Wasted days."

My dad crossed his arms. He had a cup of coffee in his hand and raised it toward the calendar.

"You know what I see, when I look at that, Mr. Pilson? All those X's?"

"What's that?"

"Relief."

Pilson turned.

"I see days when no one died," my dad went on. "No bodies found."

"Well, you know what I see?" Pilson asked. He tore the calendar off its nail and tossed it at my dad's feet. "I see a murderer getting away."

He walked past us and left the station without another word to anyone, leaving my dad to pick up the calendar and poke a new hole for the nail. I asked Marie once why she insisted on antagonizing Pilson so badly, but she only shrugged and said that with a man like him there was no winning anyway. That even if every victim had turned up alive again she would always be guilty. Guilty of wasting his time. Guilty of being poor. Of being a girl. She said from the moment she met him she could tell that all he wanted was to find a way to strap her into Nebraska's electric chair. But the joke was on him. Because she requested hanging.

CHAPTER SIXTEEN

Pilson

I CAN'T RECALL if I disliked Benjamin Pilson on sight. He had a clean-cut, good-looking face and carried himself with confidence. He looked like you would expect a DA to look: maybe he styled himself after the ones in the movies, or maybe they styled themselves after him. I do know that almost every single thing I learned about him subsequent to that first impression made me like him less. Now, maybe I hate him. So I guess I could have hated him from the start.

I was picking up cough syrup for Dawn at Anderson's Drug Store one day when he approached me in the street.

"Michael," he said. "I've been meaning to buy you lunch. Where in town can we get a good cheeseburger?"

I took him a few blocks over to the Sportsman's Café. It didn't have the best cheeseburgers, but they were decent and it was close, and I didn't want to spend any more time in his company than

I had to. We slid into one of the cream-colored booths and he ordered two cheeseburgers with fries, a soda for him, and a vanilla milkshake for me. I resented the milkshake—it seemed like he was trying to point out my youth. But maybe that was unfair. Either way, my mother raised me to be polite so I drank every drop and ate the cherry, too.

For a while we talked about innocuous things: he asked me about school and what position I played on the baseball team; I asked him how long he'd been the DA in Lincoln. His easy way felt genuine even though I knew it was practiced—putting people at ease one minute only to knock them off balance the next is something even our DA knew how to do—so I knew what he was doing when he rolled up his sleeves and loosened his expensive necktie.

"Your recorded conversations with Marie Catherine Hale have been interesting."

"They have," I said.

"Shadowy figures, caped monsters in the dark—" He flashed a grin: How ridiculous were the tales of this lying girl?

"That's not exactly what she said; she said he had tricks, and that he drank the blood."

Pilson shrugged. Same difference.

"How are you going to get her to drop that nonsense?" he asked.

"My dad says maybe I shouldn't. That I should let her tell it her way and sort it out after."

Pilson smiled. It was a mean smile. No mirth at all, just condescension, and it made me feel small. He wiped his mouth with his napkin and placed it over his plate, then pushed his plate to the edge of the table. "But your dad isn't the interviewer, is he? You are."

"Yes, sir."

"Since the judge has seen fit to place the integrity of the entire case on the shoulders of a high school student."

He reached into his briefcase and produced files not dissimilar to those I'd seen fanned out across my father's desk. They were the files on the Nebraska Bloodless Murders: Peter Knupp and Angela Hawk and Beverly Nordahl. One by one he opened them on the table, before my plate of half-eaten burger and fries.

"Have you seen the photos of the Carlson family's bodies yet?" he asked.

"No."

"Don't you think you should?"

"We aren't to that part of the interview. I want the details to be fresh."

"Well," he said, and clearly he didn't believe me, "you've got to be nearly to these. So have a look." He threw me a pile of photographs.

Peter Knupp was splayed facedown. A close-up of his face showed open eyes and parted lips. The expression conveyed no fear. It didn't convey much of anything, which was somehow worse. Pilson moved the photo of his face to reveal pictures of the wounds that killed him. Cuts, deep and smooth, opened at the edges to show the layers of skin and flesh and vein. The cut to his thigh had been done through his trousers, and the edges of the fabric were stained dark. The cut at his neck was short, and narrower than the others, and the angle of the photo focused less on it than on his face, for which I was grateful.

I'd never seen a dead body before. It was nothing like I imagined, and the vanilla milkshake sat uneasy in my stomach.

"Why are you showing me these?" I asked.

"So you remember," he said.

He opened the files on the student nurses.

"I remember," I said.

"Then why are you letting her lie? Here." He moved my plate and pushed the photographs toward me so far I had to grab them to keep them from falling into my lap.

Angela Hawk and Beverly Nordahl were seated in the front bucket seats of Angela's car. Their throats had been cut, and small rivulets of blood escaped down into their collars. Beverly's head tilted toward Angela's as if she was trying to provide comfort.

"The ME estimated they died within minutes of each other," Pilson said. "They look like they were killed while they were unconscious, don't they? Except they weren't. No traces of sedatives, no intoxicants found besides the alcohol in a bottle of beer. No ligature on the throat, no signs of asphyxia. No blows to the head. And if you look close, you can see that Angela's eyes are open."

I didn't want to look close.

"They suffered," he said. "Every one. Have you ever watched someone bleed to death, Michael?"

"No, sir."

"Marie Hale was involved in this." He turned one of the photos of Angela and Beverly to look at it. "Maybe she was even in the car."

"She didn't kill them," I said. But the blood had drained from my head. I could see Marie crouched in the back of that car. I could see her leaned across the bodies.

"Maybe she didn't do the cutting," he said. "Or maybe you don't want to believe she did. She's a pretty girl, Michael."

"What does that have to do with anything?"

"Just that you're a young man. And she's using that."

"You don't know if she's using anything. Maybe she's confused. My dad says—"

"Your dad is not the most experienced interviewer, though, is he? How many murderers do you think your dad has questioned?"

"I don't know," I said, even though I knew the answer was none.

My cheeks burned. Had I opened my mouth to say something else I might have cried out of sheer frustration. Or I might have hit him. But as it happened, I didn't need to do either, because Mr. McBride had been watching and decided to step in.

"Oh, I don't know about that," Mr. McBride said. "The things our sheriff has seen might surprise you. And besides, I don't know that you have any advantage to press over him. Lincoln may be the capital of Nebraska but it isn't exactly New York City." He held out his hand. "Matt McBride. I'm the editor of the local paper."

Pilson shook it. As quickly as he'd laid them out, he swept the photos back into his files.

"I've been meaning to make your acquaintance," Mr. McBride said. "See how you're liking the place. Maybe get a quote on the case for the *Star*."

"Sure," Pilson said. "I'll stop by your offices one of these days." He never did, of course. Pilson saved his quotes for the bigger papers.

"Great. You stop by, too, Michael. Anytime." Mr. McBride waited for me to nod, to tell him I was okay. Then he tipped his hat and walked to the lunch counter for a cup of coffee.

"Friend of yours?" Pilson asked, staring into his back.

"I delivered papers for him this summer."

"That's good." Pilson smiled. "But Michael, if you speak to him about this case, I'll press charges against you faster than you can slap a fly."

"Yes, sir."

"And don't forget," he said as he gathered his things. "The man who killed these people has to pay. And Marie Hale will have to pay, too, for standing by and letting him."

"What if she couldn't stop him?" I asked. "What if she tried?"

"I need a name," he said as if that didn't matter. "I need his name, or she dies."

CHAPTER SEVENTEEN

Debunking

I NEVER IMAGINED I'd be in the position of debunking a vampire myth, but I couldn't just let Marie get away with the story. Pilson was right about that, at least. There were real people here. Real victims. I was fairly certain that Marie wasn't using the story to pull off some kind of insanity plea—but just the same, if she was determined to stick to her blood-drinker tale, she was going to have to earn it.

So I started checking out books. A whole lot of books that I had to hide inside my coat like they were dirty. It was embarrassing to even ask our school librarian, but she didn't bat an eye, no pun intended, and I thought the elementary school rumors about her being a witch might actually be true. But if it hadn't been for her, I might have gotten nowhere. Only the investigators were privy to the blood-drinking detail of the confession by then, so I couldn't ask Mr. McBride. Though I did, later on, and he found me a pretty good book on Mercy Brown and the vampire hysteria of New England.

The next time I interviewed Marie I was armed with knowledge of vampiric tradition. We met at her cell. My dad didn't have any objections to our meeting there, though I was surprised that Mr. Pilson didn't. Looking back, it's possible that my father never even asked him. In any case, when I got there, I had to haul the cumbersome tape recorder up there with me. It was such an awkward shape that I nearly dropped it, and the only thing that saved me from spending the next several years paying my father back was that I arrived when Marie had a visitor: Nancy had come up from the reception desk. She and Marie had taken a shine to each other. I think Marie reminded her of the daughter she lost in the fire.

As I burst through the two-color door Nancy rose from her chair and said, "Michael! Let me help you!" She swooped down just in time to catch the tape recorder as it bobbled from my grip. Then she helped me carry it to the table and set it up.

"I'll give you the room," she said. "If you're still at it when I come back from my dinner break, I'll bring you some cookies and sandwiches."

"That thing sure seems heavy," Marie noted when we were alone. "Nancy must be stronger than she looks."

"You two seem pretty friendly," I said.

Marie shrugged. "Did you bring me those smokes?"

"Shoot. I forgot again; I'm sorry."

"Sure."

"No, I am. Really. I keep meaning to swipe a pack from Percy."

"Don't worry about it," she said, and then slipped a cigarette out of her sock. She smiled at me and lit it with a match struck against the cement wall.

She was wearing the same blue jeans, rolled to the ankle, and a different white shirt. Her hair looked dark and glossy in its ponytail, the ends of the black ribbon nearly as long as the strands.

Inside her cell, she seemed more at ease and in control of the space, and despite the fact that I had lived in this part of the jail for many years of my life, stepping into my old kitchen felt like Marie receiving me into her parlor.

"Where'd you get that?" I asked, and pointed to the cigarette.

"Never mind." She exhaled. "You don't think you're the only boy I'm talking to?"

"I do think that, actually. Are you keeping secrets, Marie?"

"Everything's a secret until I tell you. But I'm going to tell you everything, so I guess no, I'm not keeping secrets." She watched me a minute and then laughed. "Lighten up. I got it from Nancy. Jealous, jealous."

"I'm not jealous," I said, except that I kind of was. Marie was my secret thing—an entire world separate from my usual one. It shocked me how quickly I'd begun to think of her as mine.

She took another drag and gestured to the tape recorder so we could begin.

"How have you been?" I asked, on the record.

She gestured to the walls, to the tidy kitchen, the small writing desk in her cell. "Better here than some other places." But then she seemed to regret saying so. "I am sorry, you know. That you've gotten caught up in this mess. Your mom and dad, too."

"But are you sorry for the rest?" I asked.

She shrugged.

"What good does sorry do?" she said quietly. "They're all still dead."

"Then why tell me what happened? To avoid the death penalty? To unburden your soul?"

She laughed.

"To stop your accomplice from hurting anyone else?"

Marie cast a quick look toward her window. "He won't hurt anyone else. Not for a while anyway. And when he decides to, nothing I say is going to stop him."

"Because he's a blood drinker?"

She nodded.

"No one's stopped him before," she said.

"No one?" I asked.

"He's still alive, isn't he? Sort of."

"You know he isn't really what you say he is. You know vampires aren't real."

"Believe what you need to believe, Michael. I'm just telling you what happened."

"I'm not saying you're a liar, Marie. Just that maybe he fooled you."

"Sure. Because I'm a stupid girl." She curled her lip. "Do I seem stupid to you? Because I stopped going to school?"

I paused. No, she didn't. She seemed smart. Rough, maybe.

Fast, maybe. But not stupid or like the kind of person it would be easy to get one over on.

"Tell me about him, then," I said. "How did he find you? Were you in a graveyard? Did you stumble across his coffin?"

"You're making fun."

"Of course I am, when you tell me something ridiculous."

"Were all those empty bodies ridiculous? Where did all their blood go, Michael, if he didn't drink it?"

"Maybe he moved them. Maybe the victims were killed someplace else." Except that one of the victims, Jeff Booker, found at a service station slumped over the cash register, had been seen alive by a previous customer not thirty minutes before he was found dead.

"How could he move around in the daylight?" I asked.

"With a parasol," she said sarcastically. "He doesn't burn up in daylight, all right? And he can go into churches, too, not that we ever did. Are you done now?"

"Are you?" I asked. "DA Pilson's not happy about what you're telling me. I've heard him talking about going to his governor—getting you extradited."

"I'm sure he will."

I frowned. I didn't know it then, but Pilson had already tried. And failed. The killings had seemingly stopped, or at least paused, and in the meantime no one wanted to get in deeper with Marie—they knew what it would look like if they hauled a fifteen-year-old girl to the electric chair, lickety-split.

"Marie—if he is what you say, and he has killed before, then why haven't we seen any murders like this?"

"You probably have. You just didn't recognize them."

"These kind of strange, grisly killings?" I asked, dubious. "I doubt that we'd let them just go unsolved."

"Tell that to the Black Dahlia," she said, and snuffed out the nub of her cigarette. "Or those people in the house by the train . . . the one where all the mirrors were covered and there was a bowl of blood and some bacon on the table."

I said nothing. I'd heard of the Dahlia, but the other case was unknown to me. It certainly sounded strange enough, but I searched through the newspaper archives with our librarian for hours and was never able to identify it.

"But," I said carefully, "there's never been another spree like this. Young people . . . teenagers . . ."

"He didn't need to do it before."

"So why did he do it now?"

"I don't know!" She pulled her knees up to her chest and I took a deep breath. It was hard not to scream at her—it was hard not to give my frustration away with a clenched fist or a cracked knuckle. To appear neutral when I was sure she was making it all up as she went.

"You don't have forever, you know," I said. "You only have until they catch him. Then they won't care what your side of the story is."

She laughed a little and muttered, "Forever." Then she stretched her arms.

"You're right though, Michael, about not having all the time.

You're just wrong about how much. I have until they realize they *won't* catch him. Until they give up. That's when they'll come for me."

"How long do you think that'll be?" I asked.

"As long as he keeps them jumping," she said, and shrugged. "You're the cop's son; you would know better than I would."

I didn't know anything better than she would. None of us did. Black Deer Falls, Pilson, the deputies and my dad, we were all stumbling around in the dark.

"You said he didn't need to do it," I said quietly. "What do you mean?"

She watched me, trying to see if I was serious. Then she turned her wrist over and showed me her scars.

"He doesn't always kill," she said. "Sometimes he just feeds."

I leaned forward to look at the thin lines that ran from the palm of her hand up to the elbow to disappear into her shirt. There were so many that the skin was like a patchwork, criss-crossing, some running along the length of her arm and others cutting across it, so many, but so delicate and pink that you could miss them if you weren't really looking.

"You can come closer, if you want."

I got up, and she held her arm up to the bars. I reached through and took it. Her skin was cool, and smooth until I ran my thumb over the small raised scars. Some of them seemed tentative; they were thinner, shallower. But they gained in confidence. The largest one, tucked into the fold of her wrist, looked like it should have had stitches.

"There are others, too," she said.

"Where?" I asked, but she didn't answer, and I remembered where the other victims had been cut: at their throats or the inner thigh. Marie's throat was untouched, and the blood rushed to my cheeks.

"You have good hands," she said, and I realized I was still holding her. "Gentle. You're not the kind of boy he'd want me hanging around."

"What kind is that?" I asked.

"The good kind. Good-looking. Good-hearted. Just, good."

"I thought you said the blood drinker was handsome?"

She laughed.

"No. No, he was . . . He could have been a film star."

"Who did this to your arm, Marie?" I asked, and she jerked free.

"I told you. He did."

I withdrew and wiped my clammy hands on my jeans. "It must have hurt."

She shrugged. "It didn't hurt so much."

"Where is he now?" I cleared my throat and returned to my chair. "Is he still here? Could he hide in Black Deer Falls? As a bat?" She didn't like me teasing her and I don't know why I kept it up.

"Maybe he could and maybe he couldn't," she snapped. "Your joking about it won't change what happened."

I was getting nowhere. I considered changing tactics. Confronting her, making her mad. Except Pilson had already tried that and failed, and I couldn't imagine that I would do much better.

"Someone left a snake in my friend Percy's car," I said simply, surprised the moment the words came out. The snake and the blood drinker had not been connected in my mind until right then.

"What do you mean someone left a snake?" she asked.

"We got into his car and there was a snake on the seat between us. It was only a python, I guess, and it was in a burlap sack. But Percy nearly hit a truck."

"Your friend Percy . . . does he have many enemies?"

"No," I said. "Perce is . . . Everybody likes Percy. Even when he's annoying." I smiled a little. "It was just a joke."

"Was it?" she asked, like she thought it wasn't.

"Marie, do you know where he is?"

"No. But I always thought he might stick around to watch." She looked at me seriously. "You shouldn't go off on your own, Michael."

I almost smiled. I wasn't going to hide from a make-believe monster. But someone real had killed Steve Carlson.

"You think he'd come after me? Or my family?" I asked. But she didn't answer. I suppose she couldn't have known. "Marie, why did he leave you that night after the murders?"

She clenched her teeth.

"Because the bastard wanted me to get caught."

CHAPTER EIGHTEEN

The Blood Drinker

IN THE THIRD week of October, the Upper Midwest got hit with an early snowstorm. The farmers hated it—they had to start hay-feeding their cows sooner than planned, and Percy was worried about his buck. The one he'd been tracking all summer. So one afternoon we headed into the woods behind the Valentine house to follow a few deer trails and do a feeding run. To make sure Percy's buck didn't wander off to get shot by someone else.

"He's too pretty to wind up on Martin Greenway's stupid den wall," he said.

"But just pretty enough for yours?" I asked. "We both know you're not going to shoot it."

"Well. Next year he'll be even bigger."

"And bigger and bigger," I said. "Until he turns gray and hunched over with arthritis."

I followed Percy through the silent trees, our boots sinking into soft snow, snow that was still good, not hard and crusted from melting and refreezing. He showed me the trails the deer were moving through, and the last places he'd seen the buck, in the thicket near the swamp. I watched him shimmy up trees to cut branches down, nice twiggy branches full of buds and stuck-on acorns for the deer to find and feed on.

"Gotta keep plenty of feed out," he said as he dropped another branch, then bent another to feeding height so I could tie it down with bailing twine.

I jumped up and grabbed a branch, pulling the tender bits closer to the ground.

"You know there's still plenty of leaves on the shrubs that he can paw up," I said.

But Percy just grinned. "Trying to fatten him until he's too wide to run."

"You're just spoiling him." I was a little worried about Percy, to be honest. Bow season was already on, and if that buck wandered out of the Valentine swamp and onto someone else's property after a doe or something . . . it would have broken Percy's heart.

"Percy, do you still think about the murders?"

Ahead of me, he broke the branch he'd been hanging on to.

"I try not to," he said.

"But you do."

"Sure."

"Do you ever wonder what happened to the blood?"

"Well, yeah. Everyone wonders about that." He turned to me. "Why? Do you know?"

"No," I said. "But it's so strange. Why take it? What did he want it for?"

"What do you mean 'take it'? He was taking it? I thought it was just"—he gestured to the air—"somewhere else."

I took a deep breath. "What if he wanted to drink it?"

I expected Percy to laugh. Or to shove me and tell me to grow up. But he just shrugged.

"Sure," he said. "Like the papers call it. The Dracula Murders." He turned back to the deer trail and the trees.

"You don't think that's odd?"

"*Yeah* I think it's odd. I think it's a pile of nonsense."

We went on along the trail, pulling down branches and shaking snow off the taller bushes. For being such a loudmouth, Percy didn't like to talk much on those runs—he didn't want to spook the deer. But I had too much on my mind.

"Did you know that in Europe they believed that vampirism caused the plague? They buried women with stones in their mouths to keep them from feeding on corpses in the mass graves. And they'd bury them facedown, so they'd lose their way in the dirt if they tried to dig out."

Percy frowned at me. He slapped his hands together to get the cold bits of bark off and washed his palms with snow. "What are you on about?"

I told him what I'd been reading: disturbing tales about babies being born with full sets of teeth and about Mercy Brown, whose father let her be dug up so his neighbors could cut out her heart and burn it. When I got to the part about her brother eating the ashes, Percy swore loudly.

"Why in the jumped-up hell are you reading about stuff like that?" he asked.

"I just keep thinking about the blood. How it was all missing. And I don't know. I got to wondering if someone could be so deluded, to try and kill that way. To drink it." I hesitated. "Can you even imagine something like that?"

"No, I can't imagine," he said. "And I'd rather *not* imagine. The Dracula Murders was just a name the papers made up. How much blood do you think is in a man? Or in those two girls, those nurses? You couldn't drink that much . . . no way." He was looking at me like I'd completely lost it.

"Yeah," I said as I heard the echo of Marie's words through the trees. *Where did the blood go?* A whisper, the barest brush of her lips against my ear. "You're right. I was just thinking."

"This thing's really got you turned around," he said. "Are you sure you should . . . I mean, if you wanted to quit, your dad would understand. So would everyone else. And if they didn't, well, I'd—"

"I can't stop, Percy."

He nodded. "Yeah, yeah, I know you can't. Biggest story of the century, right? When it's over, there'll be colleges . . . scholarships. You'll go on Cronkite and I'll go over to your folks' house and watch it with them." He grinned. He was proud of me. Excited for me, even though papers and scholarships weren't what I'd meant.

"Maybe you can come along," I said.

"Yeah. Maybe I'll come to college, too. Not that I could get in. But just come along to get a place."

"Yeah."

"Nothing here that won't be here anyway when we get back." He looked up into the branches. "Not like the birdseed factory is going to close down."

"Yeah," I said softly, and he went on ahead down the trail.

When I looked up again, Percy was gone, soaked up by the trees. I must've moved slower than I'd thought, but it was okay— it's nearly impossible to get lost in the woods behind Percy and Mo's place, especially since I'd been traipsing through them since I was nine. And there were Percy's tracks in the snow, headed up the deer trail.

"Perce?" I called out, and waited. "Percy?"

He might've been too far off to hear. When he finished his feeding run, he'd double back and find me. It was disconcerting to look up and realize he was no longer four feet in front of me, but it wasn't dangerous or even that strange, considering how fast Percy moved when he stripped branches. At least that's what I told myself as I stood alone in the middle of the quiet forest.

I opened my mouth to shout again. But all of a sudden I didn't want to make any noise. A strange sensation had begun to creep up my back. Like I was being watched through the trees.

I stiffened, and my boots squeaked loudly in the snow. I held my breath and looked for birds or squirrels but there weren't any. I thought of a story my dad had told me from when he was younger and answered a burglary call. The feeling he'd had when he walked through an open door and had known that the house wasn't empty.

"Damn it, Marie," I muttered into my collar, because it was her fault; she'd filled my head with stories of murderers and a blood-drinking movie monster. An hour earlier I would have laughed out loud. But in those trees I felt what a deer must feel when a hunter is on them. I was waiting for the ambush and hoping I'd be fast enough to get away.

When Percy's dark shape stepped onto the path ahead, I must've jumped a mile. The inside of my coat collar was wet with sweat.

"Percy," I said. "I lost you for a minute."

"Yeah," he replied. "I cut in toward the swamp and then back out again." He looked at my face. "What's with you? You catching sick or something?"

"Maybe. This coat's no good." The coat was fine. If anything it felt a little too warm. I wanted to shrug out of it—I was shaking all over. Percy cocked his head like he might laugh. Then he stopped short.

"What?" I asked.

"What's that?"

"What's what?" I demanded loudly. He pointed over my shoulder and I couldn't bring myself to turn around to look. He walked back and moved past me to a tree not far off the deer path.

There was a symbol marked into it, like a sun or a flower, beneath a long upside-down T. It was above head-level: when Percy took off his glove to run his fingers in the carved grooves, he had to reach.

"Is that a T or a cross?" he asked.

"I don't know."

"It's deep." He rubbed his fingers together and sniffed them. "Sap feels fresh. But who in the hell would come out here and mark up one of our trees?" Everyone knew the land belonged to the Valentines. And everyone knew that if you poached a deer on Valentine property you were prime to catch a bullet in the leg, or so Mo liked to loudly proclaim.

"Are there tracks?"

Percy looked down and around the base of the trunk. "Oh yeah." He bent down. "And they're not old either." He looked over his shoulder, quiet. Then he looked back at me. "Did you see anyone?"

I shook my head, and Percy stood back up, shoved his hand into his glove, and came back to where I stood. The strangeness was getting to him, too.

"We should have seen that on the way in," he said. "Unless they did it after we'd gone past." He chewed the inner part of his lip. "Pop's going to be pissed if someone's been out here."

"Marie said she thinks he might still be here. In Black Deer Falls."

Percy looked at me. We were teetering on the edge, the fear flying around us like bugs. If we let it land, we would run for his house as fast as our legs would carry us, like we used to when we were kids running from an imagined cougar. Or we could do something else. We'd been afraid too many times lately. In the Carlson house. By the stream with Petunia and LuluBelle.

"So let's find the bastard."

We set off. When I was alone, the killer had become something more than flesh and blood, but with Percy back my fear changed again to anger. He was just one man, and we outnumbered him. I was tall and an athlete; Percy was a little shorter but wiry and armed with a hunting knife.

Percy took the lead. He was by far the better tracker, though not even I would have had a problem following the prints as they wove around trunks just to one side of the deer trail. They were large and deep; sometimes near a tree they would become a flurry of kicked and trampled snow, and we would find another symbol carved into the bark. We'd nearly reached the edge of Percy's backyard when the tracks doubled back on themselves and disappeared.

"Aw hell, we've been going the wrong way!"

"No we haven't."

Percy kept on looking around, but I knew he was wrong. There hadn't been any other tracks leading from the first carving we'd found. And we had followed every offshoot.

"Well, they didn't just up and disappear." He ducked and turned to peer into the trees from all directions. His voice became a hissing whisper. "It can't really be him. Can it?"

Him. The man who killed the Carlsons. That feeling was back again, that we were being watched. Back and stronger than ever.

"We've got to get out of here," Percy said. "And tell your dad."

"Tell him what? That a vampire was following us on a deer-feeding run, carving symbols into tree trunks and vanishing without a trace?"

"Well, not the vampire bit but otherwise yeah."

We hurried down the deer trail until Percy's house was visible. The sight of it made us feel safe even though it was a lie—there was no one home at Percy's house that day, and no other house around for miles.

"I don't want to tell my dad."

"But you need to, don't you?" Percy asked. "If there's any chance it could be him?"

I did tell my dad, and he had men search the woods until dusk: Bert, and Charlie, called in on his day off. My dad stopped short of getting extra help from the state police, but he did let Mo lead some of his pals into the woods: Richard Wittengren and Skinny Earl Andersen, guys who knew the forest as well as we did. They found nothing. No old fires, no campsites. And they, too, lost the trail at the last carved symbol. Mo thought whoever it was must have covered up from there. They took photos of the carvings, and my dad told me it was good that I'd let him know. But I heard it in his voice. He'd have to take every last man out for beers as a way of apologizing for wasting a day on his spooked kid.

I rode home with my dad after the search ended, fingers aching from the cold, dreading when the feeling would return to my feet. When I followed him silently up the porch, I scooped up Dawn's old cat on the way. He was good and didn't scratch me, despite my never having picked him up before. He even purred against my chest.

"Dawn!" I shouted.

"Yeah?" She came bounding down the stairs. "What are you doing to my cat?"

"I'm not doing anything to him." I set him down and he stuck his gray tail out indignantly.

"Don't just throw him down!"

"I didn't just throw him down," I said as she picked him up.

"Just keep him inside for a while," I said. "Percy heard some howling in the woods. He thinks some wolves might have come down with the snow."

CHAPTER NINETEEN

Cat and Mouse

ON SUNDAY, MY mom decided to drive the car separately to church. When I asked why, she said she wanted to drop a coconut cake by for Widow Thompson, the Carlsons' old neighbor.

"You can come with me, if you want," she said when I hung around in the kitchen.

So after church, I drove the two of us out to the Carlson farmhouse along County 23. The closer we got, the tighter my tie felt around my neck, and I could tell that my mom was nervous, too—she kept fiddling with the plastic food wrap over the top of the cake, worrying the toothpicks were going to punch through and the covering would ruin the frosting.

We pulled into Fern Thompson's driveway, which was actually an offshoot of the Carlson driveway, and parked near her front walk. I got out and opened the car door for my mom, both of us stealing solemn and nervous glances toward the Carlson farmhouse. Charlie and Bert had been by to clean things up like my dad had promised, so the chalk marks were gone and the blood-stained rug had been burned. But if that had been meant as an exorcism, it hadn't worked. The place still looked empty and inhabited at the same time.

We went up Fern Thompson's cement steps and I knocked. My mom didn't wait for a reply before trying the knob and opening it up a crack.

"Fern? Hello, Fern? It's Linda Jensen and Michael!"

We stepped into the linoleum entryway just as Widow Thompson was getting up from her living room chair. Steve's old tomcat swayed a few steps ahead of her with his tail in the air. Then he jumped up onto the kitchen table to say hello. My mom gave the cat a look, but when Mrs. Thompson gave no objections, she just said, "Michael, take care not to let the cat out."

"It's all right," Mrs. Thompson said. "He won't go. Not even if I try to shove him through the door. That's a very pretty cake."

"I hope you like coconut."

"Mmm," she said. "I'll put on some coffee for us to enjoy with."

She nodded to me and I said hello, but I think my being there made her kind of sad. Maybe I reminded her of Steve. We didn't have the same build or the same coloring, but being the same age might've been enough. She moved around her kitchen, setting out three small plates and three forks. Only two cups for coffee, figuring I was too young to drink any. She and my mother chatted, and I tried to pet Steve's cat, but it seemed shy of being touched. Not by Mrs. Thompson, though, who scooped him up with one arm and set him on the back of the sofa. I remember wishing that the old tom had been younger. So he would live longer and give her more company.

"Would you like a big slice of cake, Linda, or a smaller one?" Fern asked.

"I never say no to a big slice. I just won't have sugar in my coffee."

"Your boy will have to have a big slice, too. So I won't have so much left over."

"Yes, ma'am," I said, and wandered out to the living room while they talked about church and what my mom used to make the frosting. The Carlson house was clearly visible through the front windows, just across the small yard and driveway. Close enough to give the impression that it was looking back at me. The night of the murders, Widow Thompson would have been able to see right into the living room. Except that the curtains had been drawn closed. Earlier that evening she'd have been able to see Mr. Carlson going to and from the barns. She'd have been able to see everything they did on that last day.

When Bert had interviewed her, she'd said that Steve came home around eight thirty, which checked out—he'd had dinner over at Cathy Ferry's house that night and stayed afterward to watch a little TV.

"Come and have some cake, Michael," my mom said.

I went and took my plate and a fork, then wandered off again so they might be able to keep visiting. But when my mom excused herself to the bathroom, Mrs. Thompson asked, "Michael, how is that girlfriend of Steve's doing?"

"Cathy?" I asked. "I guess she was pretty upset. They hadn't been going out long; they weren't a couple. But I know she liked him a lot."

"I never did see him take her home that night," Mrs. Thompson said. "I must've dozed off. Like I dozed off during . . ." She looked down at her cake. But then she smiled. "She seemed like a nice girl."

"She is," I said. Then I stopped. "What do you mean you never saw Steve take her home? Cathy was never at the Carlsons' that night."

"She wasn't?" Mrs. Thompson put her fingers to her lips. "But I'm sure that she was . . . She had his jacket on over her shoulders and he took them in through the back door."

I froze. The girl she saw had to be Marie.

"Them," I said. "Who else was with Steve and Cathy?"

"Hmm?"

"You said he took them in through the back door. Who was 'them'?"

"Oh." The widow blinked a few times, like she was trying to remember. "No one," she said finally. "It was just him and his girlfriend."

But at first she hadn't been sure. That uneasy feeling crept up my collar, but she was an older lady and probably couldn't trust her memory when it came to a lot of things.

"Why didn't you tell Bert or my dad that Cathy had been here that night?" I asked.

"Oh," she said. "Well, I didn't want to bring her up. Being a young girl and out late with a boy—even a nice boy like Steven. It didn't seem like any of my business."

I would have asked more, but my mom returned from the bathroom. I turned back to the window. The Carlsons had a bright light mounted on a pole above their driveway, to light the way between the house and the barns. If it had been bright enough that night for Mrs. Carlson to see Steve and Marie and where they went, she couldn't have missed someone else. The killer must have come later, after she had already nodded off.

Except she had said, "Them." That Steve had taken *them* around the back of the house. Maybe she misspoke. But I didn't think so.

"I wish someone would move into that house," Mrs. Thompson said to us before we left. "But I suppose no one will. Come next summer, all those flowers will need to be tended."

When we got home, I told my dad what the widow had told me, and he cursed Bert under his breath and said he would reinterview her himself. My mother just stared at me, aghast that I would question Fern Thompson while she had been away in the bathroom.

"That was a sneaky thing to do, Michael," she said. But I hadn't meant to do it. It had just happened. I didn't regret it, though, because between what Mrs. Thompson had said and what Percy and I had seen in the woods, I was starting to feel like I was being toyed with.

That Monday I went back to the jail to see Marie.

"What?" she said, and I pulled out the piece of paper I had stuffed into my pocket.

I'd crudely sketched the markings we'd seen cut into Percy's trees. I've never been much of an artist and I kept messing it up—I must've drawn it thirty or forty times. In the end my bedroom was littered with symbols staring up at me in furious black ink, large and small, over and over and over.

Marie studied it, her eyes lingering on the inverted cross.

I'd already tried to explain it to myself: Percy and I could have missed those carvings on the walk out. We were distracted. We could have covered over the other footprints with our own. But none of that really stuck. And I couldn't stop thinking about something that Percy said, right before I left to go home with my dad.

"The carvings were deep," he said. "So deep those trees might never heal."

I didn't know how strong someone would have to be to stab that far into the wood; I just knew that I wouldn't have been able to do it, not even if I'd been leaning over a log on the ground.

Marie handed the paper back to me.

"They're only games."

"Games?" I asked.

"Yeah," she said. "He's just showing off. It must be quite the novelty having me locked up. I suppose he didn't figure it would take this long. I suppose he's enjoying watching, knowing I didn't get away."

I studied her quietly. The things she said about the blood drinker didn't always make sense; she made her incarceration sound like it was planned and also a fortunate surprise.

"Does he want to hurt me, Marie? Does he want to hurt my family?"

"He might want to. But he wouldn't dare."

"What do you mean?" I asked.

I assumed she meant that attacking me would be too big a risk. But the way she said it seemed to imply something else. Like she had forbidden it. Like she had that power over him.

That thought only occurred to me later. It was only when I was away from her that I could consider what she was and her role in the murders. I know everyone thinks I thought she was completely innocent. A victim. A hostage. But Marie was never as simple as that. Victim. Killer. One thing or another.

"Are you afraid of him?"

"Of course not," she said. "Why would I be afraid of him?"

"Because he killed people," I half shouted, frustrated. "Or was he ever there at all?"

Marie's eyes widened.

"How did you get to the Carlson house that night, Marie?"

"Your friend Steven picked us up. We were walking along the road and he stopped to check on us."

"We?" I asked. "Widow Thompson said she saw you go into the house with Steve. And only you."

"Widow Thompson doesn't know what she saw. I never killed anyone."

"You can't do this, you know," I said. "Tell me a killer is in my town and not tell me who he is, give me no way to protect myself besides hanging garlic in my window."

Marie laughed. "That wouldn't work."

"I know it won't. Not any more than holy water or a wooden stake. Because he's just a man."

"If he's just a man, then why didn't any of them run?" she asked. "Why didn't they fight? He never tied any of them up. Doesn't that seem odd to you, that they just lay there and let the life drain out of them?" She licked her lips. "Almost like someone had convinced them it wasn't happening."

I glanced at our old kitchen table, where the tape recorder sat, whirring. I hadn't brought my pen and paper, but I'd switched on the recorder the moment I came into the room.

"But that wasn't always true," I said. "Sometimes they ran." The truck driver, Monty LeTourneau, and the hitchhiker who was found with him. Their bodies had been found almost a mile apart. One of them must have run.

Marie shrugged and I sat down on one of the kitchen chairs. It was strange, but talking about the murders put me at ease. They were as real as the graves and the photographs in the files. They weren't an imagined monster stalking us through the woods and leaving me presents of snakes on the bench seats of cars.

"What about Stephen Hill?" I asked. "The other service station worker who was found in the field across the highway? He had run."

"Sometimes he let them run," Marie said.

"Why?"

"So he could chase them."

"What about the way Stephen Hill was found?" I asked. Stephen Hill was presumed killed on August 18, in the same attack as Jeff Booker, though his body wasn't found until a day later, abandoned in a field across from the service station. His corpse had been in a different state than the others: lying on his back with his pants around his ankles, the deep bloodless cuts in his thighs laid open to the Iowa sky. "The investigators," I said, and cleared my throat, "thought it might indicate a sexual element."

"The investigators are disgusting men," Marie spat. She lay down on her bed and rolled onto her stomach. "Are you thinking about that?"

"No."

"Sure you are. You're thinking about it and those pretty nurses. You're thinking about the other marks on me." She pushed up onto her elbows. "Have you ever gone all the way with a girl?"

"What does that have to do with anything?" I asked.

Marie rolled over again and sat up.

"You haven't. When you do, you'll realize that there are lots of other things to think about."

"So those investigators . . . you don't think they've slept with a girl either?"

Marie laughed. "You've got me there. I guess maybe men just never stop thinking about it. The way they pursue . . ." She trailed off. "My stepfather wasn't young when he met my mother, but every time he showed up at our door, you'd have thought it was to go to the senior prom."

"I thought you said he was terrible?"

"He wasn't at first. At first he was good. Kind of stupid. He used to brag that he had an ancestor who was a cowboy. One of the famous ones from those parts. But my stepfather was the least cowboy-looking man I'd ever seen. Always in a suit. Always shined shoes."

"What about your father?" I asked.

"We lived by a train yard. He was one of those railmen. Left before I was seven."

"Was he a transient?"

"No. He just had someplace else to go. He was just smart enough not to put down roots."

But you were a root, I wanted to say. You and your mother. But before I could, Marie asked, "Do you think I should die?"

"You didn't do the killing," I said quietly.

"But if I let them die, does it make a difference?"

"That's not for me to say."

"Well, it's for someone to." She reached down and touched her scars. "I cut my hand the first time he saw me. I think that's why he noticed. It was at the roadhouse where I worked. I'd been washing glasses. Sharp glass in warm water."

"Why did he pick you?" I asked. "Why did you go?

"I don't know. He said he loved me. Said I was special."

"What was special about you?"

"I don't know. Maybe he thought I'd be willing to go along with it. That would make me pretty special."

"But you didn't go along with it?"

"No, I already told you. I never killed anyone."

"Who was he, Marie?"

"I told you."

"But what was his name?"

"His name doesn't matter," she said, "because it wasn't his real one."

I sat back and eyed the tape recorder again. In the months to come I would sometimes forget that it was there and we were being recorded. I have an almost vitriolic resentment for it now and its mechanical intrusion on some of the most intimate moments of my life.

"All right," I said, "then why him? It couldn't have been just because he looked like James Dean."

"I never said he looked like James Dean. I said he looked like a film star."

"Yeah, well. Same difference."

"He was charming," she said. "I wouldn't say he was kind, but he was kind to me. And his smile was—"

"Full of fangs?" I prodded, and she gave me a look.

"If he had fangs, what would he need the straight razor for?" She pursed her lips, and I resisted the urge to mutter about what kind of a vampire didn't have fangs.

"But even if there was some kind of attraction—after you saw him kill, how could you go on with it? Did he threaten you? Promise to protect you?"

"He promised that after it was over, I would never need to be protected again."

I sat back. "Because you would be like him."

"A blood drinker like him," she said. "The Carlsons were supposed to be mine. My first. But I didn't want to do it. Only he had the baby and he kept saying—"

I shook my head and stopped her. Mr. McBride said I should let her talk, but it wasn't right.

"This is grotesque, Marie," I said. "It's indecent. These were real people. They were my friends. Stop with the monsters. Tell the truth."

Marie just sighed.

"All these bodies without blood," she said. "And you won't believe in vampires. Yet you believe in God."

"That's different."

"How?"

"Do you believe in God?" I asked her.

"I guess," she said softly. "And I'm still not scared of Him. What about this"—she held up my scrap of paper—"cut into a tree? What about everything I've told you? The tricks to fool them into not struggling? What about me, covered in the Carlsons' blood?"

"There has to be an explanation," I said.

"And I gave it to you," she said. "We didn't just slash people and leave them to bleed. Why would we do that?"

"You were fleeing. You panicked and stole cars and hitched a ride with Steve on your way to Canada."

"Who chased you and Percy through the woods?"

"Maybe no one. Maybe we mistook it all."

"Where was the blood?" she asked, and I looked away.

"You still don't believe me," she said quietly. "But you're starting to."

CHAPTER TWENTY

Black Deer Falls, November 1958

I STAYED AWAY from the jail for a while after that—for nearly a week. If Marie believed what she said, then she was deluded. But deluded or not, I knew what Pilson would eventually make of it: it was motive. She had gone along with the killings in exchange for what she thought would be eternal life.

Then again if she was making it up as she went . . . I didn't know why she would choose to tell that story. I only knew she was doing a damn fine job.

Marie and the murders had taken over my entire life. I walked through my days with my mind on nothing else—more than once I crossed the street to nearly get flattened by a passing car. I'd been speaking with Marie almost every day since the interviews began and was still no closer to finding the truth—she'd given me a description of the killer's home ("not a cave or a castle or a burrow dug into the ground if that's what you're thinking, Michael") but left out anything that would allow us to locate it. Sometimes when she talked about him she sounded dreamy. Other times her words were clipped and bitter. She had called him a bastard once, when he left her at the Carlson farmhouse. "The bastard wanted me to get caught."

All the while the search for the killer continued. Authorities were still certain of catching him. He was flustered now, the papers said. He had to be, when his flight from the Carlson house had been so fast and sloppy that he'd left his accomplice behind.

Early in the month, the FBI came in and conducted a very embarrassing series of interrogations where Marie shouted at them and called them all no-good cheats. They kept her under the lights for almost thirty-six hours, but according to Charlie, when it was over she bounced out of there like she was fresh from a feather pillow. The agents, on the other hand, looked like they'd been hit by a truck.

A reporter from the *Times* would say later that it was like Marie had us under her spell. That the heartland had been held captive by the murders all summer and now were held captive by the murderess. It was a nice turn of phrase. Made for a good story. But he was an idiot. I don't think he ever set one foot in Black Deer Falls, and if he did, he didn't spend his time talking to any of us.

On my way to the jail one afternoon, I ran into our neighbor, Mr. Vanderpool, who had managed the Buy-and-Bag before retiring a few years ago.

"How's it going over there," he asked, "at the jail?"

"I don't think I'm allowed to discuss it, sir. My dad would tan my hide."

"And right he should! But I won't lie; there are plenty of people who'd have preferred your dad had turned her over, and let that prosecutor from Nebraska handle the mess. Having her here, lingering . . . it isn't helping anyone to move on from the Carlsons' deaths."

"Yes, sir," I said, even though that was the very reason she'd had to stay. The Carlsons were ours. If my father had given up and let her go, we might have never gotten the answers we deserved. They'd have called him a coward and accused him of passing the buck.

"How much longer do you think it'll be?" Mr. Vanderpool asked.

"I really couldn't say, sir."

"I see you coming and going from Matt McBride's office over at the *Star*. . . . This'll all be written up for us, then? Everything she said? Everything she's done?" He smiled harder when he asked that, a forced smile that stretched across his face.

"I'm not sure what will be released to the papers," I said. "It's not really my story. It's Marie's story. I'm just taking it down."

"Marie's story," he said, and the corners of his mouth fell, though his teeth continued to show. "Well, you can hurry her up, can't you? And then send her on to the chair."

He tipped his hat and went home. Black Deer Falls was not under Marie's spell.

Neither was the rest of the country. The headlines that had

sprung up in the wake of Marie's arrest were in black ink and bold letters. They declared her the Blood-covered Demoness of the Bloodless Murders. The articles said she was coldhearted, an accomplice who refused to give up her man. And of course there was the picture. Always the same picture on the steps of the court-house in the capital—the one snap, the one instant, where she appeared to be smiling, with my mother's lipstick darkly crimson on her upturned mouth.

I don't know how many times I went back over my notes, over and over them, wondering if the story I would write would show a different side of her or if it would turn out the same.

Mr. Vanderpool's words rang in my ears as I walked to the jail that day. *Send her on to the chair.* I didn't know if I could face her. If I could look at the bars and the painted door. The small square of sky through the window. Suddenly everything seemed over already. And it seemed like such a waste, that she would spend the rest of her life in that cell.

I made it through the doors of the station, but I couldn't go up. Nancy saw me sort of standing there.

"Come with me," she said. "For a breath of fresh air."

She took me out around the building and I leaned against the brick wall as she lit a cigarette.

"Some breath of fresh air," I quipped. "How many packs do you think you've given to Marie by now, anyway?"

She held the pack out to me and I took one. Just one, the way I did sometimes after a few too many beers with Percy.

"Don't tell your dad," she said as she lit it for me.

"They shouldn't have made you do this," she said. "It's too much for someone your age."

"Marie's younger than I am," I said, and she took a long drag. Nancy was so pretty: bright blond hair and ruby lips. "How's Charlie?" I asked, and she shoved me lightly.

"Mind your own business."

We smoked for a while in the cold quiet.

"You've taken a shine to Marie," I said.

"I guess I have. I guess you have, too." She ashed onto the pavement and smudged it with the toe of her low-heeled shoe. "People probably think we're crazy. But she's just a kid. I don't want to see anything worse happen to her than what already has."

"You don't think she did it, then?" I asked.

"She says she didn't. And she doesn't seem like . . ." Nancy trailed off. "She just seems lost. Tough and lost."

Images of the murder victims flashed through my head. That was the week I'd finally looked at the photos of the Carlson murder—if you could call it looking. I'd sat at the desk in my room and held my breath while I flipped through the pages. When I got to the shot of Steve's body lying curled on the rug, I shut the file and sat there with my face in my hands.

"Why didn't they fight?" I asked Nancy. "Do you ever wonder about that?"

"Maybe they were afraid. Maybe he told them he was going to let them go if they didn't."

"But when he cut them—why didn't they fight then?"

Nancy shrugged. "Have you ever felt the difference between

a shallow cut and a deep one? There isn't much. Just a sense of panic. Remember William Haywood, how he died?"

"William Haywood the movie star?"

"He hit his head and cut it deep and then sat down drinking gin until he stopped breathing. Just sat there on his bedroom floor, not knowing he was bleeding to death." She stubbed out her cigarette and picked up the butt to toss in the trash. "Maybe none of the victims knew either, until it was too late. You coming in?"

"I think I'll stay out here awhile longer. Thanks for the smoke, Nancy."

"Just get the smell off before your dad sees you," she said, and went back inside.

I stood there in the cold and thought about Marie. I thought about the scars on her arms. The shallow and the deep ones. And I thought about Nancy and why she knew what they felt like.

Nancy had moved to Black Deer Falls five years before, from one of the small states out east. Looking at her now, so pretty, flirting with Charlie, you'd think she was never sad a day in her life.

The fire that had killed her husband and baby had been an accident. A freak thing. Sparks from the flue had caught on the rug, and when she woke coughing, Nancy had run out on instinct. By the time she realized what was happening, the blaze was too high for her to go back in. So she just stood in her yard and screamed and screamed until the fire truck came.

We never would have known about that, except when she first came to town she used to have drinks at the Rusty Eagle, the old army bar between the butcher and the bus garage. And when she'd had enough, the whole story came out. How much she'd lost. How much she hated herself. It wasn't her fault, of course. It could have happened to anyone.

But there are women in town who to this day refuse to speak to Nancy. They think it's indecent that she could dare go on. That she smiles. That she flirts with Charlie. I used to think they were just being ugly. Now, after knowing Marie, I just think they're mistaken.

The woman they condemn doesn't even exist. The mother, the young wife, she died in the fire with her husband and baby. Whoever Nancy is now had to leave that all behind.

Since the carvings in the woods behind Percy's house, there had been no further signs of the blood drinker, and I had almost begun to believe we had imagined the whole of it. Weeks had passed, and Mo had finally stopped sitting by the fire in his backyard pit with a pile of beer cans built into a pyramid and a rifle in the crook of his arm, and Percy said they hadn't seen anything but does and squirrels in their woods since the day of the search. He also kicked slush at my shoes because I'd scared off his buck.

But if the buck had moved on, all the better for it. Those woods weren't safe.

For my part, I wasn't taking any chances. I still made Dawn keep her cat in, and I still walked her home from school.

"Can we stop and get an ice cream soda?" she asked as we cut down Main Street.

"Only you would want an ice cream in November," I said. Dawn was made for Minnesota: she kicked her blankets off year-round. She'd been that way since she was a baby. My mom said she'd had a real time of it, keeping her tiny feet in socks.

We started up the block to Anderson's Drug Store, where the soda fountain was. Dawn wanted a chocolate soda topped with a scoop of butter brickle. I was after a hot dog with extra mustard and a root beer float. The streets were busy for a weekday afternoon—probably because the sun was out and made town look warmer, even though it wasn't—and full of unfamiliar faces. Black Deer Falls was never so small that I knew everyone, but lately, the people I didn't know seemed to know me, and that was an uncomfortable feeling.

"Maybe not today, Dawn, okay?" I said, and stopped walking.

She frowned, and when I looked up the street again, I saw Mr. McBride and his wife. They were arm-in-arm, and brown paper bags of groceries were tucked in each of their outer elbows like bookends. Mrs. McBride saw us first and whispered, and Mr. McBride looked up and shouted hello. He gave a little wave with the hand holding his groceries and almost spilled them in the process.

I took my hand out of my pocket and waved back, then put my arm around Dawn to hurry her along home. I felt guilty repaying his warm greeting with something so brief, but I wasn't up to talking. I thought about it the rest of the short walk to our house, wondering whether he'd taken it personally or if I'd just flat out hurt his feelings.

"What's that on our door?" Dawn asked.

"What?"

She pointed with a red mitten. Something was hanging on our front door, like a wreath hung for Christmas—except whatever this was hung straight down. It was three-feet long and narrowed at the bottom. And it was dripping.

I knew what it was before Dawn did, but my legs kept moving forward like in a dream as I tried to make sense of what it was doing there. I kept on walking toward it, like a fool, until Dawn finally put her hands to her face and started to scream.

"Dawn, Dawn!" I shouted, and bent down to take her by the shoulders. I tried to pull her in close but she fought me. She wouldn't stop screaming. In the corner of my eye I saw our neighbor's door open up and Mrs. Schuman step out to see what was wrong. Others would join her soon enough—Dawn's screams must have been audible for at least two blocks. But all I kept thinking was that my mother was inside. My mother was inside, and I didn't want her to open the door.

It was a snake hanging down the white wood. The same snake that someone had left in a sack on Percy's front seat. Someone had taken her and nailed her to our front door, right below the brass door knocker.

"Good God."

I heard Mr. McBride's gasped words as his running footsteps came to a halt. Mrs. Schuman approached on the other side, hands over her open mouth. Mrs. Spanaway and the Misses Monson—the spinster sisters who live two houses down—crept toward us with wide eyes. They made me sick to my stomach, those eyes. They made me cold all over. The snake was terrible, and here we were, my family, in the middle of it again. And then my mother came to the door.

"What's going on?" she asked. The door swung in, and as it did, the snake's dead body swung in toward her like a fat length of rope. Her mouth made a surprised O and she screamed and slammed the door back shut, disappearing from view to shriek inside the house while the snake thumped heavily against the wood.

"Someone call Sheriff Jensen," Mr. McBride said to the growing crowd of neighbors. He looked down at Dawn and placed a hand on top of her red knitted hat. "It's all right, sweetheart. It can't hurt you."

At his words, Dawn started to cry. Dawn never was afraid of snakes. That wasn't why she had screamed. She had screamed because someone had killed the poor thing.

"Tell him not to bring Bert," I called to Mrs. Schuman, who was hurrying back to her house to call my dad. "Tell him that no matter what, he needs to keep Bert away!"

"It was Bert's snake," I explained to Mr. McBride. "He took it in after someone left it in the front seat of Percy's car."

He blinked at me and looked at the snake. It had nearly stopped swaying after being disturbed, but the movement had made the scene more gruesome; she had slid and rolled through her own dripped blood and smeared it in an arc.

"How do you know it's the same one?" he asked.

I didn't respond. I couldn't be sure, not then. I just knew that it was. Later, poor Bert would confirm it when he found her tank empty, though he couldn't say how she'd been taken. There was no evidence of forced entry. He figured that one of his window latches was faulty or that someone had picked the lock to the back door. Poor Bert. He hadn't had her long, but he loved that snake.

While we waited for my dad, Dawn and I lingered on the lawn with our backs to the door. My mom chose to remain in the house on the other side of it. I don't think she wanted to face the crowd. I saw her peering out at us through the curtains in the kitchen and gave her a small nod. Then I tugged Dawn closer. I had her. My mother didn't need to worry.

Behind us, I heard a familiar click and whir and caught the light of a flashbulb. Mr. McBride was kneeling at the base of our front porch steps and taking photographs.

"I didn't know you had your camera," I said.

"I asked Maggie to get it from the car." He gestured back toward town. "We're parked not far up Pine." He snapped off a few more photos and changed the angle, stepping up onto the porch like I had given him permission.

"Are those for my father?" I asked.

He lowered the camera. "Well, yes. He's welcome to them. But they're also for the paper."

"The paper? You'd publish this—our house—in the paper?"

He looked down.

"Mr. McBride, Dawn's already having trouble at school because of the case, and if I get one more suspicious glance from my neighbors, I'm going to turn to salt."

"Lot's wife was turned to salt for looking," he said with a small smile. "Not for being looked at. But I know what you mean, Michael. I know what you've been going through." He put the camera away, slinging it over his shoulder by the leather strap.

Not long after that my dad arrived. He pried the nail free of the door and placed the snake into a sack to bring to the station. Then he broke up the crowd and brought Dawn in to my mom around the back. After that he came to stand with me and Mr. McBride.

"Do you think this was a prank, Sheriff Jensen?" Mr. McBride asked.

"One hell of a nasty prank," my dad replied.

"Too nasty for those same folks who came to the jail the other day?"

"What folks?" I asked. My dad hadn't told me that there had been a group at the station, protesting Marie being kept there.

"Hard to say," he said, ignoring me. "Hard to judge the limits of anyone, after the things we've seen lately."

Mr. McBride asked a few more questions, but my dad wouldn't comment further. So he nodded and tipped his hat. "I hope that little girl of yours is okay," he said, and walked back to his wife, slipping his arm around her thin waist. I hadn't noticed before, but she looked near frozen to the bone, and they broke into a jog as soon as they were back on the sidewalk, in a hurry to get to their car.

"Do you want me to scrub the door?" I asked.

"It's too cold. Let's go inside. I'll get a bucket of soapy water and come back out while your mom finishes up supper."

"He was taking photographs," I said when we got into the warmth of our mudroom. "Mr. McBride, I mean. He said you could use them for the investigation."

"So I can use them. And so he can use them."

"He said he wouldn't," I said, though looking back, I guess he'd said no such thing.

"Listen." My father grabbed my shoulder. "I like Mr. McBride. I really do. I know some folks think he and his wife are a little strange but I've always found them pleasant enough. But his obligation is to that newspaper. His loyalty is to that newspaper. Not to what's decent. And don't you forget it."

Before the events of that fall and winter, I would not have understood what my father meant. How could an obligation to the truth be anything but decent? But now I know. Matt McBride ran the photographs in the *Star* a week later. When I confronted him about it in his office, he said he'd held them back as long as he could. But too many people had seen him take them, and he was beholden to them to write the story. Because it might have been a prank, sure. Or it might have been a threat, and if it was, the public had a right to know. He said he wished he hadn't had to run it. Or that it hadn't been my house. He wished it hadn't been the same snake that had been left once for me already. But I was still angry. And I still felt betrayed.

"You're a journalist, Michael," he said to me. "You understand these choices."

I did understand. And his running the story didn't stop me from thinking of him as a mentor. But it did change things between us, and I knew he regretted that even if he didn't regret printing the photographs. Sometimes choices bear a price. Even the right ones.

One day a long time afterward, I told him I still thought he was a good man. "So does my sister," I said. "She says she knew it the day we found the snake. Because when you waved to us in the street you did it with your hand full of groceries even though it would have been easier to let go of your wife's arm. She said she knew it then."

I remember thinking once that I wasn't sure if the McBrides were happy together. I remember I thought of them as distant. But I must not have been paying very much attention.

CHAPTER TWENTY-ONE

The Carlson Graves

MY DAD ASKED around to all of our neighbors about the snake, but no one could say how it got there, despite it happening in the middle of the day and the fact that my mom had been home the whole time. She had been in the kitchen, yet she swears she didn't hear anyone come up the walk, and she certainly didn't hear a nail being driven through our front door.

I stood with my dad in our backyard, beside the fence and winter shrubs. He was holding the nail we'd removed from the snake's head. Her body he'd given back to Bert, who would keep her in the freezer until he could bury her in the spring.

"Someone must have seen something," I said, eyeing in particular Mrs. Schuman's front windows that lined up nearly perfectly with ours right across the street.

"If they did, no one's talking." He rubbed the nail back and forth between his fingers. All the blood was gone; it looked like a brand-new nail. "If you hear anyone whispering about it at school, you let me know."

"We should have dusted the door for prints. But I was just so eager to—"

"It was only a prank, Michael. I wasn't going to pull prints for a prank."

"How did they get it out of Bert's house, though? How did they keep from being seen?"

My dad looked at me, thinking I was getting spooked. And worried I was starting to buy into everything Marie was telling me.

"He was seen," he said. "Whoever saw him is just lying about it. And I don't know why."

"It must've been someone from school," I said. "Or there are plenty of people around town, I guess." I glanced at him. By then my dad walked around with a slight hunch, like he was ready to fend off something thrown at him. Dawn, who had always loved school, didn't want to go anymore because of the things the other kids were saying about us. And Steve and his parents were lying cold in boxes under the ground.

"We'll be all right," my dad said. "This will pass, and everything will go back to the way it was."

Except that was the problem. The hostility had taken hold of Black Deer Falls so fast and with such ease that it was hard to pretend that it hadn't always been there.

On the way to the jail to see Marie, Charlie rolled past me in his patrol car. He nodded from behind the wheel, but he was grim. Because he wasn't just driving by on the way to see my dad. He was on duty and keeping an extra eye on our house.

I'd thought the interviews were my ticket into any journalism program in the country, but that ambition had started to feel foolish. I'd been thoroughly humiliated and made to look like an idiot—chasing symbols through the woods, reading about vampires. My family was being harassed. By the time I knocked at the door to the women's cell I was angry, and I threw open the door.

"It's not a game now," I said. "What's he playing at?"

Marie stood, fists clenched. She looked at the door still banging against the wall.

"I don't know! I've been stuck in here, if you haven't noticed."

"You're going to be stuck in here for the rest of your life if you don't start telling the truth!"

"They can't keep me forever," she said. "Not when I didn't do anything."

"Even if you didn't kill them, you were there."

"Only because he made me! Because he said I needed to if I wanted to—" She cut off abruptly. I was mad but so was she. I could tell by the bright shine in her eyes and the way her chest rose and fell under her sweater.

"If you wanted to be like him," I said, disgusted.

"What's gotten into you?" she asked. "I mean, I heard about what happened to Bert's snake . . . but that could have been anybody who did that."

"But it wasn't just anybody, was it?"

"I told you, I don't know."

"Sometimes I wish you'd never come here," I said.

"Only sometimes?"

"They hate you, you know. Everyone. And they hate us, too—me, my dad, my little sister—because they think we're . . . we're—"

"They're going to think what they want to think. They don't *know*."

"They know what you brought with you," I said. "All this mess."

Marie relaxed. She slipped another cigarette out of her sleeve and lit it, even though she'd been smoking one just before I came in. I could still smell it hanging in the closed air.

"Not everyone hates me," she said, and puffed. "Nancy doesn't. You don't.

"What would you do," she asked, "if someone told you you could live forever?"

"That's not possible."

"What if it was? What would you do for it? What would you give?"

"Nothing," I said. "I only want the life God gave me."

"That's only because He gave you a good one," Marie whispered.

"Marie, I just want you to—" I stopped. Standing there, watching her smoke, the anger just dropped through my feet. I couldn't say all the things I wanted. I wanted things I couldn't even admit to myself. And I wanted for her to be innocent.

"I just want you to tell the truth. I just want him in the chair where he belongs. If he comes near my family, I'll take him in myself."

"Don't do that," Marie said.

"Why not? I'm not afraid of a knife, Marie. I'm not afraid of a straight razor."

"Don't be stupid, Michael!"

Marie was tough—tougher than most, boys or girls. But she was so frustrated with me, she could hardly speak. "Look, I don't want anything to happen to you, okay?"

"Nothing's going to happen to me," I said, and left.

That night, Percy dragged me out. Away from my notes, away from Marie. "Just come and have a few," he said. "A bunch of us are going down to the lake. It'll be fun."

We drove down the dirt roads that edged Eyeglass Lake and stopped when we got to the row of cars parked along the shoulder. Then we got out and made our way down to the boat landing.

"This doesn't sound like a small party," I said.

"I never said it was," said Percy.

The road was hard-packed with snow, and the air was crisp and clean. Orange light flickered in the trees from the fire someone had started by the shore but we'd have been able to see without it: out there the moon reflected off all that snow and made it bright enough to see the happy grin on Percy's face. The night was warm, all the way up to the low thirties. Which may not sound like much, but when temps drop regularly into the single digits, twenty-five starts to feel downright balmy.

We were late, or so it seemed, though it couldn't have been past ten o'clock. When we reached the party, Percy asked me for a few dollars and headed off; when he came back, he had two six-packs tucked under his arm. He popped off two cans and put one in each of my hands. To catch up.

I don't know who put the party together. I never asked. Percy always seemed to know about those kinds of things, what was happening where and who was going. I saw a few guys from our baseball team, mostly the ones who played football, too. And a few of the girls were there: Sandy Millpoint and Jackie and Violet Stuart, Rebecca Knox and a few of her friends, standing by the fire, looking nice with scarves wrapped over their ears.

I did as Percy asked and drank a few, and then I drank a few more. I helped the guys unload more firewood. Nobody seemed to mind that I was there, and if they looked at me funny, after the first four beers I didn't notice. I sang the school fight song with everyone but mostly I kept to myself and let Percy do the entertaining. He'd had quite a bit to drink but he kept on looping back to me.

"You feeling okay? You out of beer?"

"Nope, I'm fine."

"Jackie Stuart looks cold. Maybe you should go see about warming her up."

"I think Morgan's doing a good job of that already." I gestured to a car parked near the road with the taillights on and the rear window all fogged up, and Percy made this disappointed face, like he hadn't known she'd gone in there.

After a while it got pretty late, and the girls went home, and the guys started horsing around on the ice. Sliding around and snowball bowling, but everybody was too drunk to be any good. I was pretty drunk, too, so when the fire died down and someone said they had an idea, Percy and I didn't ask questions.

We got into our cars and drove along the snow-packed dirt roads, too fast and too loud. There was a bunch of us but I can't say with certainty who was there. Morgan, for sure. He and Paul Buell rode in Percy's car. I thought I'd seen Joe Conley earlier, but I think he'd gone home by then.

There weren't any houses out that way so we turned our radios up and rolled down the windows. One of the guys in the car in front of us pulled down his pants and flashed a full moon through the back; Percy hung his head out the driver's side and howled at it. By the time we stopped we were out of breath from laughing. I don't think Percy even knew where he'd driven us. But we'd wound up at the Methodist cemetery.

The Methodist cemetery isn't very big, and it's pretty far out. The parking lot only had enough space for four cars. Funeral parties had to pull off and park along the ditch down the road.

"What are we doing here?" Percy asked. But I think he knew. The Methodist cemetery was where the Carlsons were buried.

A few of the guys tugged open the short iron gate. It had been half ajar already, and even if it had been locked, we could've jumped it. I hadn't noticed when we left the lake but the only boys who'd come with us were Steve's friends. His best friend, Rudy Bartholomew—who everyone called Bart or Rudy Bart! when he came onto the football field—tossed me a fresh beer and said to come on.

"You wanna go home?" Percy asked.

I looked at the guys. They were still laughing, maybe swaying a little on their feet. I didn't feel like going home. It felt like I should go in, like I should've gone already.

They led us through the cemetery, up the little hills, past the grave markers—most of them small, some of them old and leaning crookedly, partially sunk into the dirt. Some clouds had rolled in and it was darker there than by the lake. I tucked the beer into my coat pocket and pulled my collar up. Ahead, the guys were shouting. They shouted "RUDY BART!" all at once, like they did when he took the field during home games. "RUDY BART!" like "TEN HUT!" in the army.

Percy tripped over something and swore.

"Someone got a light?" he called, and ahead, one of them switched on a flashlight.

"Don't yell in the cemetery!" someone whisper-hollered, and we heard them laughing.

"This doesn't feel right," Percy said. "Let's go back."

"What about Morgan and Paul?"

"They can pile into one of the other cars. They'll be all right."

But it was too late. They'd stopped at a flat patch of ground, under a copse of bare winter trees. The Carlsons' graves.

Their headstones weren't like the others in the cemetery. The town had taken up a collection and purchased all three: large rectangular monuments in white granite. They sat in a row: Bob, and Sarah, and Steve in between them, and against the snow, the white of the granite looked dirty and gray.

I crept closer, shoes sinking into the snow. It was different seeing them there than seeing their caskets. Buried under all that dirt, and all that snow, resting beneath the heavy headstones, the Carlsons felt like a memory.

The first full can of beer hit me in the back, between the shoulder blades. The next one caught me in the side of the head, by my ear. I barely felt the cold of the snow on my hands when I fell.

"Hey!" Percy shouted.

The hit near my ear made my head ring, but I could still see two guys grab Percy from behind. They yanked his arms back hard enough to put him up on his toes.

"Knock it off, you guys; that's not funny!"

"It's not supposed to be funny," said Paul, and threw another can. It was open already, and half-gone. It hit me in the chest and splashed beer up onto my chin.

"Hey, let go of him," I said, and got up on my knees. In the fog of the beer, I thought they were going after Percy. But they were just holding him back.

A few more cans hit, catching me in the face. Or maybe someone hit me. I'd never been in a real fight before, and I suppose that wasn't much of one either. I just knew the blood was warm coming out of my nose and tasted bad, and my split lip was stinging already. I knew I'd had too much to drink, and I thought if I laid down a while whatever was happening would stop.

"Cut it out," Rudy said. "It's a waste of beer."

The cans and hits stopped. It was just Rudy standing there with his dad's pistol.

"You better leave off!" Percy shouted. "He's a Jensen and you'll catch hell!"

But they knew that already. They'd known that before they started.

"You planned this," I said, and Rudy pointed the gun in my face.

"Shut up," he said. "You've got this coming."

I was on my knees in the snow beside the Carlsons' headstones. Percy was screaming, asking them what they were doing, warning them off. I was going to let her get away with it, they said. I was a traitor.

"Don't," I said. "Rudy, don't."

"You think you're so smart," he said. Then he screamed in my face, and I shut my eyes.

I knew that they meant to do it. That they would lose the last of their tempers and pull the trigger. I knew they'd kill Percy, too.

"Keep the light on him," Rudy shouted. Then he pointed the gun at Percy, who had started to call for help.

"Leave him alone!" I screamed, and straightened up, still on my knees in the snow.

The gun swung back, and Rudy rushed forward and pressed the barrel against my forehead. I closed my eyes again.

"Keep it on him," I heard him saying. "Keep it—"

He stopped.

"What is that?" I heard him ask.

"I don't know," said Morgan.

"Give me the light!"

I opened my eyes and looked at Percy as the beam of the flashlight moved behind me. The guys holding him had let their arms go slack, and Percy had nearly sunk down to the ground. They looked less certain.

"What is it?" Paul asked. He went around with Morgan to Rudy. They were behind the graves, the flashlight trained on the back of Steve's headstone.

"What is that?" Morgan asked. "Jesus Christ, what is that?"

The guys holding Percy let go as the flashlight beam swung wildly into the trees, like Mo's had the night of the search party, and Percy scrambled over to me.

"Let's get out of here," he whispered. "Let's go!"

He started to help me up, but Paul and Morgan started screeching the same thing.

"Let's get out of here, Rudy! Come on!"

Then they ran off and took the flashlight with them, leaving Percy and me in the dark. After a few minutes we heard their cars start up and their tires spin as they drove out of the parking lot.

"You okay?" Percy asked. "Christ, you're bleeding."

"I'm okay."

"Christ, let's get out of here."

But I was looking at Steve's headstone in the scant moonlight. They'd seen something there. Something had stopped them.

"Hang on," I said.

"*Hang on*? For what?"

"Percy, give me your lighter."

He grumbled and handed it over, and we moved around the

graves. I flipped the lighter open, and flicked it on. "What in the jumping hells," Percy whispered.

The same symbol that had been carved into the trees in the woods had been cut into the back of Steve's headstone.

I held the flame closer. It wasn't just one symbol this time. It was dozens, etched into the granite, so tightly packed that one bled into the next, large and small, some so shallow it could have been done with a penknife, others so deep it was a wonder that the whole headstone hadn't cracked into pieces.

I cast the light out into the trees, just like Rudy had with the flashlight, and Percy jumped. Whoever had done it wasn't there anymore. The marks had taken time, and could have been done any night after the headstones had been installed. Just the same, I expected to see that pale face.

"Hey," Percy said, "can we just go now? Can we just go?"

"Yeah. Let's go." We backed away from the graves and walked out of the cemetery, and I didn't flip the lighter shut until we were inside his car.

We spent the night at Percy's place, in his room with the lights on and pretending to read comics after I'd washed all the blood from my face.

"What are we going to tell your dad?" Percy asked.

"The truth, I guess. Just . . . not all of it. We were fooling around at the lake and decided to visit the cemetery. We saw the marks on the headstone and got into a fight."

"With who?" he asked.

"With everyone. We were all upset. It all happened fast."

"You're just going to let them get away with it? Morgan and Rudy Bart and those guys—"

"They didn't mean anything by it," I said.

"They had a gun."

"They weren't going to use it." But they were. And he knew they were, too; I could see it on his face.

"I guess it was lucky for us the killer decided to mark up Steve's headstone," he said. "That's a strange thing to have to say."

"Yeah," I said. But I knew what he meant.

The blood drinker, or whoever had carved up Steve's headstone before we got there, had saved us by accident. Over the next few months, I thought about that a lot. I wondered if there were other symbols just waiting to be found.

"Well," Percy said, and sighed. "You want to punch me in the eye? Mo's going to do it anyway, when he hears you got beat up and I came out with not even a scratch."

Mo would never do that, of course. But I told Percy I would hit him with a board before we went to school, if that would make him feel better.

CHAPTER TWENTY-TWO

Lasting Cuts

PERCY AND I reported the defacing of Steve's headstone to my dad, and it didn't take long for pictures to be splashed across the papers. The photo that Mr. McBride took of it was reprinted nationally, and the interstate manhunt refocused on Black Deer Falls. For a few days the town was once more swarmed by state patrol and federal agents, knocking on doors and searching attics and storage sheds. And they inspected every inch of our cemeteries, looking for more marks.

When I went by the women's cell, Marie was up on her toes, staring down through her window. She was watching the extra patrol cars come and go from the parking lot.

"Dummies," she said. "Driving all the way out here, guns blazing, like they don't know that headstone could have been carved up as soon as it went in."

That's just what I had thought, but I just said, "You must be pleased. He's keeping them jumping." The headlines were all about the killer again, and for a little while she would be forgotten. He'd bought her more time.

"Why would he want to?" I asked. "I thought you said he wanted you caught. That he wanted it over."

"I said I didn't think he figured it would take this long. But as for what he wants . . . I don't always know." She turned and saw my face, covered in bruises with my lip scabbed in the middle.

"What happened?"

"Just some guys from school."

She came to the bars and wrapped her fingers around them. "Tell me."

So I did. I played it off as a joke. As a scuffle.

"They were just fooling around," I said.

"They pointed a gun at your face," said Marie.

"It wasn't like that. I'm okay. Percy's okay."

"They're bullies," she spat. She let go of the bars and dug her fingernails into her palm. Then she let go and did it again.

"Rudy Bartholomew," she said. "Morgan Todd." She repeated the names I'd told her and dug her nails into her fist.

"Marie," I said.

"I don't want to talk today, Michael."

"Marie." The tips of her fingernails had broken the skin; they came away red. "Marie, stop that." I opened the door to the rest of the jail and called for Nancy.

"Everything's fine," Marie said.

I left when Nancy got there. Later she told me that Marie

willingly stuck her arm through the bars and let her clean and bandage the wounds. And Nancy trimmed Marie's nails down on both hands, to the quick.

"She did that?" Percy asked when I told him. "Christ."

We were sitting in the school parking lot, the Monday after the cemetery. As had become usual, we were in no hurry to go in. My face was still bruised, and you could still see the cut on my lower lip. We'd seen Morgan go in earlier and he'd seen us. He sort of looked scared, and maybe a little sorry. Percy said he didn't look sorry enough.

"Is she—" Percy asked, and twirled his finger beside his ear to ask if she was crazy.

"No," I said. "She was just upset." But her reaction had disturbed me, too. I'd never seen anyone behave that way.

"Well she's not the only one," he said. "They'll get their payback."

"No. Let it go, Perce."

"You can't be serious."

"I am." But inside, I was boiling. If I could have whisked my classmates away with a thought, they would have disappeared. Morgan. Rudy Bartholomew. Even Carol. Those guys had done what they did because they were angry. Because they were scared, of the killer and of Marie. But they'd been able to do it to me because to them I *was* Marie. I was an outsider. I'd never quite fit in. Never found my place, except with Percy.

"I'm not staying here, Percy," I said. "After this is over, after graduation, I'm getting out."

"I know," he said. "I always knew that." He stared out the window, watching the last of the students hurry inside, wrapped up in their coats, their books clutched to their chests as they ducked against the cold morning wind. "It used to make me mad, you know? You always had one foot out the door. On to bigger and better things. Better than this. Better than me."

"Not better than you."

"Well, this town is me," he said, and pointed to himself. "So how was it supposed to feel? But now I think I really would go with you. Now it feels like Black Deer Falls isn't such a good place.

"He must like it," Percy said, and I knew he wasn't talking about Morgan or Rudy. "He must like what he's done to us."

Sometimes it was hard getting Marie to talk about the murders. She would wander off or daydream. She would ask about Percy or Nancy or Dawn. Other times it was easy. I'd ask, and she'd answer.

"My mother and stepfather. Peter Knupp. The student nurses. The Taylors. The truck driver and his hitchhiker. The guys at the gas station. Cheryl, the waitress at the truck stop. The students, Stacy Lee and Richard. And the Carlsons."

"So that's everyone," I said. "And no undiscovered victims in between?"

"Nope," she said, and looked at my empty pockets. I'd yet again forgotten to bring her any cigarettes.

"So the Taylors were killed right after the nurses?" I asked for clarification. Because they lived alone and kept to themselves, the

Taylors' bodies hadn't been found until after the discovery of the next victims: the truck driver Monty LeTourneau and his unidentified drifter.

"Yes. It was August eighth."

"You're sure?"

"I'm sure. He was careful about dates. I thought it was dumb: when you had forever, what did the date matter?" Marie rolled her eyes. "But he said that was precisely why it did."

"And it was after the killings at the Taylor house that you came upon Monty LeTourneau and his hitchhiker?"

"Monty first. And he picked up the hitchhiker later."

"Who? Monty or . . ."

"The blood drinker," she said, and her eyes widened when I grimaced. "What? You gave him that name."

"All right," I said. "What happened with the hitchhiker? How did his and Monty LeTourneau's bodies wind up so far away from each other?"

"Because they ran."

"Like Stephen Hill ran. Why them and not the others?"

"Maybe he let them," Marie said. "I don't know." She fidgeted sometimes, running her fingers through the ends of her long brown hair. "He liked Stephen Hill. Stephen Hill was good-looking. Better-looking than he was, even."

"Is that why he was stripped?"

Marie shook her head. "It was just a game."

"What kind of game?"

"Like a cat with a bird," she said, and looked up. She seemed a little angry, frustrated with me.

"So he liked it? The running?"

"And the screaming. They were all quiet at first. Peter Knupp, the Taylors. Those nurses were like two swoony church mice. But by the time he got to Cheryl . . ." Cheryl Warrens, the waitress at the truck stop where Monty LeTourneau's truck was found abandoned, "Cheryl screamed so loud my ears hurt."

For a moment, Marie's eyes clouded, and we sat in silence. On the tape it goes on for fifty seconds.

"It didn't seem so bad, you know? Not at first. Some of them even smiled. Peter Knupp was smiling until he was dead."

"Smiling," I noted, and jotted it down.

"Listen," Marie said. "I'm going to tell you this, but I don't want you making fun. I need you to believe that everything I say is true, even if you only keep on believing it until I'm done. Got it?"

"I got it. I won't make fun."

When Marie had seen the picture of Steve's headstone, she wasn't surprised. But no one else knew what to make of it. In the end they called it unexplained. An unexplained prank. But I'd had enough of the unexplained. I was ready to believe.

"I told you he had tricks," she said. "To make people see what he wanted them to see. He used them all the time, if there was something he wanted. He said all kinds of things to get people to invite him in. He told Walter and Evangeline Taylor that we were their grandchildren. Evangeline kept saying how sorry she was— that she didn't have any sweets for us or any presents. And she said her house was a mess—but it wasn't.

"Are you close to your grandparents, Michael?"

"I was."

Marie nodded. "I never knew mine. Not even my mother's. She had an older sister, but I never met her either."

"So you tricked them," I said, putting her back on topic. "But how did you kill them?"

"I didn't kill them. I never killed anyone."

"Then how did he?"

She took a deep breath.

"We stayed with them all night, playing the game. Then we put them to bed. Into their nightclothes. I shaved Walter's face with the razor."

"The same razor?"

She nodded.

"He drank Walter first. He slit his wrist. Evangeline didn't even notice. She just kept looking at Walter like he was talking to her."

"And you never considered letting them go?"

"He wouldn't have let them."

"But what about you? Why didn't you run? Did he carry a weapon? Did he have the razor in his hand the whole time?"

"No."

"Then why didn't you go for help?"

But Marie didn't answer. "You can check everything I told you against what they found. It'll match."

"Marie," I said. "Why did you go with him? Was it really just because he was good-looking? Was he so good-looking that it made it okay?"

"No!" She looked at me sharply. "You wouldn't understand.

"Everyone said I was a bad girl. He said that I wasn't."

CHAPTER TWENTY-THREE

A Welcome Departure

AFTER MARIE RECOUNTED the murders of the Taylors, I tried to do what she asked and believe that her story was true. That the blood drinker was real and everything occurred just the way she said. But I couldn't. The idea of the blood drinker was a block—a blank spot. So instead I imagined it in all the different ways it could have happened.

I imagined the Taylors terrorized and slaughtered. Trying to run and dying in fear, still slightly alive as they were placed in bed and the scene was staged. I imagined Cheryl's screams. I imagined the smile slowly relaxing off Peter Knupp's face.

I was starting to worry that something was wrong with me. It was odd how detached I could be, how detached we could both be when she was talking about the killings, as if we were older and harder boiled.

"It's a coping method," Mr. McBride said to me. "A tactic.

Every good journalist has to have it."

"I still care about them," I said. "About the victims. About the Carlsons, and Steve."

"But you care about her, too."

We were sitting in his office at the *Star* with his crowded desk between us. Since the murders came to Black Deer Falls, he'd gotten messier; practically every surface was covered in coffee-stained papers and photographs, editions of other, bigger newspapers. There was so much that the picture of his wedding had been moved to the top of a filing cabinet.

"It's fine if you do," he said. "You can't spend that much time with a person and not see their humanity."

I reached out and dug around in the mess until I found a paperweight. It had a similar heft to a baseball and I tossed it back and forth between my hands.

"I do care about her," I said. "And I care about the story."

"That's okay, too." He smiled with closed lips. "She chose you to tell it."

"She chose me to hear it. I don't even know if she understands that I want to use it. Write it."

"She seems too smart to me," he said, "not to. Does she care about you?"

I looked at the wall behind him, at the framed diploma from the University of Pittsburgh School of Journalism.

"Why did you come out here?" I asked. "When you could have stayed and written out there?"

"I see you've learned the art of deflection."

I sighed.

"Yes. I think she does care about me."

"Then she's probably glad."

But I wasn't sure. I was no longer sure about anything. I only knew that the interviews were almost over. Soon she would tell me what happened the night that the Carlsons were killed, and after that she would go to trial or jail—and it would be up to me to put it all together.

"Don't be afraid of your involvement in the story," said Mr. McBride. "Don't be afraid to show your heart."

"What does heart have to do with the truth?" I asked.

"More than you'd think. You'll know what I mean, when you're writing."

"I don't know why you're so confident," I said, and he grinned.

"Call it a reporter's instinct."

It was a day toward the middle of December that I went by the jail and Bert told me I had to wait.

"Wait for what?" I asked.

"Mr. Pilson is up there with her and Ed." By Ed he meant Mr. Porter, Marie's defense attorney.

"What's Pilson doing up there?" I asked. Benjamin Pilson had been in Black Deer Falls all that time, through all those strange occurrences and wild tales that must have infuriated him. He'd still been there, plotting, huddled over a pile of Marie's taped sessions in his room at Mrs. B.'s. I really don't know why he'd stayed. He had almost never interfered.

"Nancy, do you know what he's up to?" I asked. But before Nancy could guess, we heard Marie's shout, carrying from all the way upstairs.

"You can't do that!" she hollered. "You can't kill me if I'm not the one who did it!"

I bolted for the women's cell, and raced through the station in what seemed like three strides. I burst through the door to our old kitchen just in time to hear Mr. Porter say, "You'll never get the death penalty for an accomplice. Not for one who didn't do the killing. And who's a fifteen-year-old girl!"

"Sixteen, isn't she?" Pilson said, and looked at Marie. "Sixteen, now that December's here. And yes I will. That little nurse they killed? Angela Hawk? She wasn't just anybody. She was the niece of the governor's wife." He picked up his briefcase and turned to go. "Felony murder, Mr. Porter. Look it up. In the state of Nebraska you do not have to wield the knife to be found guilty."

He strode out of there, leaving Mr. Porter to try and calm Marie, who looked like she might climb up the bars.

"Mr. Pilson, wait!"

I chased him all the way through the station, out into the cold parking lot where his car was idling. The entire back seat of his sedan was full with boxes of case files, satchels, and suitcases, dress shirts hung ingeniously from hangers hooked onto the edge of a cracked-open window.

"You're leaving?"

"I'm going back to Lincoln until the trial."

"You can't," I said. "You can't do this. You can't just kill her!"

"She was there and she's protecting him," he said. "Yes, I can."

"But she's telling the truth!"

He stopped, and looked at me like I'd gone crazy.

"She's telling the truth," I said again, more quietly. "I know how it sounds. But I've seen things, and what she's told me—"

"I knew this was a mistake. You're just a kid." He opened his door and threw his briefcase inside. "Marie Hale was advised of the potential consequences during the district court hearing. And so were you. Yet for months you've let her play out this fantasy. When she goes to the chair, it'll be your fault as much as her own."

"Wait, Mr. Pilson—"

"You just have to look at the facts—"

"I am looking at the facts," I said. "And all the facts that you can't explain." He opened his door and made to get in but I cut him off.

"The fingerprints found at the scene. The footprints. Why are they only hers? The people you've shown her picture to in Loup City, in Norfolk, in Grand Junction—why is hers the only face they remember? Unless you think she did it alone?"

He turned away and put his hands on the hood of the car. I could see him thinking about it, that she was the one, and I regretted floating the idea. But a moment later he shook it off: no jury would buy that once they saw Marie, so young and so little. So female. A woman couldn't commit murders like that. She could only help a man do it.

"She doesn't deserve to die," I said quietly.

"It's not for you or I to decide. But the judge. And the governor. And the Lord."

"But it is you deciding. If you ask for mercy, they'll listen to you."

"So I guess it's true," he said. "About how close you two have become. You do know she never really wanted to confess? That if you hadn't been there, all of this would have gone another way. But a nice-looking boy like you? From an upstanding family? Marie Hale has never been alone in a room with someone like you, let alone have him listen to her. Part of her probably even believes that if she can convince you she's innocent . . . then she really will be innocent."

"That's not what she's doing, Mr. Pilson."

"I know you're not recording everything," he said. "Sometimes the tape will start and you're already in the middle of a conversation."

"Sometimes I forget to start it," I said. "But I'm not missing anything important. Just shooting the breeze. She'll ask me for smokes, things like that."

"Smokes," Pilson repeated. "And maybe things of a more delicate nature? Things you might not think are appropriate to record on tape?"

I stared at him blankly.

"Like sexual things?"

"I—"

"Do you know if they had sexual intercourse? Do you know how many times? How about if they engaged in deviant sexual behavior? Did she maybe let him put it in her mouth?"

"Why does that matter?" I asked.

"Insight into her level of involvement." His eyes had gone mean—he was enjoying how uncomfortable he was making me. "Come on now, you don't think that she's a virgin?"

"I guess I don't. But I still don't see why it matters."

"It matters because she's got you fooled."

"Where was the blood?" I asked as he got inside the car. "Where was the blood, Mr. Pilson?" I raised my voice over the sound of the shutting door, the revving engine. "Where was it, if it wasn't like she says it was?"

"I have a lead on something, Michael," he said. "I didn't want to say so in there in case it doesn't pan out. But if it does, I'll be back. And then everything is going to change.

"You know, most of the so-called mysterious anomalies of these cases can be explained by institutional foul-ups. You say they never tried to get away? Never tried to call for help? Except the Covey kid in Madison did try to call for help."

Richard Covey, the graduate student who was killed in an abandoned house with his fiancée, Stacy Lee Brandberg. The last killings before the Carlsons were murdered in Black Deer Falls.

"What do you mean?" I asked.

"He dropped textbooks out the window of a car with his name and messages to police written in them. Someone even picked them up and reported them. Only no one made the connection until after the bodies were found. Madison PD kept it out of the papers." He looked at me one more time. "Just get her to tell the truth," he said. Then he put the car in gear and drove away.

That evening, my dad stopped by the jail to give me a lift home for supper. On the way he looped around to the service station and the small store across the train tracks, and left me in the truck while he went in and bought cherry-vanilla pipe tobacco and some bubblegum for Dawn. He got back in and tossed me a box of Mike and Ikes.

"Toxicology reports came back on the Carlsons," he said as I opened the box and he backed the pickup out of the parking lot, sliding a little on the ugly, half-melted ice. "They came back clean.

"I'd hoped," he said softly, "since they did the autopsy so fast, that they'd be able to find something. But if there was poison or sedatives, it was nothing that could be identified."

"Why weren't they bound?" I asked. "Wouldn't it make more sense for them to be bound? It wouldn't be hard to do it if there were two perpetrators. One to hold the razor, the other to tie them up?"

My dad shrugged. "Maybe he didn't trust her knots."

"Or maybe she was unwilling."

I caught his glance at me from the side of my eye.

"Maybe."

"Pilson thinks he has something," I said.

"*Mr.* Pilson," my dad corrected, even though he thought about as much of him as I did. "And what's that?"

"He wouldn't say."

"That why he's going back to Lincoln?"

I shrugged.

"Richard Covey tried to signal for help," I said. "He dropped textbooks along the highway with his name on them."

"Where did you hear that?"

"Mr. Pilson."

My dad glanced at me.

"Michael, do you want to stop?"

"I can't stop, Dad," I said. "Even if she did what she did, I don't want Marie to die. I don't even really want her to be gone." I shoved Mike and Ikes into my mouth to keep from crying and my dad shifted in his seat and let me chew.

"I'm sorry, son."

"I don't know how to help her."

"There's only one way to help her," he said. "Pilson doesn't really want Marie. He wants *him*. She has to give him up."

"What if there's no one to give up?" I asked.

But he shook his head. "There has to be. I don't believe that little girl ever hurt anyone."

CHAPTER TWENTY-FOUR

Winter

PILSON WAS GONE from Black Deer Falls for the rest of December, and all the blessed month of January. And for a while it was as if his leaving had freed us—in the absence of him peering down the backs of our necks, we forgot where we were. We forgot, for a little while, why we were there and that our time was borrowed. We refused to believe that it wouldn't just go on that way forever.

But when I was away from Marie, I knew it was almost up. The blood drinker was no longer keeping folks jumping. The roadblocks, the extra patrols and searches still went on, but in fewer and fewer numbers. For weeks, there had been no new trace, no new clue. There had been no trail to pick up, not so much as a gas station knocked over for cash. And there'd been a subtle shift in the dwindling number of newspaper articles, too: just a few carefully placed questions about what Marie knew and what she could have done.

The day after Christmas, I brought Marie a few gifts from my family, and a plate of leftover Christmas dinner: roasted goose and mashed potatoes and my mom's wild-rice stuffing. I figured we had at least through the holidays before I had to push. But after she'd opened the card Dawn made, and unwrapped the skirt and the length of green ribbon from my mother, she asked,

"How long do you think we have left?"

"I don't know. Not long. To be honest I thought we'd have heard from Pilson already." I reached through the bars of her cell and picked up the ribbon. "What do you think he knows? What lead was he following?"

"He can't know anything," Marie said. "He's bluffing."

"Do you think he's bluffing about the death penalty?"

I didn't want to talk about it that day. It was Christmas, and I figured it would upset her.

"No," she said. "That was always what he hoped for. He's so damned lucky that Pilson showed up."

I was confused. I'd thought she was talking about Pilson.

"You mean the blood drinker," I said. "He wants you to die?"

"Has to happen somehow. If he can't do it himself."

It took me a moment to figure out what she meant: to die and be raised from the dead. That was how it went in the legends and the lore.

"Oh," I said. "Because of the vampire stuff."

Marie's mood lightened, and she smiled.

"Right. Because of the vampire stuff." She smoothed the skirt where it lay across her knees. "This is really nice, Michael. It's the nicest Christmas I ever had."

I want to recount one more thing that happened before Pilson returned in February.

It was a night in January. A school night, but I was up late, and the rest of my family was fast asleep. I'd been up in my room, looking over a book on vampire lore or maybe just reading a comic, when something hit my window. A pebble, like I was a girl and someone had come calling. At first I took it for a branch from a tree or a leaf, even though it wasn't windy out. Except it kept on. One pebble. Then a second. Then a third, and that one hard enough to leave a chip in the glass.

I got up and looked, expecting to see Percy, or a friend of Dawn's. But there was no one. No one below my window. No one on the front porch or standing in our driveway.

He was standing in the street. Hidden mostly in shadows, only his lower half and left shoulder illuminated by the Schumans' outdoor garage light. For a minute I thought I was seeing things and blinked hard—but when I opened my eyes he was still there. Looking up at my window.

I was scared at first. Then I filled with jittery excitement. It was him. The one who'd dragged Marie into hell. Who had murdered Steve and his parents and a dozen others. And he was right there.

My dad was asleep down the hall and he kept his service pistol in there with him, hung up in the closet, but it had been locked since I was a kid. So I grabbed my baseball bat instead.

I don't know what I was planning. I would run him down and break his legs. I would hit him until he didn't wake up. All of the odd things that occurred to me later—that he had managed to throw rocks at my window from the street, that he was standing in the middle of the night in the dead of winter with no coat on— didn't occur to me then. I just wanted to catch him.

I would've been a hero. Marie would've been safe. And it would have been over.

The time it took to turn from the window, grab the bat, and run downstairs couldn't have been more than five seconds. I know my front door was locked and that I didn't hear the knob or the heavy jangle of the holiday wreath. But when I charged off the last stair, the door was already open.

He was standing in the middle of our living room. The exact same shape he'd been in the street, as if he was a statue that someone had moved. And despite our living room being lit by the moon and the clean white snow—I couldn't make out anything about his face.

I raised the bat.

"Ask her how much she drank," he said.

I started screaming at the sound of his voice. It wasn't like any voice I'd ever heard. And his face hadn't moved with his words.

I screamed for my mom; I screamed for my dad. Maybe I even screamed for Dawn. I was still screaming when my dad came down the stairs, half stumbling from sleep, and flipped on the lights.

"Michael, Michael! What's going on?"

I was standing in the entryway in front of the open door. The living room was empty.

They were scared. They said I'd been sleepwalking. I got a short lecture about how my dad could have shot me even though he hadn't brought his gun. And another after my mom had to field phone calls from nearby neighbors whom I'd woken.

"It's that girl, isn't it?" she said.

"No. It wasn't her at all."

"She's manipulating you, Michael. All those days the two of you alone. A girl like that knows how to get what she wants."

"Is that what people are saying?" I asked. "Is that what you think?"

"All I know is that before you met her, this would never have happened."

People blamed Marie, they suspected her, they even hated her. Those who were kind pitied her. But no one believed her, and maybe that's why I had to.

We found no trace of the intruder—no snowy footprints or wet spots on the carpet, nothing out of place. By the next afternoon, my family had all but forgotten about it. My mother apologized for what she'd said and made me some meat loaf sandwiches to take to the jail.

But there was still a crack in the glass of my window. And I have never been a sleepwalker. I asked Marie about it, in a round-about way, but even she said I was imagining things.

"He couldn't have come inside your house unless you'd invited him, Michael. And you didn't invite him. Did you?"

I hadn't. But it was funny how the bastard only followed vampiric rules when following them made me look crazy.

A few days later, my dad came up to my room and made me get rid of everything vampire related. The books went back to the library, and he confiscated a few of my notebooks. He pulled down the sketches of the symbol Percy and I had seen in the woods.

Maybe it worked. Maybe it was all in my head. In any case, the blood drinker never tried to contact me again, in my dreams or otherwise. And then, a week later, Pilson returned with news.

CHAPTER TWENTY-FIVE

The Discovery

I BET WHEN Benjamin Pilson first heard about Marie, he was excited. A young girl like that at the scene of the crime? I bet he thought he'd lucked out. She would be easy to lean on and easy to fool—the entire case had to have felt like a golden egg cracked right onto his plate.

I remember the day he came back: walking into the station smiling like a game-show host.

I was on the main floor, helping Bert clean up his desk. It was always a mess—food wrappings and napkins from hurried lunches, coffee rings everywhere—and my dad harped on him sometimes, so I wanted to help. We all still felt bad about what had happened to his snake. Later that spring, as soon as the snow melted, my dad drove to the big pet shop in Brainerd to get him a new python, a trip that made for a few rare moments of levity: my dad had never looked so nervous during any prisoner transport as he did driving around with that snake.

Pilson came in as I was carrying out the trash. He glanced at me and I just sort of nodded, surprised to see him. He didn't bother nodding back and went in to speak with my dad. They must have made some calls because before long our prosecutor, Mr. Norquist, arrived, and then Mr. Porter a few minutes later.

"What in the world's he starting now?" Bert asked as we stood beside his desk.

Pilson wanted everyone to march up to Marie's cell.

"She's just finishing her lunch, Rick," Bert said. "Why don't you let me go up and fetch her?" My dad nodded, and Bert got up with the keys.

"What's going on, Dad?" I asked, but he motioned for me to be quiet.

Bert brought Marie down uncuffed. He kept a hand on her shoulder.

"Into the interrogation room, please," Pilson said.

Marie frowned. "It'll be pretty damned crowded. Can't you just tell me out here?"

At first Pilson seemed annoyed; the line in his forehead creased deep. Then that smile came back, and that was even worse.

"If that's what you want, Miss Hale," he said. "Or should I say, Miss Mewes?"

"Miss Mewes?" my dad asked.

"Her name isn't really Marie Catherine Hale," Pilson said. "It's Marie Catherine Mewes. She was born in Greeley County, Nebraska, to one Audrey Cody—formerly Mewes—of North

Platte. Mrs. Cody was reported missing some months ago. Along with her husband, Nathaniel."

I looked at Marie. I'd never seen her afraid, not even when she was drenched in the Carlsons' blood. But every time Pilson said the name Mewes she flinched like he'd hit her.

"Isn't that them?" he asked. "Your parents? Audrey and Nathaniel Cody? Missing since early summer. And dead, according to you."

"Yes," Marie said. "They're both dead."

"But they aren't, are they? Or at least he isn't."

"What do you mean he isn't?" I asked.

"I mean that Nathaniel Cody is our killer." He told us how he'd found them. It was a clue from the taped interviews. He'd been trying to trace Marie for months, calling orphanages and halfway houses and combing through reports on missing girls. Then one night he was listening to the interviews and heard Marie say her stepfather claimed lineage to a famous local cowboy. It didn't take long for him to learn that Buffalo Bill Cody's Wild West Show had been founded in North Platte. And once he had the name Cody, the rest was easy.

"Mr. Cody's employer had thought it odd when he failed to report for work on a Monday morning, but after he asked around and discovered that his wife and stepdaughter were also nowhere to be found, he assumed that the family had picked up and moved on, as some folks do. It wasn't for another week that the landlady went by the house and noticed that nothing had been packed. Clothes still in the dresser. Jewelry and family photographs all left behind.

"I always thought it was strange," he went on, "that no one came forward to claim you after your picture was all over the papers and shown on the news. But you looked a little different back then. Meeker, and your hair longer and dull. Flawed skin. And no smile, even for a photograph." He pulled a photo out of his jacket and flashed it at us: it was taken not more than a few years ago and in it her hair was lighter and thinner. Dark spots marred her forehead and chin. It was different, but it was her.

Marie looked like she wanted to claw his eyes out.

"Is that true?" I asked.

"I already told you it was," she said. "I already told you they were dead."

"They were dead," Pilson went on. "Isn't that what you said? *They.* But people in North Platte had a lot to say about your step-father after they found out you were the one being held up here. Troubling things."

"You shut your mouth."

"What kind of troubling things?" Mr. Porter asked.

"Nathaniel Cody had a proclivity for young girls."

Marie's jaw and fists clenched. My dad caught on sooner than I did, and whispered, "Good God."

"He made a sort of pet of you, didn't he, Marie?" Pilson said. "Buying you little presents. New outfits. You were plain and he spruced you up. Maybe it was innocent enough at first. But then it changed. That's what your landlady said. Mrs. Marshall. She said maybe it was never your mother he was interested in in the first place."

"Shut up."

"Looking at you now, I can hardly blame him."

"Shut up, shut up, shut up!" Marie lunged for Pilson with hooked fingers. Bert had to haul her back. He and my dad had to pin her to the floor and put her in cuffs. And she kept screaming, these awful animal screams.

"Put her in the interrogation room," Pilson said. "I'm not done with her yet."

"No," Mr. Porter said. "You are. You're done."

"Take her back up, Bert," my dad said. "Keep the cuffs on and stay with her until I tell you different!"

Bert nodded. He looked terrified, wrestling her toward the stairs. She was furious, screaming and kicking.

"Did you seduce him?" Pilson called. "Did you help him kill your mother? Tell us where he is, Miss Mewes! Don't you want her body found? Don't you want her to have a Christian burial?"

He smiled the same smile he had on when he came in. Until my dad put an arm across his chest and shoved him into the wall.

"That is enough out of you, Mr. Pilson."

"Get your hands off me!"

"You come into my station and let all hell out?" My dad shoved him one more time. Pilson's tie hung askew and his top button had come loose; he straightened the tie angrily as my dad pointed for him to go through his office door.

I followed them inside.

Pilson slapped a thin file folder onto my father's desk. My father picked it up and leafed through the pages.

"Once we found her, everything fell into place," Pilson said. "She and the stepfather embarked on some kind of affair that resulted in the death of the mother. From there things spun out of control."

My father cast him a disgusted look. "Around here, when a grown man takes up with a fifteen-year-old girl, we don't call it 'embarking on an affair,'" he said. "Where is he? Have you found him?"

"Not yet. We've put out a bulletin. The Federal Bureau is sending men. Now that we know who we're looking for, he won't be able to hide for long."

I stood to one side like wood. I had never heard the name Nathaniel Cody but now I couldn't stop hearing it, and imagining what he looked like: tall and dark, handsome like a movie star.

My dad closed the folder.

"It's disturbing," Pilson said. "But at least it's an explanation."

But it wasn't the real explanation. Everything about it was wrong, even her name: Marie Catherine Mewes. It was like they were talking about a different person.

"Listen, Rick," Pilson said, "you have to give me another run at her. Now, before she comes up with something new. We've already lost too much time."

They glanced at me. They were embarrassed at having let the interviews go on for so long and listening to all that silly vampire talk. Only it wasn't silly. Nathaniel Cody hadn't been standing outside of my window. He hadn't been scaling trees and carving symbols into them.

But my dad gave in. "Mr. Porter will need to be present."

"Dad," I protested.

"It'll be all right, Michael."

"It won't be," I said quietly. I could've slugged Pilson in the gut. Yet he still had the gall to look at me with sympathy, and to give my shoulder a squeeze. Then he went into the interrogation room.

Pilson questioned Marie for two hours. She shouted through most of it. But it was worse when she was quiet. I didn't want to think about the questions he was asking, filthy questions like he'd put to me before he'd left town. And I didn't want to think about the answers.

When it was over, she came out looking like a ghost. I said her name but she just walked through the station with Bert back up to her cell. To be fair, Pilson came out not looking much better: he'd taken off his suit coat and his underarms were dark with sweat.

"So?" my father asked. "Is it like you said?"

He nodded, and wiped his face. "But she's not cooperating. She won't give him up."

"It's been months," I said. "She doesn't know where he is."

Pilson looked at me, annoyed. "The interviews will stop. There's no need for the expense of the tape recordings. And we can arrange for transport to Lincoln as soon as next week."

"Hang on," my dad said. "There's been no new hearing."

"And she's not finished," I said. "There's still more—"

"If she needs to confess more," Pilson said, "she'll have a priest."

"You can't just take her."

"With this new information—her identity, the main suspect—Nebraska has the better claim."

"With all due respect, Mr. Pilson, that's for a judge to say. And the people of Black Deer Falls will disagree. We still don't know what went on in that farmhouse that night."

Pilson sighed, but then he nodded. "You're right. You do need answers. I know that I'm not the only one with an election to think about."

CHAPTER TWENTY-SIX

The Dracula Murders

SHORTLY AFTER MR. Pilson returned to Black Deer Falls, he leaked the details of Marie's confession to the press. In the interest of journalistic integrity I can't say for certain that it was him, but who else would it have been? He'd kept it quiet all this time, fearing ridicule, but he didn't need to now that he had a "reasonable explanation." So he let it out: about the blood drinker, and about the nature of Nathaniel Cody and Marie's relationship. Cody instantly became the most wanted man in America. Marie became a joke.

The papers took to calling the murders the Dracula Murders again and this time as farce: they ridiculed Marie for girlish silliness in the same article that condemned her to death.

My father and I weren't spared either. They called us rubes. They said we'd rushed through our forests armed with rifles and wooden crosses, hunting monsters, too stupid to realize that Marie probably took the idea from their very own headlines. Hadn't they coined them the Dracula Murders all the way back in August?

The reporters took the explanation of Marie's stepfather and ran with it, forgetting all about the missing blood, the missing prints, the symbols carved into Steve Carlson's headstone, and the other questions about the case that still remained. To the public at large, the mystery of the Bloodless Murders had been solved and attention turned to other things. In Black Deer Falls that meant things like transferring Marie out of our jail for trial and sentencing, and holding a special recall election for county sheriff. The whole town was ashamed of us for listening to her story. And my father didn't defend himself. He didn't tell them why he thought it was worth listening to. I guess it just wasn't his way.

At school, kids laughed at me. They threw things. They'd trip me in a crowd, or someone would run up from behind and shove me before running off again. And Percy showed up in the cafeteria with a blackening eye.

"Never mind it," he said before I could ask. "It was a fair fight. You could even say I won."

"Who was it?" I demanded.

"Never mind, I said. Just keep your head down. Let me take care of it."

"*I* can take care of it."

"No you can't. If you did, they'd say . . . I don't know. But you'd be the one in trouble, and your dad, too. They're all watching you."

He didn't say who he meant by "they." There were eyes

everywhere again, reporters gathering like crows, in dark winter coats and hats, freshly purchased scarves and gloves that weren't warm enough for our winters. Over on 9th, Mrs. B.'s was full to bursting, and so was the motel out by the highway. The diners and bars were crowded every night with "nosy reporters" and Charlie had started to grumble that it was hard to get in and out of the Sportsman's Café for his lunch break.

I sat at our table in the cafeteria, tray untouched as Percy ate his meat loaf and cottage cheese. Around us all was quiet. No chatter. Only whispers. I felt eyes in the back of my head and wished I could be more like Percy, still able to fake a good appetite with his face swollen. I even wished I was more like Pilson, who stood in the center of the reporters ever ready with a quote or a quip, every photograph taken a portrait of a grim man of the law, the crease in his forehead nearly too deep for the ink to capture.

"He says it brings him no personal joy," I said, and Percy stopped eating. "That Marie will face the electric chair. He says it's his responsibility as a prosecutor to the victims and their families. To us, the good, honest citizens afraid to turn off our lights."

"Did he say it with a straight face?" Percy asked.

"I don't know. It was in the paper."

I chanced a glance around the lunchroom and caught Carol's eye. She was sitting with her friends. The other girls were a gaggle of furtive glances and murmurs, but Carol simply looked at me, and I imagined for a second that I could lay my head on her shoulder until the reporters left. Until Marie was gone. Until everybody forgot that it was me in that room taking shorthand about vampires.

I stood.

"Where you going?" Percy asked.

"Not hungry."

I took my lunch tray and dumped the food into the trash, and Rudy Bartholomew yelled, "Going back to the jail?"

"I'm going back to class," I said without turning around.

"Steve's murder gave you a heck of a story, I guess."

I made a pair of fists and looked. Rudy Bart stood near the center of his table, wearing the letter jacket he never seemed to take off. I was a little surprised he had the nerve after what he'd done to us in the cemetery. But that was our fault, I guess. We'd kept quiet, so we'd been the ones to teach him that he could get away with it.

Percy jumped up and came over to stand with me.

"You think Michael wants to be in the papers? He's not the one following the reporters around, constantly combing his hair in case one of them wants a picture. I've seen you all do that." Percy pointed around the cafeteria.

"He's going to make everybody feel sorry for her! Don't you care?"

"I suppose you'd kill her with your bare hands," I said, a little louder than I meant to. I looked into their eyes. I glared at them. Kids I'd grown up with. Kids I knew. But I didn't know any of them as well as I'd come to know Marie. I bet if I did, they would have their secrets, too.

Percy and I walked out. Behind us the cafeteria ladies found their voices and told Rudy to sit down and go on eating.

"I don't know what your old man was thinking, making you keep on coming to school," Percy said. "Mo's not the best dad but even he would have me locked up at home with the curtains closed until this blew over."

"This isn't going to blow over."

We walked though the halls, feeling lousy, and someone shoved a newspaper in my face. Marie's photograph was on the front page—the picture of her at the courthouse in my mother's red lipstick—beneath the headline "16-year-old Lolita or Bride of Dracula?"

The kid holding it was Nick Clinton, a decent enough fellow and a sort of friend of mine. It wasn't his fault. He'd just had bad timing.

"My mom's making a scrapbook," he said. "Of the articles. She says someday we'll want to remember the days when Black Deer Falls was famous."

I hit Nick in the face. Then I hit him again when he fell, over and over, so when Percy finally pulled me off, his face was marked red and his lip was bleeding.

"Have you lost it?" he cried as he struggled to one knee. He had his hands up to catch the blood dripping down his chin.

"I'm sorry," I said numbly, and let Percy pull me away before I could throw up all over the linoleum floor.

"No one'll blame you," Percy kept saying. "But we should cut for the rest of the day just to be safe."

"I don't want you to get in trouble, Perce."

He waved his hand. "I won't get into any trouble. This my old man will understand."

Percy slowed the car to a crawl as we approached the parking lot of the sheriff's station. The lot was peppered with strange cars, most of them running to stave off the cold, and inside each was a reporter or a pair of them, ready to leap out at the first sign of movement.

"Are you sure I shouldn't just drive on by? We could hide out at my place or head over to the bowling alley in the Rapids."

I shook my head. I couldn't avoid it forever, and there was really nowhere to run. He pulled in, and I looked at him gratefully as he parked.

"You haven't asked me anything since the story about the confession came out."

"I figured you'd been questioned enough."

"But it's different," I said. "You're my friend. I don't mind you asking."

He sat and considered it, his eye shifty over his swollen cheek.

"Do you believe it?" he asked. "What she told you?"

"I don't know," I said. "Should I?"

He shook his head. Of course I shouldn't. But what he said was, "I just keep thinking of the marks in our trees and on Steve's headstone. What it felt like out there in the woods." He looked at me. "That thing you said, about that girl in New England. Those people digging her up and cutting her heart out. Was that true?"

"Yeah," I said. "That was true."

He gave a big sigh.

"Then I guess I wouldn't put anything past anybody." He looked out the window Three reporters had gotten out of their cars and were headed our way. "Here they come," he said. "Good luck."

"Thanks, Perce."

I kept my head down and said nothing as I made my way inside. Not even so much as a "no comment."

Inside the station, Nancy sat behind the booking desk, typing.

"You should have called first," she said glumly. "I'd have had Bert go out and order them to stay in their cars."

"Would that have worked?"

She shrugged and went back to typing.

It was oddly quiet inside compared to the commotion in the parking lot. My father had gone home for lunch and Bert was at a loss about what to do with the reporters; he peered out at them from behind the deputy's desk like he was trying to decide how he was going to get to his patrol cruiser. As I passed the hallway that led to the jail, I got a heavy feeling, like I sometimes got when the cells weren't empty.

"Just a few drunk and disorderlies from last night," said Nancy. "Charlie had to bring them in after a fight broke out at the Eagle. They were scuffling with the out-of-towners."

"Has anyone been up to see Marie?"

"No one but me, and I've been here since nine."

I went up and knocked on the door that led to our old kitchen and the women's cell.

"Come in," she said.

"You should've asked if it was me. It could have been anyone, with so many folks in town."

"No one else would've knocked."

"How are you?" I asked.

"I'm fine." She was seated on her cot like normal, her dark hair tied back with black ribbon. A lunch tray sat on her writing desk, the food untouched. It wasn't much, just a sandwich and a macaroni salad. But it was uncommon for Marie not to eat.

"What are you doing back here, Michael? I thought they'd keep you away now that they've got their story."

"Is it true what he said?" I asked.

"What who said?"

"What Pilson said. About your stepfather."

For a moment she seemed angry, and her jaw tightened. She curled her lip. "Which part?"

"That he's the killer."

"Of course not." She made a dismissive sound. "He lacked the nerve, among other things."

"You sound like you hate him."

"I do. He deserves to be hated."

"When you spoke of him before, you didn't seem to care much one way or the other."

"Well, that was when he was dead. Now he's back and ruining everything." She cast her eyes to the empty table in the kitchen, where the tape recorder usually sat. "They took it yesterday morning."

"So what?" I held up my notebook and pen. "The tape was never for us anyway." I drew my usual chair away from the wall and sat down.

"Why do you still want to talk to me?"

"If you say he wasn't the killer, then I believe you."

She smiled with such relief that I felt bad about what I had to ask next.

"But what about the rest of it?"

She tucked her knees up to her chest. She seemed so young, all of a sudden. I remembered how I had thought she was a fast girl. I remembered thinking that she seemed older, and felt disgusted with myself. And I felt guilty for thinking about her the way I sometimes did when we were alone. There was only a year difference between our ages. But she didn't need anyone thinking about her like that.

"Nathaniel Cody," she said, "was a filthy bastard."

"So it's true."

"No, it's not true. Why does it matter?"

"Because it matters."

"It doesn't. I told you."

But I knew that she was lying. She wouldn't look at me. She hunched her shoulders.

"Tell me the truth."

"I am."

"What have you left out?"

"What does it matter?" Marie shouted, the only time she ever raised her voice to me. "Even if it was true it doesn't mean the rest of it's a lie! I told you he was terrible and you were happy enough. But now you want to know it all. Every dirty detail. As if that's the only part that's important."

"Marie, what he did—it is important."

"No it isn't. It only is if I say it is. And I don't."

I sat back quietly. I didn't understand. I still don't, and I suppose that I never will. But I did understand this: if she gave them anything on her stepfather, they would let her live. But everything she had told me—her story—would be erased as if it never was.

"Okay," I said. "Then keep going. Finish it."

"I can't. He's tainted it," she said, and I couldn't tell whether she meant Nathaniel Cody or Benjamin Pilson.

"Well, isn't there a way to 'untaint' it?" I asked. "If Cody didn't do it, there must be a way to prove that he didn't."

She looked down and toyed with her shoelaces.

"Marie? There must be a way."

"There is," she said. "But I don't want to ask you to do it." She took a deep breath, and I leaned forward so she could tell me what she wanted me to do. When she was through, I won't say I wasn't nervous. But I agreed.

"Okay, then," she said. "Go get Pilson. Tell him I'm ready to tell him where my stepfather is."

I rang Pilson and caught him at Mrs. B.'s. He said he would be there within the hour but he showed up not ten minutes later, storming through the station like he owned it—which he only got away with because my father wasn't there. When I heard him on the stairs, I made sure to step back to avoid catching the swinging door in my face.

"Miss Mewes," he said.

"Don't call me that," Marie said, and scowled.

"It is your name, isn't it?"

"So is Marie."

"How about I just call you 'Miss,' then?"

Marie shrugged.

"Well, then, what did you want to tell me?"

"I wanted to tell you that Nathaniel Cody didn't kill Peter Knupp. Or Angela Hawk or Beverly Nordahl, or any of the others. He never even met them."

"I think we both know that he did."

"He didn't. He wasn't innocent of much, but he's innocent of that."

"That story won't hold up for much longer. I'm circulating photographs of your stepfather around Grand Junction and Loup City, even around the University at Madison."

"It won't amount to anything."

Pilson looked at me and laughed. A short bark. "We'll see."

"We will see, you horse's ass!"

"Marie," I cautioned, and she clamped her mouth shut.

"Why don't you tell me where the blood went," she said, "if you're so set on things?"

"Cody will tell me himself when we catch him."

"No one's going to find Nathaniel Cody unless I tell you where he is."

"We're broadening the search daily."

But so far they'd come up with squat. Pilson's eyes hardened. He wanted Marie to fear him, but the truth was that he feared her: Marie was someone he couldn't intimidate. No matter which of his many faces he presented her with, Marie remained the same. Unflappable and threatening.

"All right, then. Where is he?"

"He's just where I said he was." Marie crossed her arms. "He's dead and buried with my mother. And since there's no other way to make you believe me, I'm going to let you dig them up. I'm going to tell you where they are."

Pilson shifted his weight, impatient or maybe nervous. If she was lying, she was getting better at it.

"And where is that?"

"Oh, I'm not telling you," Marie said. "But as usual I will tell Michael."

CHAPTER TWENTY-SEVEN

Hatching a Plan

MARIE'S PLAN WAS for me to go with Pilson to find the bodies. Pilson agreed to it, because what choice did he have? It took only a few hours for him to assemble a team of local police officers and even federal agents to aid in the recovery of the bodies of Marie's mother and stepfather. I would be with them all the way. I would show them the route to take. And not even I would know exactly where we were going—Marie wanted to be sure they couldn't shake it out of me and go ahead on their own. She gave us the name of the town, and when we got there, I would phone her at the jail for the final location.

We were to leave that afternoon. I had only to go home and pack a bag—and get permission from my mother.

"Pot roast with carrots," my mother said when I walked through the door. She often did that—announced the evening meal in lieu of an actual greeting. "I didn't expect you home so early." When

I didn't say anything and hovered near the door, she turned and asked, "What is it? What's the matter?"

"I can't stay for dinner," I said. "They need me to go to Nebraska."

"Nebraska? For what?"

"Marie's going to tell us where some bodies are buried."

She blinked. "What's your father say?"

"He says I need to check with you."

"Then no. Of course not. It's too far. And on a school night."

"Mom—"

"And it isn't right. It's . . . morbid. You're not even eighteen yet."

"But—"

"I said no, Michael. Now set the table and call your sister. There's Jell-O for dessert."

I pursed my lips, but I called Dawn, and we sat down to eat, even though it was more than an hour early and the roast was still tough. It was an awkward meal, cuts of meat slapped down on my plate and sloshed with gravy, extra carrots because she knew I wasn't fond of them. Dawn giving me wide eyes and mouthing, "What did you *do*?" And I did not get any Jell-O. I figured I would take the matter up again while we did the dishes. After she'd had more time to think it over. But as luck would have it, I didn't need to. Because before we cleared the table, my dad came home with Pilson.

When they came in, I stood up hopefully, and was immediately ordered upstairs. But I heard everything they said.

"Absolutely not," my mother said. "It's not right to take a boy his age. Dead bodies? After a killer?" She kept on like that for a long time, even speaking over my dad. So I crept back downstairs.

"I have to go. Marie won't have it any other way."

"I don't see why she has to get her way. It seems like she's always getting her way."

"She's sitting in a jail cell," I said. "And this isn't just a body. It's her mother."

My mom made a sad, frustrated sound. In the end both Pilson and my dad had to swear that I would be in no danger and wouldn't be there for the actual discovery. They were lying on both counts, as it happened, but they didn't know that at the time.

Back at the jail a caravan was waiting to take us to Nebraska and the city of North Platte. For reasons of jurisdiction, it was decided that my father would stay behind, so I would be on my own.

"Can I talk to Marie before we go?" I asked.

"No time," Pilson said. "You can speak to her on the phone when we get there."

He didn't want us cooking up any more schemes. Despite having access to all of our recordings, he'd become paranoid. We rode together in the same car all the way to Nebraska and he stopped to eat supper on the way. But there were no more milkshakes and easy smiles. Pilson scrutinized my every movement like he was trying to crack a code.

We stayed in a motel near North Platte, off the interstate—the kind with a detached lobby where an old woman parsed out room keys from a wooden pegboard and offered you a warm-up from an hours-old pot of coffee. Our cars filled up the otherwise empty parking lot, but the woman who ran the place didn't snoop, as if she saw a troop of investigators and federal agents pass through every month. When I asked her about it, she squinted at me.

"Government workers. They're clean and their money's always good. Some of them even make the beds up before they check out, tight enough to bounce a quarter off."

"Yeah," I said. "Every one of them is tight enough to bounce a quarter off."

She chuckled. "I won't ask," she said, "but I imagine this is something to do with those murders last summer. I can't guess what you're doing caught up in it."

"I'm Michael Jensen," I said, and shook her hand. I could tell she recognized my name. "I'm taking Marie Hale's confession up in Minnesota."

"Well, I'm not asking. But you'll tell me, won't you? If I need to start keeping my shotgun behind the desk again?"

I couldn't think of what to say. During those weeks when bodies were showing up in Nebraska, she must have been terrified. A woman alone, right off the highway.

"Maybe I ought to just keep it out from now on," she said.

I went back to my room, a room that I shared with—of course—Pilson. I kept expecting him to try to get at me about Marie, or to change tactics and sweet-talk me again, but he barely said a word. In fact I don't think our sharing a room was part of his strategy at all; I just don't think anyone else would have me.

In the end, though, I was sort of glad. I was nervous that night and couldn't sleep. Had I been in a room with anyone other than Pilson I might've spilled my guts just for someone to talk to. Instead I lay on my side, facing the wall, and thought about the bodies lying dead somewhere nearby. Bodies that Marie had buried or helped to bury. Sometime before dawn I must've fallen asleep, because the next thing I knew Pilson was shaking me awake, saying it was time to get dressed and call Marie.

The man in charge of the operation was with the FBI: Agent Daniel McCabe. He was a slender man of medium height and wore the same dark suit as the others except that his necktie was oddly thin. He had dark hair, speckled but not yet peppered with gray. He never smiled, and despite his diminutive size it was obvious that he was in command. I've described him as slender but really he was a twig, skinny but skinny in the mean, dangerous way, like a winter wolf. By the time we'd assembled in his room that morning to make the phone call, twelve agents and three cars of local police had joined us at the motel. They stood around drinking coffee from paper cups and watching me curiously. Pilson moved the phone from the bedside table onto the bed and pointed at me to sit.

"Is this normal?" I asked. "This many men"—and more to join us at the location (I had overheard a few of them speaking)—"for a body recovery?"

"We can't know for certain what we'll find," Agent McCabe replied. "Or what we're being led into."

"Nothing, is my guess," said Pilson. He picked up the receiver and dialed the jail back home. His jaw was tight, and after having shared a room with him and lying awake half the night, I knew that he hadn't slept much either.

"What will you do after we find him," I asked, "long dead and just where she says he would be? Then who will you blame?"

He glanced at me, irritated. Then my dad must have picked up.

"Sheriff Jensen," Pilson said. "We're ready when you are. All right. Put her on." A pause. "Miss Mewes?" Another pause and a grimace. "Miss Hale. I have Michael here, as requested."

He handed me the phone.

"Hello, Michael," Marie said.

"Hi, Marie." I looked at Agent McCabe, who gestured for me to hold the receiver away from my ear so they could hear both sides. I did it, and he nodded. "We're in North Platte."

"Where?"

"The Sunshine Motel and Motor Lodge off the interstate."

There was a pause.

"Good," she said. "That's not far."

"Where are we going, Miss Mewes?" Pilson asked loudly, and received a roomful of dirty looks.

"Follow Highway eighty-three down to the lake," she said, and at a snap of Agent McCabe's fingers, three men fell over themselves trying to get him an unfolded map. "Take a right and follow the lake road until it turns off from the river, then go right again heading north. After three miles there will be an unmarked dirt road on your left. Take it. The house sits off in the middle of a field. There's a bright red mailbox and an oak tree in the side of the yard taller than the house."

"Is there a house number on the mailbox?" Agent McCabe asked.

"No."

"What color is the house?"

"Gray."

"Where will we find the bodies?"

"Have Michael put the phone back to his ear."

McCabe frowned and backed off—he'd come so close listening that he could've puckered up and given me a kiss. He gave me another nod, and I placed the receiver back securely against my ear.

"They still listening?" Marie asked.

"They're still listening but I don't think they can hear," I said.

"I'm surprised they didn't try to hook us up to one of those tape recorders."

"So am I."

"I'm going to tell only you where the bodies are buried," she said. "So they'll have to bring you with."

"They could just search the property themselves," I said, and she chuckled.

"Don't give them any ideas. But they won't. The property's too big."

"All right. So where are they?"

She paused.

"Listen, Michael. I want to say that I'm sorry."

"About what?"

"About you having to see them. My mother and stepfather, I mean."

"It's okay." I swallowed. I didn't know if it was. I'd never actually seen a dead body up close.

"Can you do something for me?"

"What's that?" I asked.

"I need you to tell me if my stepfather's body is unmarked."

"Unmarked?"

"Uncut. Full of blood."

"Sure," I said, and licked my lips nervously. "Sure, I will. But why?"

"Because I made him swear to leave just that one alone. Will you make sure? Will you promise?"

"I will. I promise."

She sighed, heavy, and lowered her voice. "The bodies are in the basement. Near the west wall. It will be work, to bring them up. Will you call me when it's finished?"

"I'll try, Marie."

"Okay. Goodbye."

We hung up, and I looked into the faces of a dozen waiting agents.

"I'll take you to them when we get to the house," I said.

Pilson might have groaned; I know he made a face. But Agent McCabe just asked, "But the bodies are inside the house?"

When I nodded, a ripple of relief passed through the men. If they'd been buried elsewhere the whole operation might have stalled until the spring thaw.

"Very good," he said. "Let's get the warrant."

Not an hour later, we loaded into our caravan of cars and police cruisers and I did my best not to compare the precise, practiced movements of the agents to the slow and often haphazard antics of Charlie and Bert. Still, I couldn't help but be impressed by the efficiency with which the agents moved: Agent McCabe coordinated with the local authorities in the span of two or three sentences and within minutes we were pulling out of the motel parking lot as smoothly as floats in a parade.

Pilson and I rode in the lead car with Agent McCabe and another agent whose name I didn't get. We sped down the highway and turned off at a lake, where the pace slowed as McCabe tried to follow Marie's directions. A few times we had to stop and McCabe hung his arm out the window with a *what now?* gesture, and an agent in the car behind us had to hang most of himself out to shout whether he thought this was the turn or that was or that we hadn't gone far enough. But once we reached the unmarked road, the house itself was easy to find: it stood in the middle of not just one field but many—huge stretches of unplanted and untended land. Huge stretches of nothing, and beside the house a bare winter oak. As we passed the red mailbox, I shivered and pretended like a draft of wind had snuck down my collar. But it wasn't that. It was the house: flat, gray paint and white, peeling trim and obviously abandoned. And it looked to me like nothing but a grave.

We parked in the area that should have been a driveway,

though it was clear that no car had come through all winter; our car floundered and spun tires a few times. We got out and stared up at the house. Our breath rose white in the still. It was cold, bitter cold even without any wind, and as the men unloaded, thermoses of hot coffee came out with the picks and shovels. Agent McCabe looked around uneasily. Our party had descended upon the house like a cluster of flies and we were out in the open. Our presence wouldn't go unnoticed for long.

"Well, Mr. Jensen," he said. "Where do we begin?"

CHAPTER TWENTY-EIGHT

The Bodies

"AFTER YOU, MR. Jensen." McCabe gestured to the porch and I stepped up. I wasn't the first one in; two other agents had been inside already and done a sweep before emerging and calling, "Clear!" A small crowd of men followed Agent McCabe and me into the house. Mr. Pilson stayed behind, looking cold and out of place, and I'm unashamed to say I did not feel sorry for him.

The front door of the house opened directly into the main room. It had indeed been abandoned, but it had been abandoned with care: the sofa, chair, and large dining table had been covered over with sheets, by then lightly coated with dust. And though the main furnishings were spare, the rest of the house was littered with possessions. Over the mantel was a long row of books, with more stacked along the wall. There were shelves and glass cases filled with all manner of things: figurines and ceramics, jeweled hat pins and jewelry boxes—one box held a fancy, painted egg. The glass cases lined the entirety of the dining room and the far wall of the living room. One shelf was nothing but piles and piles of silver spoons, tiny and ornate, the kind that were never meant to be eaten off. The house felt, oddly, like a shrine or maybe like storage. I couldn't help wondering whether Marie had ever been there. Whether she had touched some of the strange objects. Whether some of them were hers.

"Send somebody outside down to the clerk's office," said McCabe. "See if they can find the owner of record."

A few of the agents frowned. Not a man there thought that the owner of record had been the last person in residence. Or that they were still alive. We wandered the ground floor for a few minutes more, studying the items here and there—a typewriter resting against the wall of the hallway, a doll in a dress of blue silk—and I paused before a dark red door, nearly the same shade of red as the mailbox.

"Tell us where to go, Mr. Jensen," said McCabe loudly, startling everyone. "And then, if you like, you can go and wait in one of the cars. Or an agent can take you back to the motel."

"Aren't Mr. Pilson and I driving back tonight?" I asked.

"Yes, but I think the federal government can afford to pay for another day's room."

I hesitated.

"Marie asked me to be there. She wants me to verify something about her stepfather's body."

"What did she want you to verify?"

"I'd rather not say. Or I guess, I'd rather tell you what it is when we find him."

"Fair enough." He held out his hand again, like he had when he was motioning me to step into the house, so I walked past him to a second set of stairs that led to the basement. The door had already been opened by the agents who conducted the sweep.

"They're down here."

We walked down single-file. The light from upstairs illuminated an eight-by-six-foot patch of plank wood flooring, which was lucky—I'd expected a lot of frozen dirt and agents toiling away with pickaxes. We stepped onto the floor and our feet rang out against hollowness. The corpses had been sealed up beneath the floorboards.

"Near the west wall," I said.

The agents commenced with the recovery at once, nearly trampling over me as they carried down tools and hung lamps from the low ceiling. In contrast with the crowded floor above, the basement was almost entirely empty, the walls an amalgamation of stone and dirt, supported by thick wooden beams. It did not run the full length of the house—only a forty-by-twenty rectangle, crudely shaped—and the only thing in it was a broken rocking chair huddled like a ghost in the corner.

With so many men in the small space, the air began to warm and give rise to all of the smells that the cold had made dormant. I hung back near the stairs to stay out of the way but also to keep from being too close when the first of the boards was pried up.

The bodies would be frozen now, or nearly so, but the corpses would have been decaying in the basement all through the long hot summer. I feared that they would have a scent and that it would make me turn away, or get sick all over my shoes.

"It's coming loose," one of the agents said. He'd been at the board with a pry bar and reached down to lever his fingers into the opening he'd made. The board came up with a dry creak. Every head in the room craned forward as he stepped back, one hand covering his mouth and nose seemingly out of habit.

There she was. Marie's mother. I couldn't see anything besides a flash of her dress—white cotton with a pattern of small brown flowers—but when I rose up on my toes, I saw that the removed board had revealed her lower half and her left leg. The skin of her calf was gray and withered, shrunken down to a foot that looked like it could never have filled that dusty black shoe.

The mood in the basement had been irritable at first; it changed immediately to one of practiced grimness. The agents had been through all this before.

"Get the cameras," McCabe ordered. More boards came up. Within minutes the whole of Marie's mother's corpse was exposed. Her hands had been folded on her chest, the fabric underneath stained dark from the last trickles of blood from cuts at her wrists. Her hair had been a deep brown, like Marie's, and in death it had been laid out over her shoulders. I looked into her face to find traces of the girl I knew. But it had been altered too much by decay.

"Not much blood," said the agent leaning over the body. Not

even on the dress. But at least in this case that was expected. We knew that Marie's mother had been killed somewhere else and brought here to be buried.

Bursts from flashbulbs cut through the yellow light of the lamps. Then the photographer stepped back so the agents could resume tearing up the floor. I waited, tensing as every new board was pulled away. Marie's stepfather would be there, right beside her.

"Another body," an agent said. "It's not the stepfather."

I broke through the barrier of agents and looked down. Marie's mother's body was tucked perfectly between two support beams. On the other side of her, where Nathaniel Cody should have been, was instead the corpse of an old woman.

"Who is she?" McCabe asked me.

"It was supposed to be Nathaniel Cody."

"Pull up more boards," Agent McCabe ordered.

"Seems like a waste," said one of the men. "These are the only new boards. See here—" he held one up. "Different wood." He pointed at the exposed edges of the adjoining floorboards, which were noticeably different, warped and weathered.

I kept on staring. The body beside Marie's mother looked like it had been dead longer. The skin was tighter, more wrinkled. I couldn't see any bloodstains, but she was wearing black, kind of like Widow Thompson, who still wore only black after all these years.

"Pull them up anyway," McCabe said, but his voice was dull. "Kid, why don't you give us some space."

"But—"

"If we find anything else, we'll call you back down. You have my word."

I looked back at the opened grave. More men came down with bags to transport the bodies out of the house.

I went back upstairs feeling dazed. I'd been so certain that we would find him. Why had Marie sent me so far on a wild-goose chase? Why had she been so triumphant with Pilson if she'd known she would only be proven a liar?

I couldn't bear going outside and seeing Pilson's smug face, so I wandered around the house, continually returning to the closed red door. It seemed odd that it would be closed—that the agents would shut it again after doing their sweep. But I figured there was no reason I shouldn't open it and go through.

The red door was unlocked and came open with a soft sound, barely a creak. I looked over my shoulder, through the main room to the agents walking back and forth through the kitchen, but none seemed to notice. The agents in the basement were bound to be a while, and I'd be able to hear them if they called. Sound carried through the house like it was made of paper. So I walked down the hallway that had been blocked by the red door, listening to the house creak and trying to figure out what Marie had been up to, sending me there.

I wondered why she had lied and what else she'd lied about. Had she lied about everything? Maybe Pilson was right and it was in her nature. Maybe she couldn't even help herself.

In the creaking house, with the smells of dirt and death fresh in my nose, the unreality of her story landed hard. Seeing those bodies had been like turning the lights on after a nightmare; I was far from home, far away from carved symbols and spectral figures in the night. Far away from Marie and her strange, steady voice. Of course there was an explanation for the missing blood. Just because we didn't know what it was didn't mean an explanation didn't exist. And it certainly didn't make it a vampire.

The late winter sun had begun to slant, and I followed it west into a bedroom. It had soft blue walls, and the floorboards had been painted white. There was one large window, and above it a brass curtain rod hung bare. The bed beside it was still covered in a blue-and-green checkered quilt, while in the corner a vanity dressing table sat idle, missing its mirror. There was a large walk-in closet full of women's clothes: dresses in plain colors of yellow and gray, the style a little old-fashioned.

As I walked around, making lines through the dust with my fingertips, I heard a voice from the main room note that the floors seemed too clean.

"Like, freshly cleaned," he said, and a chill crept up the back of my neck. I hadn't noticed anything odd about the floors. But once he mentioned it, I realized he was right: the floors in the main room and the kitchen had shone. They'd been completely free of dust. Yet the rest of the house looked like no one had been there in a year.

"Did you check the entire house?" an agent asked.

"Wasn't that red door closed?"

The red door, I thought. The red door I was currently on the other side of. I walked out of the bedroom and back into the hall.

The door had drifted mostly shut again, and I was about to say it was me, that I had opened it, when I took a step, and the floor squeaked. The next thing I knew, the door was thrown open and a gun swung into view. I ducked, right before it went off and shot two holes into the wall.

"It's me, it's me!"

"Shit! Goddamn it, kid, are you okay?"

The shots had been so loud that my ears felt stuffed with cotton. More agents crowded into the door with their guns drawn and I put my hands up.

The guy who'd shot at me—a local police officer, not an agent—was shaking all over. He came and helped me to my feet.

"Kid," he asked, "are you sure I didn't get you?"

CHAPTER TWENTY-NINE

The Findings

"**KID, ARE YOU** sure I didn't get you?"

Even now, what that officer said almost makes me laugh. *Are you sure I didn't get you? Are you sure you're not shot plain through?*

The bullet holes in the wall where I'd been standing were at head level. Yes, I was sure he didn't get me.

After the agents had completed the search of the house—and after my brush with danger courtesy of the nervous deputy—Agent McCabe designated the house a crime scene and ordered it processed: more photos taken, every item cataloged, and an extensive search of the grounds once the snow cleared and the dirt softened. The body of Marie's mother was transferred to a coroner for examination. After that it was released to the next of kin: not Marie but an aunt, Marie's great-aunt, some sixty years old. Marie had never met her.

The body discovered beside her was later identified as a

previous owner of the house but not the current one: she was a woman named Lorraine Dusquene. Five years earlier she had sold the property to a man named Peter Quince. As of this writing, no other records of Peter Quince have been located, and I do not believe that any will be. Nor does Mr. McBride. When I mentioned the difficulty in finding him, he wasn't surprised.

"When you told me the name I thought it sounded made-up," he said. "Peter Quince is a character in a Shakespeare play. *A Midsummer Night's Dream*."

And of course, poor Mrs. Dusquene was just like all the others: cut at the neck and emptied of blood. The medical examiner stated that she had been dead for a number of years. I could guess that number was five.

Pilson couldn't wait until we got back to the jail to tell Marie that we hadn't found her stepfather's body. He called her to gloat as soon as he found a telephone, and he did it in front of everyone. I heard only one half of the conversation at first.

"He wasn't where you said he was." A pause. "Oh, there was a body; it just wasn't him. Your mother was there, buried in the floorboards beside an older woman. Who was that older woman, Miss Mewes?" A longer pause. "He wasn't there, I said. The entire house was searched. Come on, Miss Mewes. You knew all along what we were going to find."

That's when Marie started shouting, and he pulled the phone away from his ear. He feigned a wince but really he wanted us to hear what she said, how unhinged she sounded.

"I don't know about any woman! Just my mother and him,

Nathaniel Cody, right there under the boards, in the dirt, so you look again, you son of a bitch! You look again!"

Pilson grinned at us, at me and the FBI agents, before he hung up the phone.

"She may be a liar," he said. "But she's a committed liar, I'll give her that."

Days later, when she was transferred from our jail to the one in Lincoln for her trial, Pilson was her escort. As she was loaded into the police car, she resisted a little. Her eyes moved over the walls of the sheriff's office to the window where she'd spent so much time looking out. She lingered with us as long as she could, until Pilson finally snapped that she'd stolen enough time, but she wouldn't be stealing away with her life.

"I was never trying to 'steal away with my life,'" Marie said. "I was trying to steal away with my soul."

I told my father later that she had almost gotten to Pilson, that I saw his brow uncrease at those plaintive, Christian words. But my father only frowned and said the truest thing I'd ever heard.

"Benjamin Pilson is no real Christian."

CHAPTER THIRTY

The Things We Have to Do

THE DRIVE BACK to Black Deer Falls with Pilson was tense. I couldn't stand the man, how he kept humming along to the radio, and how friendly he'd become again now that things had gone his way. He'd even seemed truly concerned that I'd almost gotten shot. Though maybe he really was—I guess if I'd been killed he'd have been in a heap of trouble for bringing me along.

"Mr. Pilson," I said, and the humming paused.

"Yes, Michael?"

We'd just passed a highway sign saying we were thirteen miles from St. Cloud. There were only two more hours left in the trip.

"You have to change your mind."

"About what?" he asked.

"About asking for the death penalty."

"That is what the State will ask for. I've already spoken to the judge, and he's amenable."

"But she's just a kid," I said quietly.

"And who were the sixteen people she killed? They were also someone's kids. Marie Catherine Mewes murdered her own mother. No one will weep for this." Then he sighed. "But I am sorry for you, son. I know you care about her. Maybe foolishly, but I can't say that the same thing has never happened to me."

I stared out into the darkness past our headlights. I didn't believe for one minute that the same thing had ever happened to him.

"I don't understand why she has to die. I don't know why you won't believe her."

"Why I won't believe her?"

"There are too many holes in your story," I said. "If Nathaniel Cody was the killer and they killed her mother, then what? It's weeks from the Codys' disappearance before the murder of Peter Knupp—"

"So they were hiding. Honeymooning."

"But why kill him at all?"

"Their interaction with Knupp went wrong. They panicked. Then they go right on killing as they run to Canada."

"None of the victims were robbed."

"Witness disposal, then. Or they'd just acquired a taste for it." His cheek tensed. "Your theory is a campfire story. A monster that drains people of blood and flaps away into the night."

I gritted my teeth. I wanted to say that I never said he turned into a bat, but that seemed counterproductive.

"What about the blood?" I asked. All those murders, whether

the victims had lain nice and docile or whether they had run and been chased down—all of their blood had been missing. Exsanguination. Severe loss of blood. It's what had killed each and every one. Yet there were no pools or stains around the bodies. No arterial spray across the dash and steering wheel of Angela Hawk's car.

"She was there," Pilson said. "She knew what would happen, and by her own admission, she helped Cody carry out these crimes."

"You say Cody like you know for sure, but you don't. Where was the blood?" I asked, and he looked away. "What about her fingerprints? Why were they the only ones?"

"He was careful," Pilson said. "He directed her."

"And the blood on her the night of the Carlson murders. Soaked through every inch of her clothes, like it had been poured over her head—how do you explain that?"

"It was collected. And poured over her, just like you said."

But I was barely listening anymore. I was running roughshod over the top of him and his unanswered questions.

"The house in North Platte. The cleaned floors. Someone had been there before us. Someone could have moved Nathaniel Cody's body—"

"Who?" he demanded. "How would he have known to move it? No one knew we were coming. How would he have beaten us there?"

"Maybe he went back and moved it when you released Cody's name to the press."

"And why would 'he' do that?"

"Because you gave him someone to lay it on. And moving the body would make sure Marie couldn't disprove it. It made Marie look guiltier."

Pilson barked laughter. He bore down on the accelerator.

"There's doubt," I said. "I'm just saying there's doubt."

"Not *reasonable* doubt. And Miss Mewes has only herself to blame for that."

He dropped me in front of my house just past eleven p.m. and didn't go inside to speak to my father, despite seeing the lights on in our living room. My dad opened the door to let me in and gave a half-hearted wave to Pilson's taillights.

"Are you all right?" my dad asked.

"How's Marie?"

"That's not what I asked." But when I didn't budge, he said, "She's fine. She's resting. We had to bring the doc in—"

"The doc?"

"After Mr. Pilson's phone call she wouldn't calm down. She didn't believe that the body hadn't been found. So eventually Dr. Rouse came in and gave her a little something."

"It should have been me who told her," I said. "Not Pilson."

"She might have taken it better," he said.

"She was upset."

"She was angry. Almost like she really believed that his body would be there."

"She did believe it, Dad. She did."

"Michael." He looked at me with a kind of pity and seemed to search for his words for a while. "Sometimes . . . when something is really bad . . . like what happened to Marie, a person will—"

"Make something up?"

"Not because they're a liar. Just so they won't have to face what really happened."

"You think that's what Marie's doing?" I asked.

"I think so."

"Do you think the judge will understand that?"

"I don't know. I'm not a judge. Or a jury."

"I want to see her. I want to see Marie."

"You can see her in the morning," my dad said, and squeezed my shoulder. "She did lead them to a body. Maybe that will be enough."

But I knew it wouldn't be. And I knew that with the Cody story, Pilson would be able to avail the judge to move the first trial out of Minnesota and into Nebraska. Marie had bought herself a few days, with the body search, but Pilson would be at the court as soon as he'd had enough sleep to get up and type the motion.

I went up to my room and set my bag on the floor, then lay on my bed. They would never catch the one who really did it—he was gone, disappeared like smoke—but they would make someone pay. And I couldn't let them do that.

She wasn't innocent. But she wasn't alone in the crimes. And I never believed she was a killer.

I waited until I heard my dad go to bed and then waited another hour after that. I'd never snuck out of my house before. Never tried to go out through the window or creep through the downstairs without making noise. I thought about that before I did it, how my parents would never believe I had broken the rules. When they found my bed empty in the morning, they would probably check underneath it first. And they would be scared. And disappointed. But there was nothing I could do about that.

Considering my lack of experience and the light sleeping habits of my father, it was a wonder that I made it out the front door. But I did, with a fresh bag of clothes and some food from the pantry and all of my savings folded into my wallet. In my right hand, I had my father's keys.

I unlocked the back door at the jail and went up to find Marie in her cell. But she wasn't alone—Nancy was sitting on the bed holding Marie's head in her lap.

"Michael," Nancy whispered. "What are you doing here?" She saw my coat and my bag—the keys. "Oh no. You can't do this."

I unlocked the cell door.

"I can't let her stay."

Marie stirred. When she saw me, she came awake all at once, her eyes a little glazed, probably from the effects of what the doctor had given her. But when she saw my bag, she turned over and got up.

"You'll get into trouble," said Nancy. "You'll get caught; you'll never make it."

"We'll take one of the cruisers. Drive until dawn. Then we'll hide it and go on hitching. Come on, Marie."

"You mean it?" Marie asked.

I held out my hand and she smiled and came to me. She wrapped her arms around me and buried her face in my shoulder.

She felt cold and small.

"Nancy, do I need to tie you up?"

"I guess not." She looked at Marie sadly. "I'll just say I never saw you."

I tugged Marie out of the cell. She was going to need a coat and better shoes and I had no idea where to get them.

"Michael, wait," Marie said.

"Wait for what?" I asked.

She slipped her fingers down my arm and held my hand. She looked around at the same walls she'd stared at for months.

"You would really do this," she said. "For me."

"I have to," I said. "So let's hurry and get it done." She still had a hold of me, so steady. I was trembling like a leaf.

"I can't go," she said quietly. "But I appreciate the gesture."

"Marie—we have to. They're going to kill you."

She didn't let go of my hand, but she gave it a little shake, like she was trying to wake me up.

"I have one more thing I need to tell you, before they come to take me away. Since you're here anyway, would you mind taking it down?"

CHAPTER THIRTY-ONE

The Murders of Bob, Sarah, and Steven Carlson: September 18, 1958

THE TAPE RECORDER was gone, but Nancy brought me a pen and one of my dad's notebooks. She said since it was only us there we could move down to the interrogation room, or I could sit with Marie inside the cell. But Marie joked that she would miss the bars and wouldn't recognize me if she could see all of my face at once. I don't think she wanted anything to change. It's difficult to explain. She hadn't been free for a long time. But at least her incarceration with us had been on her own terms, and I'd like to think that it wasn't all terrible.

So we sat like we always had: her on her cot and me at the kitchen table, though we left the cell door open and Nancy brought us cups of coffee. It didn't feel official, without my father there and without the tape recorder. Without Pilson looking over my shoulder. But I was glad that it happened that way. This part of the story belonged to Black Deer Falls—it was ours the way that Steve and his parents had been ours, and it was right that we would know it first, before the rest of the world.

Marie's accounting of the events of September 18 were difficult to hear. Her story was at times disjointed. Some parts she narrated as well as any storyteller. Other times she got stuck and needed me to nudge her along with questions. She repeated the conversations of that night like she was reciting lines from a play—I had to stop her a few times and ask who was speaking. But I took everything down.

This is what she told me.

They had begun to quarrel on the road. It started in Madison, Wisconsin, when Marie had refused to kill Richard Covey and his fiancée, Stacy Lee Brandberg. They were supposed to be for her: Marie's first kills. Carefully selected. So when she refused, he got angry.

"They seemed so resolute," she said. "Holding on to each other in that empty house. They'd heard about us on the radio and read about us in the papers. They knew what was going to happen. But still they didn't scream or try to run. They didn't panic.

"I said it wasn't like he'd promised. They knew what we were going to do; he hadn't used his tricks on them. But he said, 'The first time can never be easy. The first time you leave everything behind.'

"But I wouldn't. So he did it himself.

"And he did it mean: he made the boy watch when he cut her

throat. Made him keep his eyes open. Then he cut him twice in one wrist. Made him bleed out slower."

How long did it take Richard Covey to die?

"At least a half hour. Much longer than the rest.

"He was mad all the time after that. He said I'd been lying to him, playing a part. That I lacked courage and he'd made a mistake. I said he could go ahead and kill me then and start over, but he said we'd already come too far. My mother was already dead. He'd killed her for me, and he'd killed Nathaniel, and as much as I wanted Nathaniel dead, I loved my mother and cried and cried."

Do you want to tell me more about what happened to your mother? How she died?

"No. But I wish I hadn't told you where she was buried. She didn't deserve to be dug up like that. Photographed."

She paused for a long time here and then spoke at length about how they came to Black Deer Falls.

They came into Black Deer Falls on foot and wandered the back roads through dusk, until the sun went down. There had been no hunt, no plan until the headlights of Steve's Chevy caught them walking on the side of the road. It had all been by chance; it could have been me in my dad's old truck, or it could have been Percy. Steve hit the brakes and pulled over, and Marie and her companion walked in the red of his taillights right up to the passenger door. I can imagine it as if I had been there: Steve, leaning over to get a better look and then reaching to pop the door open. He'd have been in his varsity letter jacket, but it wasn't cold yet, so it would've been unbuttoned. He'd have smiled and asked them where they were headed.

"It was easy to tell him our car had broken down and ask if we could use his family's telephone. He was nice—so nice—and I thought, He'll never try to make me kill this one, when he's so similar to Richard Covey. But when we got to his house and spoke with his family, I knew I was wrong."

Steve parked the car in the usual place in the empty side of one of the large red barns, and walked them inside. I stopped here to ask if Marie was sure.

Widow Thompson saw you walk into the house together but only you and Steve. Are you sure it was the three of you?

"I am."

You're sure he didn't go on ahead or trail behind?

"He was right there, on Steven's other side."

I let her go on.

Inside the house, Mrs. Carlson had just finished cleaning up the kitchen from supper. Mr. Carlson was in the living room, settling down with a newspaper. Steve said he'd been at his girlfriend's house, eating dinner and watching television with her family. Cathy Ferry, though they had not been going steady and she didn't call herself his girlfriend after he died.

The house was warm and lived-in—the rich smell of that evening's stewed beef and potatoes hung in the air and permeated every room. Mrs. Carlson said there was still some left, if they hadn't eaten yet.

"You look like you could use some color in your cheeks," Sarah said. "How about some coffee? Or I could get a pie into the oven.

It's no trouble: I can make a crust with my eyes closed, and there are a dozen jars of filling in the pantry."

"Just coffee, please," said Marie. "Thank you."

Sarah poured a cup for Marie and set it on the table. Marie heard Steve and his father in the living room, conversing with him and laughing.

"I knew it was a trick, to keep them from being put off by his appearance in the light."

Sarah decided to start a pie anyway and asked if Marie was partial to apple or cherry.

"She didn't think anything of getting bowls out and flour and making a mess of her kitchen, even though it was plain that she'd just finished tidying up. She said she thought I looked like an apple girl. That's when I heard the baby. She started to fuss from her crib in a room just off the kitchen."

"You have a baby?" Marie asked.

"Yes, ma'am." Sarah fetched the child up out of the crib. "Patricia. A surprise for everyone, believe me, after all those years of hoping when Steve was little. But here she is. Our little Patty. Steven," she called, "come and get this pile of folded laundry and bring it up to your room before the pie's done!"

He came and took it, and from the living room Marie heard a voice: "Don't go up the stairs. . . . That will be fine. Set it just there." And Steve set the laundry on the step and went back to sit on the couch.

"I got up and went in there—they were all sitting around, chatting, chuckling at nothing like they had known each other for ages. I said, 'There's a child. A baby.' And he said, 'Crueler to leave her alive, don't you think, than to send her along with her family?'"

Steve and his father, his mother, didn't seem to hear this exchange at all. Neither man had looked up when Marie approached, and in the kitchen Sarah had put Patricia into a high chair and gone back to making the dough.

"He had this look in his eyes and it made me angry. I don't know at what. I didn't want to do it, but I felt like I needed to prove it to him that I could. I was mad about the baby. I was angry that they were such nice people."

"Well, if you're going to do it," Marie said, "don't make her go to the trouble of a whole goddamned pie."

"I was shaking. I was shaking all over, and he said, 'Sarah, will you and the child come in here, please.'"

He called, and she obeyed, even with a smile on her face, and the baby on her hip. He took the straight razor out of his pocket and opened it.

"What's that there now?" Bob asked.

"Nothing you need to worry about," he said. "Nothing at all. It's just something for her." He held it up, the blade shining in the yellow light cast by the two humble lamps.

"I stared at it and then noticed the curtains had been pulled shut, and I asked him if he'd done it."

"No, dear, I did that," said Sarah. "Our neighbor lives alone and likes to look in on us. She's a sweet old thing, but sometimes we need a little privacy." Then she went back to cooing at the baby.

"I walked over to him and took the razor. I asked him if we needed all three; it seemed like a lot. And he said, 'You could have had two, back in Madison.'

"So I looked down at Steve, who was sitting next to him on the couch. I asked if they had to be looking."

"Look away," he said, and Steve did. Marie turned away from him, though, and went to his father. Slowly, she touched the razor to the skin of his throat.

"I kept expecting him to leap up. To realize what was happening. The blade had to feel cold and strange, but he didn't even flinch. He didn't seem to notice at all. So I just leaned down and did it."

You did it?

She didn't answer me. She wasn't looking me in the eye; throughout the recounting she'd looked over my shoulder or toward the floor. Sometimes she watched the movements of my pen.

"It was easier than I thought, but I went too deep and it got on me. I tried to drink it but there was a lot. He tried to help. Moved my head, and that was better."

When she couldn't do any more, he got off the couch and nudged her aside to clean up her mess. Then he let Bob Carlson slide down from the chair and onto the rug.

"Mrs. Carlson . . . she didn't know, really, what was happening. But just the same she had started to shush the baby like she was fussing something awful, even though she wasn't making a sound. She just kept shushing her and bouncing her, and not looking at her husband on the floor. I said, 'That's enough, that's plenty,' and he said, 'It's not. You need more.'"

"I'm full."

"You're not."

"He told Steve to come and take the baby. Then he went to Mrs. Carlson and—and he did it and I just went along, I guess, like in a dream. It all felt like a dream by then and there was so much and the *taste* . . . But that was it. That was all I could do."

What do you mean, Marie?

"I mean I knew the boy and the baby would be next. So while he was finishing off Mrs. Carlson, I clenched my stomach until I threw up. I didn't think it would ever come out. I thought, Out, out, out, and I knew it wouldn't, but I threw my head back and all of a sudden it did, right out of my mouth."

It bubbled up over her face, and over her hair—so much that it soaked through her clothes and ran down all the way down to her shoes. I remembered how she looked, sticky and red from head to toe.

"I told Steve to run, to take the baby and get out of the house, but he didn't move. The baby started to cry and he set her down on the rug. I yelled, 'Get out now! You have to!'

"But he said, 'He won't.' So I said, 'You go, then. I'm not coming with you.'"

Did he seem surprised? Angry?

"No. He didn't seem surprised by any of it, not even the sight of me like I was. I thought for a minute he might just kill me, too. Kill me and disappear, and I would become part of the mystery.

But he didn't. I stood between him and the baby and then he left. But not before he shot past me and killed Steve."

Marie said she stayed between him and Patricia after he dropped Steve to the floor, and I pictured her there: teeth bared, covered in red.

"And that's how Charlie and your dad found me: standing on the rug with the baby. She had nearly cried herself out by then. But I couldn't pick her up and comfort her. It wouldn't have been right."

It was late by the time we finished. Our cups of coffee were empty. It was quiet in the jail. Still. Outside the window the sky was black.

"So Mr. and Mrs. Carlson," I said. "You killed them."

"I killed them," she said.

She reached her hand through the bars, and I leaned forward and took it, and she closed her eyes and cried.

CHAPTER THIRTY-TWO

Leaving Black Deer Falls

THE NEXT MORNING, my dad burst in and found me asleep in his office. He looked pretty relieved to see me, even though I don't think he really believed that I would help Marie break out of jail. He let me clean up in the bathroom and got Charlie to bring in fresh coffee and some donuts from the diner. Nancy came in, too, even though her shift was over and it was her day off. I told them what had happened, and what Marie had confessed.

"Why would she say that?" Nancy asked after I'd finished. "She couldn't have. She always said she never hurt anyone."

"What does her story matter, anyhow?" asked Charlie. "If it's not true? If she's still going on with that blood-drinking nonsense?"

"Because it was the truth," my dad replied. "Take out the wild tales and I reckon it is just what happened. The Carlsons still have family here, and they deserve to know everything there is to know, if they want to."

He looked at me. The fact that Marie had killed circled in the air, along with the knowledge that this strange story was nearing its end. Soon there would be no more letters to the *Star* about our mishandling of the case. No more phone calls to my mother about how ashamed I should be for cheapening the Carlsons' memory. No more Marie, sitting quietly upstairs.

Later that day we got word that Pilson had petitioned to have Marie brought to Nebraska for trial. Now that he had her identity and the body of her mother, his claim was at least as strong as ours. So the lawyers came and got her again and brought her back to the capital. This time I wasn't allowed to attend. I was sick all that day, thinking I would never see Marie again, that she would be given over immediately and moved to Lincoln. But she came back that night.

"What are you doing here?" I asked. "You won?"

But they hadn't won. It was plain in Marie's sad smile, on the defeated, exhausted faces of Mr. Norquist and Mr. Porter.

"They're trying her in Lincoln for the murder of Audrey Cody," Mr. Norquist said. "They're coming to transfer her in two days."

"Then why are you back?" I asked. "She's here just long enough to plead guilty to the Carlson murders," Mr. Porter said. "And she's here because the judge didn't care for Mr. Pilson."

I didn't know what to say. Neither did Marie. I think she figured there was never any other way it could go.

The State of Nebraska didn't charge her with the murders of Peter Knupp, Angela Hawk, or Beverly Nordahl. Pilson didn't have the evidence, I guess, to feel confident about prosecuting the rest. Or maybe he figured that her mother would be enough. People were mad at first. They wanted justice on all counts. But eventually they resigned themselves to his decision. It was, after all, like I heard some say: you could only electrocute her once.

I didn't go home much in the two days before Marie was taken away. I ate my meals with her up in our old kitchen. When I had to, I would go home and get cleaned up and come right back. School was forgotten. At night, Nancy or Bert would let me into Marie's cell, and I would sleep curled against her on the narrow cot. When I woke in the morning, I would find her arm around me, gripping my shirt, the fabric wrinkled between her tight slender fingers.

The morning of the day that Pilson was to arrive, Marie asked if my mom would come and cut her hair into a bob, so my mom came with her scissors and did it while Marie was seated at our old kitchen table.

"Perfect," my mom said when she was finished. At that length the waves in it stood out more, and truthfully it looked less perfect than wild. My mom tried to tie it back with green ribbon and then immediately pulled it out again. It wouldn't all stay, and the ribbon made Marie look too young for any of us to bear.

"I'll keep the ribbon anyway," said Marie.

My mom smoothed Marie's hair back and tucked it behind her ear. Then she left, and Bert came up to put Marie back into her cell.

"You know I'd let you stay out," he said.

"It's all right, Bert," she said, and he swung the cell door shut between us and left us to ourselves.

"Are you afraid?" I asked.

"I suppose."

"Do you want me to be there? I'll come, to the trial and to what happens after, if you want me to. I'll have my dad—"

"No." She knew what was going to happen. She knew she was going to lose. "I don't want that. You have to promise me that you won't."

So I promised. Much of that last day together we spent in silence. We sat in our quiet, familiar place and listened to the clock tick away the minutes. I listened to her breathe and knew I would remember the sound.

"You don't have any more questions?" she asked.

"What do you think is left to tell?"

She leaned back against the bars, and her new shorter hair made her neck look bare and long.

"Nothing, I guess," she said. "But anyone but you would be asking for more."

She looked at me and smiled a little.

"I wish I'd met you first," she said, and I wished for that, too, even though I knew it could have never been—it was the murders that had brought her to me and without them we never would have met. It was a terrible thought, and it was terrible knowing that I didn't entirely regret it.

Pilson came to collect her with a caravan of state police. Reporters swarmed the station—even Mr. McBride had staked out the building since morning, not wanting to miss the moment she was brought out. My dad put the handcuffs on her and walked her down, and he let me walk with them.

"I don't know what there is to be done," he said to her, "but I think you could still save yourself if you just told them where he went. And I really wish you would."

We walked through the station and through the front doors to the parking lot, where Pilson waited. Charlie and Bert were on hand to keep the reporters at a respectable distance, and the state patrol that Pilson had brought did their best to help out. When Pilson saw Marie, he nodded grimly and said, "You've got a moment." Then he ducked into the front passenger seat of the car.

Marie took a deep breath and looked around. It was the first time she'd been allowed to linger outside in months, the most fresh air she'd breathed. I was glad the day was warm—it wasn't spring yet but it was one of those early days where the scent and the feel of it were in the breeze.

She turned to me. I searched for something smart to say. She was wearing her familiar blue jeans, rolled at the ankles, and her white buttoned shirt. Instead of her usual green sweater she wore a blue one that Nancy had gotten for her—Nancy, who stood to one side with Charlie and quietly cried into a handkerchief.

Marie lifted her cuffed hands and looped them over my head. She pulled me close, and I hugged her gently, and she whispered into my ear, her voice too low and close for anyone to hear.

She whispered what she felt. She whispered her regrets. Then she took her hands back over my head and pressed them flat against my chest.

"You never did bring me those smokes," she said.

And then Pilson got back out of the car, and they pulled us apart, and the reporters closed in like a flock of crows.

And then Marie Catherine Hale was gone.

Marie's trial lasted for two weeks. As expected, she didn't change her story, and the headlines blazed. Doctors and psychiatrists were brought in to evaluate her, and she was found to be competent. They said that she was willfully making it up.

The papers said that the jurors were released at 5:25 p.m. on Thursday night to deliberate. They broke for supper at 6:30 and would not bring back a verdict until Friday evening. They found her guilty, with a recommendation of death.

According to witnesses in the courtroom, Pilson had been right. There were several gasps of shocked surprise, but no one wept.

After Marie's sentencing, the mood in Black Deer Falls—and across the nation—shifted. Groups came out in support of her, asking for mercy; those same people who for all the weeks and months before had called her a seductress now said she was a child. Mr. McBride published a Letter to the Editor in the *Star* titled, "Who but God Has the Right to Vengeance?" submitted by one Mrs. Veronica Macready, who my dad said had once come to the station to complain about Marie being held there.

Even in Nebraska, the outcry was such that Pilson held a press conference. It was unprecedented, reporters said, sentencing a girl to death who would have been in the tenth grade. And Pilson's reply made headlines of its own.

"Even fifteen-year-old girls must realize that they cannot go on sixteen-victim murder sprees."

After the furor had settled down, Agent McCabe quietly suspended the search for Nathaniel Cody. He'd not been seen or heard from since the murders ended, and it was reasoned that he had long gone over the border to Canada.

Marie Catherine Hale was set to be executed by hanging in Lincoln, Nebraska, on May 8, 1959. It was expected to go on as scheduled, as she had no intent to file an appeal.

After the trial, everyone seemed to forget all about Marie's blood-drinker story. In the same way that they forgot about the missing blood and the symbols carved into the trees and Steve Carlson's headstone. The same way they forgot about the snake nailed to my door and the man who stood in my family's living room in the middle of the night. That was just a hallucination anyway. A bad dream. Even Marie said so, since he couldn't have come in without being invited.

But I never had the chance to tell Marie about a conversation I had with Dawn.

About a week after Marie left for Nebraska, I asked Dawn if she'd seen anyone strange around town.

"No," she said. "Except for the man who was lost."

"Who was lost?" I asked.

"He came by the house one afternoon. He looked cold so I

asked him to come in and made him a cup of coffee and let him use the telephone."

"You invited him in," I said. "Dawn, what was his name?"

She couldn't remember, even though she'd sat right by him and called him by it.

"Was it before or after I'd been sleepwalking?" I asked.

"Before."

She wasn't bothered by her lapse in memory. And when I asked her what he looked like, she smiled and said, "Like a film star."

Like a film star. Not "like a movie star" or "a handsome prince" or any other phrase she might have been more likely to say. But those exact words, the same words that Marie had used, like they had been planted in both of their heads.

In the days leading up to Marie's execution I thought often about the other victims: Cheryl Warrens, Richard Covey, and Stacy Lee Brandberg. I thought about the woman buried with Marie's mother in the abandoned house: Lorraine Dusquene. I thought about the made-up property owner, Peter Quince. Five years he had owned that house, according to the county records. Five years of not living there, of coming and going from other places. Five years of filling it with strange objects. I wondered if they had come with the house. I wondered if he had known Lorraine Dusquene before he killed her.

But there will be no answers to those questions. The investigations have stopped. This is all there is. Marie's accounting of the events. We can only know what she knew and what she believed to be true.

Maybe it doesn't matter. The people who were killed will remain dead. Steve and his parents, Peter Knupp—there is no bringing them back, no matter what answers we think we find or what mysteries we think we solve.

The vampire got away.

The vampire never was.

Dear Mr. McBride,

Dear Matt,

I hope you don't mind my calling you that. You always said I could, but I could never tell if that was just you being friendly. I know I never felt comfortable doing it, and even now, after all that's happened, I can only do it on paper.

In the package that accompanies this letter you'll find everything I have compiled about the Bloodless Murders, and about Marie Catherine Hale. Pages and pages chronicling the interviews and our time together. I took it down, just like you said to. And I did my best to tell it like she would have wanted.

I hope it's all right that I turn it over to you now. Take it and run. Make what you can out of it. I know that's what I was supposed to do, to sift through it all and find the truth, but I guess I don't have the heart for it anymore.

The story I wrote isn't the story you figured on, and after you finish reading it, I'm sure you'll be disappointed. I'm sorry about that. And I don't want you to think that I'm not grateful for all your advice or that I wasn't listening. You're a great reporter,

Mr. McBride, and a better mentor than I could have ever hoped to find, in Black Deer Falls or anywhere. Last summer when I was delivering papers for you, I took your diploma down off the wall and the nail got stuck—I scratched the hell out of the paint behind it so I'm sorry about that, too. I just wanted to get a better look at it. The ivory paper and the stark black lettering. The school seal from the University of Pittsburgh. I imagined it was my name on it instead of yours. I really did want to know what brought you out here to us from there, but I should have asked sooner. I guess I never was much of a journalist.

By the time you get this package, I'll be headed out of town. I got a letter from Marie, you see, and it contained a sort of last request. She'd carefully timed the sending of it, and I like to imagine the determined look on her face when she wrote it, and how she must have hidden her nerves, worrying about whether it would reach me or be intercepted by my mom or dad, or even picked off by a prison guard looking to make a buck by selling it to the national papers. I kept the original for myself, but this is what she wrote.

Dear Michael,

I'm writing to you now to ask you what I couldn't ask then. Because I lacked the nerve. And because I was afraid you would say no. So I waited until it's almost too late, hoping that will mean you won't.

Do you remember the story of Mercy Brown? Do you

remember what they did to her?

Those first days, I bet you can't read that shorthand, your pen was shaking so bad. I imagine you looking back on those papers and seeing nothing but wavy lines. But I know you were listening.

And I know this is a lot to ask. But I don't want to come back. So I need your help. I know you remember what to do.

So I'm asking. If you ever cared about me. Like I cared about you.

I'm sorry, Michael. I want you to know that I'm not the same as I was then. But it doesn't matter because I did what I did. My confession was for who I used to be. Do you believe that? That I could change? I hope you do. And I hope that you believe me.

xo,

Marie

Once upon a time, there was a girl named Mercy Brown, who they thought was a vampire, and whose grave they unearthed, whose head they severed and whose heart they burned to ashes upon a stone. Of course I remember that. And I know what it is that Marie wants me to do.

By the time you read this it'll be too late to stop us. We'll already be there.

The cemetery of Nebraska State Penitentiary is located in southwest Lincoln, on a slowly sloping hill that rises above the prison grounds. Grasshopper Hill, they call it, on account of the

*locusts in summer. The main prison is a ways away, but there are
still lookout towers, and even at night guards will be making their
rounds. We'll be lucky if we don't get shot.*

*Funny, my mother always thought that journalism was the
safer choice. She was never wild about my dad trying to get me to
follow in his footsteps. Before the murders, he used to ask me about
it at least once a month. Now I doubt that he'll ever ask me again.*

*I know this sounds like a goodbye letter, but it isn't. I don't
know what I'm going to do. I just know she asked me to do it, so I
have to try. I guess I'll decide when I get there.*

*So I guess we both have some decisions to make. I trust you
to decide what to do with this story. It was never really my story
anyway.*

*You know, before Marie left I asked her why it was so
important that the killer not be her stepfather. I didn't understand
why she wouldn't just take the out and lay it all on him. Save
herself. Then the papers started to run stories about him being the
killer and them being on the run.*

*"They're saying I was abused," she said. "They're saying I was
raped, I was molded, I was a victim." She was angry. And angry
at me because I couldn't see how that was worse. But I think the
whole reason that Marie wanted to confess was so she would have
the final say. Marie would not be defined, not by the reporters,
not by the blood drinker, or Nathaniel Cody. Not by me.*

*If the articles are to be believed, she didn't give any last words
at her execution. And she didn't pray, unless you count telling the
priest to "go ahead if it makes you feel better." Marie Catherine*

Hale. Tough to the end.

I'm going to miss her voice. I'm going to miss her. I suppose you'll think that's strange, but it's the truth.

Tell the truth and shame the devil. When I started that seemed like an easy enough thing. Find out what really happened, Michael, because the truth is the truth. Except it isn't, is it? Facts, maybe. But the truth is our own. It's tied up with belief. And belief is harder to hold down.

I want to thank you for everything, Matt. And if something goes wrong at the cemetery, I hope you'll give this to my parents and let them read it so maybe they'll understand.

Yours Truly,
Michael Jensen

May 9, 1959

When I asked Percy to drive me down to Lincoln, he didn't seem surprised. He just snuck out early and picked me up, as if we'd done it a hundred times.

"I guess I don't have to ask you why," he said when I got in. "I guess I've known for a while. But she was a killer, right?"

"Yeah," I said. "She was a killer. But that's not all she was."

We drove out of town down Main Street, watching lights turn on as the shops opened up, the sidewalks still dark and empty.

"You know I do love this place," I said. "Just because I think I might wind up somewhere else, it doesn't mean I don't. It doesn't mean it isn't home."

Percy looked at me. Some people say the Valentines aren't the cleverest of people, but I find them downright intuitive.

"Yeah," he said, and smiled. "I know."

Hours later, outside the car window, a whole lot of nothing breezes past as Percy carefully drives the byways. We've crossed well into eastern Nebraska and the springtime remnants of tall-grass prairies. As I stare into them, the pale tops rustle in the wind and in my mind, I see Stephen Hill, running for his life as the grasses snarl around his legs. In my mind the grass is green—high summer grass to his waist, and behind him the dark shapes of Marie and the blood drinker dart through it like fish through underwater weeds. I can almost hear his panicked breathing. I can almost hear her laughing.

Only that isn't the way it happened. Stephen Hill was killed far away, in a regular flat field next to a service station between Grand Junction and Mason City, Iowa.

"Can you reach back and grab Pop's atlas?" Percy asks. "I think our next turn is coming up."

I reach back for the atlas—which is really not an atlas but a collection of individual maps secured with a tie—and unfold the map of Nebraska.

"About how long?" he asks.

"Ten miles to the turn. We should be there before dark."

We drive past the cemetery just before sunset, when it's still light enough to see the rows of white grave markers and crosses. We park down the road and wait until the sun goes down. We wait until after the prison will have called lights-out.

"You shouldn't come with me," I say. "This isn't like just ditching class or swiping beers from Mo."

"Come this far, haven't I?" he says. "Can't very well let you go the rest of the way alone."

We get out of the car and he opens the trunk—there are things inside we need: shovels, a sharpened hatchet. They all feel cold in my hands. The moon is out, and the night is brighter than I would like. I tell Percy to button his jacket up over his white shirt.

We go quick and quiet along the dirt road until we reach the edge of the cemetery. Ahead in the blackness I can just make out the ghostly shapes of the crosses in row after neat row.

Percy touches the fence, and wraps his hand around the strand of barbed wire hammered into the old wood posts.

"Stay low," I say. "Stay covered."

"Not much cover to be had."

"I'm sorry about this, Perce."

"I don't know why you're doing this," he says. "I don't believe you're really going to do it."

I tighten my grip on the hatchet.

It takes some time to find her grave, stumbling around in the moonlight, sometimes on our hands and knees and feeling our way across the ground for fresh dirt. But it takes even longer to dig her up. Percy helps, and we work side-by-side until our shovels strike something firm, of wood, and he looks at me before climbing out. This part I have to do alone. The top half of her casket is exposed. It's just a plain pine box, and above it in the grass the small rectangular stone bears no name, only the date. I don't know if I have the nerve for this. If I can pry open the casket and look upon her face. If I can cut out her heart.

I kneel down. She hasn't been in the ground long. I lean in close.

"Come back, Marie. I want you to come back."

I wait.

Against the wood, the hatchet in my hand shakes.

AUTHOR'S NOTE

Though the character of Marie Catherine Hale and the killings known as the Bloodless Murders are inventions of fiction, they were inspired in part by actual events. In 1958, nineteen-year-old Charles Starkweather and his fourteen-year-old girlfriend, Caril Ann Fugate, embarked upon a murder spree that left eleven people dead throughout Nebraska and Wyoming. Eventually apprehended, Charles was convicted and executed for his crimes on June 25, 1959. Though Caril Ann's level of involvement in the killings has come into question, she was also convicted and sentenced to life in prison.

The murders of Michael's friend Steve Carlson and his parents were inspired in large part by the murders of the Clutter family in Holcomb, Kansas, on November 15, 1959, which were famously profiled by Truman Capote in his novel *In Cold Blood*.

Any quotes taken from the actual investigations have been paraphrased and otherwise altered for the sake of Marie's story, and though some of the criminal justice elements are similar to the real cases, Marie's case is different and fictionalized. All inaccuracies and liberties taken with procedure are mine.

ACKNOWLEDGMENTS

This book owes many things to many people, but let's start at the beginning, with my agent, Adriann Ranta Zurhellen, at Folio Literary Management. She kindly listened and kept an open mind as I pitched her this weird story. She also wisely told me I should write the Three Dark Crowns series first.

As usual, I am completely indebted to my editor, Alexandra Cooper, at Quill Tree Books. I handed her a painstakingly crafted birdhouse made of words, and she deftly pointed out where I'd meant to put the door, and where it needed more paint, and how to shore it up so the words wouldn't collapse and murder every bird inside.

Thank you to Rosemary Brosnan, Jon Howard, and the entire team at HarperCollins/Quill Tree: art director Erin Fitzsimmons, who designed the cover; the talented artist Miranda Meeks; the publicity dynamo Mitchell Thorpe; copyeditor Robin Roy; and of course the amazing marketing stylings of Michael D'Angelo.

Eternal high fives to Allison Weintraub and Marin Takikawa, who keep me in line and in the know. Big heart eyes to power-house publicity trio Crystal Patriarche, Keely Platte, and Paige Herbert at BookSparks.

Thanks to my two dogs and two cats for taking long naps so Mama could work. Thanks to Susan Murray, whose Father (capitalization deliberate) was a small-town detective and whose expertise in criminology, forensic psychology, and criminal justice really came in handy. Now if you would be willing to obtain an advanced degree in ancient warfare before my next book that would be just aces.

Thank you to the talented writers Marissa Meyer, Lish McBride, Sajni Patel, Rori Shay, Alexa Donne, Kaylyn Witt, Alyssa Colman, and Jessica Brody for camaraderie, good food, brainstorms, and wine.

And thank you to Dylan Zoerb, for luck.